The Nightmare Was Just Beginning

This can't be right, Jill thought, as panic merged with the pain of labor.

Oh no, this isn't right. This is not right at all!

Her legs began to shake as her body was seized by a fierce nausea. She leaned over the side of the gurney and began to vomit violently.

"What kind of nurse are you?" Jill called out as she struggled onto her back from her side.

"Why have you brought me here?" Jill screamed. *"What is going . . ."*

An icy hand clamped over Jill's mouth. The nurse, her face covered by a surgical mask, peered down at Jill. Her eyes were deadly cold, maniacal . . .

THE BABY

STEPHANIE KEGAN

CHARTER/DIAMOND BOOKS, NEW YORK

THE BABY

A Charter/Diamond Book / published by arrangement with
the author

PRINTING HISTORY
Charter/Diamond edition / October 1990

ISBN: 1-55773-397-X

Charter/Diamond Books are published by The Berkley Publishing
Group, 200 Madison Avenue, New York, New York 10016. The name
''CHARTER/DIAMOND'' and its logo are trademarks belonging to
Charter Communications, Inc.

PRINTED IN THE UNITED STATES OF AMERICA

10 9 8 7 6 5 4 3 2 1

For my parents
And for Ed

I wish to thank Paul Gillette, Carolyn Coker and Elizabeth Pomada for their invaluable help and encouragement.

Prologue

DORA MILES AWOKE DEEP IN THE NIGHT WITH THE HEART-stopping awareness that someone was in her bedroom. Careful to move as little as possible, Dora eased one eye open and saw that the prowler was her husband searching for something in the dark room.

Dora bolted upright and began to scream. Her husband had been dead for more than forty years.

Her screams brought two uniformed maids scurrying down the second-floor hall. But instead of entering the bedroom, the young girls just stood in the open doorway laughing at Dora.

Live-in help are useless, Dora thought wildly. A moment later she realized that she did not have live-in help anymore. Finding them useless, she had gotten rid of her help years ago.

Dora covered her eyes and sank back on the bed. She was having a nightmare. That was all. A nightmare. An old woman living alone in a big house was bound to have bad dreams from time to time. But Dora was tough. As she often told herself, the things she had been through would have broken a lesser woman. She was not going to let a nightmare get the best of her. She would take charge, end this awful dream the way she always ended bad dreams: by reaching out and turning on the lamp next to her bed.

She stretched an arm out from under her blankets, groped for the cord, and gave it a firm tug. As her eyes adjusted to the light, the old woman began to shake and then sob, driving a fist against her mouth. The nightmare wasn't over. She was not in her own bedroom.

Yet the room was not completely strange. Her picture was on the bedside table. And the floral print chaise lounge by the window looked familiar. She had had a chaise just like that one years ago—years ago, when she had slept in the bedroom on the other side of the hall. This room!

Slowly each piece of furniture, each object, became recognizable. That was the dresser she had given to her brother Ben and his wife when she had tired of using it. This was the carpet she had gotten rid of just before the war. That was the jewelry box that had been stolen from her years ago.

Terrified, the old woman slid deeper into bed, and pulled the blankets over her head. She would wait the dream out, stay under the covers until morning.

Then, suddenly, a baby began to cry.

Dora covered her ears. There was no baby in the house, any more than she was back in the room she had slept in years ago. Why couldn't she get this dream to end like the others?

Dora's covered ears could not shut out the baby's cries. The crying was so insistent, so unbearably piercing that Dora found herself compelled to respond. She got out of bed and walked down the hall to the room where the nursery once had been.

The moon shone brightly into the small room. Dora did not turn on the light. Even in the semi-dark, it was obvious that everything in the nursery was as it always used to be.

Afraid to pick the baby up, Dora hesitated for a moment above the crib, watching the tightly wrapped bundle squirm demandingly. Then, unable to stand by helplessly any longer, she reached into the crib and picked up the tiny infant.

"There, there," Dora cooed, "don't cry. Mommy will take you down to the kitchen and fix you a nice, warm bottle of milk."

Gently holding the infant, she carried him out of the nursery. He felt warm and cuddly in her arms, and she held him tightly, her hands caressing the smooth flannel of his blanket. Her breasts tingled from his closeness.

She had to look at him—had to gaze once again at the perfection of his delightful little face. Pausing at the top of the staircase, she lifted the baby off her shoulder, placed him in the crook of her arm, and gently pulled the blanket back from his face.

Her screams were heard by no one—her terror seen by no one. The baby's ears were gaping holes; his eyes had long ago been devoured by the worms that now slithered from his empty eye sockets onto Dora's hands and up her arms.

The old woman's legs gave way and she fell screaming down the stairs. But even the pain of that long tumble was not enough to wipe the sight of the baby's worm-infested skull from her mind. It was the final image of her life.

Chapter One

JILL DOUGLAS SAT IN THE PASSENGER SEAT OF THE RENTED Mustang, rubbing her stomach to feel for the baby that was much too small to feel. Her husband, Dr. Tom Douglas, looked straight ahead, his eyes intent on the private road winding higher and higher into the wooded hills. Below them stretched the rugged coastal terrain of Northern California.

Jill took a deep breath of ocean-scented air and thought: An original Greene and Greene craftsman house—we're going to be living in a work of art. The house was the first promising thing to come out of their move from Manhattan to California—a move that Jill had not wanted to make.

The couple had come across country so that Tom could fulfill a long-standing desire to take over his father's small-town medical practice. Jill had accepted the move stoically—after all, Tom had talked about it for years. But her acceptance meant giving up the job she loved, her friends, and the city she had lived in all her life.

The Greene and Greene house had belonged to Tom's aunt Dora, who had left it to Tom's father when she died. There was no reason that Tom and Jill should not take it for their own, Tom's father had argued. Jill had been lukewarm about the idea. She wanted to pick out her own house. And, as eager as she was to leave her in-laws—she and Tom were staying with them temporarily—she certainly did not want to end her visit indebted to them for a house. Yet, when she learned the house being offered was an original Greene and Greene—one of the few that the famous Pasadena architects had designed in Northern California—Jill's reservation had given way to guarded excitement.

Tom had not been able to tell her anything about his aunt's house. Although he had grown up a mere ten miles away, he had never been there—indeed, he had met his aunt only a few times in his life. His mother's and his aunt's mutual dislike had been so intense that Tom's father had kept his relationship with his sister separate from his wife and child. His father almost never spoke of Dora to his family and Tom seldom thought of her.

"Ohhh, Tom!" Jill gasped in astonished delight as the rental car made its final turn and the house majestically came into view. Sitting on top of the hill, framed by a large, tree-studded lawn and the curve of a red brick driveway, the massive house looked like an elegant ocean liner poised to sail away. It was covered with moss-green shingles and detailed with wood and stone. The upper-story rooms, capped by overhanging eaves, jutted out at pleasing angles. A wide veranda circling the house drew the eye to the front door, which was hand-carved of oak and crowned with a magnificent stained-glass window. The house was almost ori-

ental in design; it reminded Jill of a beautiful
nineteenth-century Japanese inn.

"Are you sure this is the *right* house?" Jill asked when
her excitement subsided enough to let her say something.

"I don't believe it either," Tom said, shaking his head
and laughing.

"Well, it's probably a wreck on the inside," Jill said,
steeling herself for disappointment. "I mean, there has to
be a catch."

Tom nodded as he began considering the old house's
potential for repair bills.

Sensing what Tom was thinking, Jill nudged his arm
playfully. "Hey, what are we so worried about? This house
might just be the luckiest deal that has ever come our
way."

Daring to hope that what she had just said was true, Jill
got out of the car and dashed up the wide front steps ahead
of Tom. The exhaustion that had dogged the first four
months of her pregnancy was completely gone. She was
up for anything and she could not wait to get a look inside
the house.

Tom unlocked the front door. He pushed it open, then
stepped aside so Jill could enter first. A long hall, finished
entirely in teakwood, stretched before them. Sunlight filtered into it from the stained-glass window above the front
door and from a glass door at the opposite end of the
corridor. An exquisite staircase with hand-carved balusters
led upstairs from the center of the hall. Elegant light fix-
tures, styled like Japanese lanterns, hung in a line down
the ceiling.

The effect was somber and imposing and also very
beautiful. There was no doubt that the house was the work
of the melancholy Greene brothers—two architects about
whom Jill knew a very great deal.

For the past twelve years, Jill had worked as a writer and researcher for Beckman Ink in New York. One of the largest companies of its kind in the country, Beckman Ink supplied research on any subject to business and professional people, corporations, and textbook companies. Sometimes clients requested a finished article, or even a book, that would be published under their own names.

While most of the writers for Beckman Ink specialized in a field, Jill preferred to work as a generalist. The only problem with her job, Jill often thought, was that she wound up knowing a whole lot about minute segments of totally unrelated subjects. She loved her work, however, and one very pleasant assignment had left her a connoisseur of the turn-of-the-century Craftsman movement in architecture exemplified by Greene and Greene.

"Let's go upstairs first," Jill said, unable to contain her excitement. She bounded up the stairs with Tom following, but about halfway up her sneaker slipped on the edge of a highly polished step. For one horrible moment, Jill thought she was going to fall backwards. She caught her balance by grabbing the handrail at the same moment that Tom caught her from behind.

"Hey, you are going to have to learn to take it easier," Tom said gently.

Jill was suddenly sickened by an image of herself falling down the stairs and losing her baby in a flood of blood. She took a deep breath and pushed the image from her mind.

The baby was fine. Everything was going to be fine. Any day now, her doctor would call from Manhattan with the results of her amniocentesis. He gave all pregnant woman over thirty-five the test. Even though Jill had just turned thirty-five, in the doctor's eyes she was over the line separating the "young" mothers from the high-risk "older" mothers. Had she conceived just six months earlier, she would still be in the group with the young mothers. But here she was, in the words of the medical establishment, an elderly primigravida.

At the top of the stairs, Jill and Tom were confronted by seven closed doors—one at the end of the corridor and three on each side. Taking the lead again, Jill strode to the end of the hall and opened the first door on the right.

Before her was a magnificent bedroom. The spacious room was elegantly furnished in the art-deco style. Large windows on the two exterior walls provided a spectacular view of the wooded coastal terrain. A glass door led to a sleeping porch off one side of the room, and a beautiful but unobtrusive stone fireplace stood in the center of one wall.

Jill sucked in her breath. The room exceeded her fantasies. She explored the bedroom almost gingerly, as if frightened that she might wake herself. Her dreamy enchantment lasted until she opened the closet. "It's full of clothes!" she said, startled.

"My aunt's been dead only a few months," Tom said softly. "Most of her stuff is still in the house. I'm afraid it's going to be a big job to go through it all."

Jill felt foolish and a little ashamed—as if she had just been caught eyeing the jewels around the neck of an elderly relative. "I'm sorry, I seem to have forgotten all about your poor aunt in my lust for her house. You said she fell. Had she been ill?"

"She wasn't ill at all," Tom said gently. "She broke her neck falling down the hall stairs in the middle of the night."

"Oh, my God!" Jill gasped. "I didn't realize. I just assumed . . ."

"I didn't realize her death was so horrible either. Dora was such a painful topic of conversation in my family that I barely knew anything about her. My father hadn't seemed to want to talk about her death, so I didn't press him. He just told me the whole story last night, after you and my mother went to bed."

Jill stared at her husband transfixed, waiting for him to continue.

"Apparently," he said, looking pained, "Dora was such an obsessive housekeeper that she would actually get up in the night to clean. My father's theory is that she couldn't sleep on the night she died and she was going downstairs to dust. They found some sort of old blanket clutched in her hand."

"A blanket? She was going to dust with a blanket?"

"It was a little blanket," Tom said, indicating its size with his hands.

"You mean a baby blanket?"

"I guess," Tom lied, immediately regretting having told Jill the story. Pregnant women were so easily spooked. Yet, the night before *he* had been a little spooked as he listened to his father describe Dora's death—the way her dead body had looked, the hideous angle of her head. His father had described the baby blanket quite vividly, too. It had rows of faded pink storks carrying rows of faded babies in their beaks—a final morbid detail that Tom's father needed to get off his chest in the safety of a late-night conversation with his only son.

Ten miles inland from Dora's estate, Tom's mother Peggy put her small bag of groceries on her kitchen counter. Sick people's groceries, she thought as she lifted out the small cans of Campbell's Chicken Soup, the cartons of plain yogurt, and the potatoes she would later mash for her husband Ben's dinner. Ben's lack of appetite worried her. It had been four months since his heart attack; surely his appetite should be getting better by now.

Peggy pushed the persistent worry from her mind and walked over to the window to check on her husband. Ben was sleeping on a chaise lounge under the old elm tree in their back yard, a book face-down on his lap. Peggy watched him sleep. Even now, at seventy years old, after being so sick, Ben was still the most handsome man she knew, even more handsome than her son Tom.

She was being a silly old goose spending so much time worrying. Ben was going to be fine. And her son was home.

Peggy's stomach suddenly contracted with a new anxiety: The kids were going to live in Dora's old house. Nothing good could ever come from anything that had to do with Dora Miles. The house was surely a firetrap, and it was so isolated. Peggy just didn't feel right about the thought of Jill being there alone during the day with a tiny baby and no neighbors nearby.

But would anybody listen to her objections? No! The men thought it was so practical, what with the title free and clear, and Jill seemed to like the idea of living farther from town. She probably thinks her old mother-in-law would drop over every day if she lived in town, Peggy thought, sighing.

Peggy finished putting away the groceries. After a quick look to make sure that Ben was still sleeping, she pulled the last item from her bag—a folded copy of the *National Enquirer*. Ben could not tolerate the tabloid and he could not understand why in the world Peggy would buy it. But Peggy enjoyed reading it every week. She liked knowing which top movie stars were dating which other top movie stars. She liked the fantasy that there might be a miracle diet out there that just might work for her. But most of all, she liked to keep up with the latest information about psychic phenomena.

Ben would never listen to her dreams that foretold the future. He was a doctor, a man of science, and if you couldn't dissect it or put it under a microscope, he wouldn't accept it. But Peggy's prescient dreams were a central part of her life.

The dreams were strongest about Tom. When he was small, Peggy had had a recurring nightmare about a driverless new green-and-white Chevrolet that followed Tom everywhere he went. In the dream, Peggy told Tom to watch out for the car, but it beckoned him, and she saw him run toward it. She chased him as fast as she could, but she couldn't catch up with him. Little Tommy got in the car and slammed the door. Suddenly, to her horror, she saw that the car was no longer a Chevrolet, but a hearse. Screaming, she continued to run after it. Finally she saw the hearse turn into the cemetery and deliver Tommy dead in a coffin.

Years later, when Tom was seventeen, he came home with his first car. It was the same car, a green-and-white Chevrolet—the exact year and model as in her dream. Peggy got hysterical. She made Tom sell the car and get another one. The boy to whom Tom sold the Chevy got drunk one night, drove into a brick wall and killed himself.

Peggy poured a cup of coffee and sat down at the kitchen table with the *Enquirer*. Maybe Jill won't like the house now that she's seen it, Peggy thought without much hope.

A baby blanket. Jill stared into the massive bedroom. In the institution where her mother had been kept, there had been an old lady who carried around a doll as if it were a real baby. The old lady had shown it to Jill once all wrapped up in a little pink blanket. How old had she been then? Twelve? Thirteen?

"Jill, are you all right?"

"Yes," Jill said, focusing her attention back to the present, "but what an awful story. That poor woman!"

Tom nodded in awkward agreement, worried that he had spoiled Jill's pleasure in the house.

Jill smiled up at him, pushing away her vague uneasiness. Everything was going to be fine. She looked around the bedroom and remarked brightly, "You know, in New York this room would be subdivided into four apartments."

Tom laughed, feeling relieved at Jill's return to her former lighthearted mood. "Come on," he said, pulling her by the hand toward the open bathroom door. "Let's see the rest of our family heirloom."

Jill clasped her hand to her mouth to suppress a delighted giggle when she saw the bathroom. Tiled in small pink and grey hexagons, it was the size of a master bedroom in a normal house. There was an enormous combination tub-shower within an arched, tiled area, a free-standing sink with a wide pedestal, a mirrored dressing table opposite the sink, and floor-to-ceiling closets. A second door led from the bathroom into the hall.

Next to the bedroom Tom and Jill found a much smaller room with a sloping, atticlike ceiling. The room was musty and filled to the brim with old sewing equipment and other junk; yet Jill could envision it transformed by yellow wallpaper, white paint and lacy curtains into a perfect nursery. A lovely vision floated into Jill's head of breast-feeding their baby in a rocking chair in front of the window. Had she herself been breast-fed as an infant? She would never know. But she did know this: The child that she was carrying would have a far better childhood than the one she had known.

Jill's earliest memory—and her only memory of her mother at home—was of finding her mother crouched on the floor in the corner of the kitchen, staring blankly into space, unresponsive to Jill's desperate pleas.

Jill was three when her mother went to the hospital and never came back. She would later learn that her mother—who by all accounts seemed perfectly normal until she became pregnant with Jill—had suffered from a severe postpartum depression. The depression deepened into a psychosis from which Jill's mother never recovered. Her illness kept her institutionalized for the rest of her life.

Jill and Tom finished exploring the upstairs, which consisted of three more large bedrooms and a walk-in linen closet, before heading downstairs. Jill navigated the stairs to the first floor carefully, trying not to think about Tom's aunt.

To the left of the staircase downstairs, at the front of the house, they discovered—to Jill's absolute delight—a library. The room was comfortably sized, like a well-planned living room, with floor-to-ceiling mahogany bookshelves. Large windows looked out onto the front lawn, and a polished stone fireplace stood elegantly against the wall. Best of all, the bookshelves were crammed with books, ranging from fairly recent bestsellers to volumes that appeared to have been purchased new in the 1920s.

This must be how it feels to win the lottery, Jill thought, as she and Tom made their way down the hall to the living room. The heavy sliding doors shutting off the living room were stuck. When Tom managed finally to push the doors apart, Jill was disappointed for the first time since seeing the house. The gloomy side of the Greene brothers had clearly found expression in this solemn and rather foreboding room. The ceiling, floor and walls of the massive room were all constructed of a dark hardwood that had grown even darker with age. A somber redwood frieze circled the walls just above the ceiling. The windows were shaded so completely by the overhanging eaves of the roof that precious little sunlight could get in to brighten the room.

Still, Jill had to admit, the room had an austere beauty. Although dark, the woodwork was nonetheless elegant. Most of the furniture had been hand-crafted to compliment the architectural lines of the room. The attention to detail was carried to the smallest feature; even the electrical outlets were plated with intricately carved wood. A large, beautifully designed stone fireplace graced the interior wall of the room.

The only vivid color in the room was provided by a large portrait, set into an indentation in the fireplace, of a woman in a 1930s-style clinging gown.

"Aunt Dora?" Jill asked.

"None other."

Dora was indeed beautiful. She shared Ben's and Tom's classic features, but her eyes—unlike those of the blue-eyed father and son—were very dark and shaded by thick eyebrows.

On each side of the fireplace were shelves lined with Tiffany-glass vases and silver-framed photographs. Most of the photographs were glamor shots of Dora or photos of her posing affectionately with an equally handsome young man. Jill looked more closely.

"These are pictures of your father!"

Tom peered at the photos. "My God, was my father ever that young?"

Jill was fascinated by the images the photographs presented. The self-consciousness and awkward affection usually captured in photographs of brothers and sisters was completely absent. The stunningly attractive pair caught in these photographs looked for all the world like young lovers.

"Well," Jill said, finally, "I can see why your mother and your aunt didn't care much for each other."

Tom nodded, looking slightly perplexed. Jill decided to change the subject.

"Where did your aunt get her money?"

"Married it. Her husband was much older. I think he might have been a congressman at one time. I don't think they were married all that long before he died. Anyhow, that was long before I was born."

The rest of the downstairs rooms were much cheerier than the living room. The dining room across the hall looked like a spread from *Architectural Digest*. On the outside wall, a three-panel stained-glass tableau of beautiful wood nymphs filled the room with shades of amber and gold. Opposite the stained glass was another polished stone 'fireplace. A built-in teakwood buffet occupied the entire far wall. The center of the room was dominated by a teak dining set, which, although obviously quite old, was so stunningly designed that it could have just arrived from an exclusive showroom.

A pantry, larger than Jill's Manhattan kitchen, stood between the dining room and the kitchen. Even in the pantry, the finest building materials had been used and the highest-quality craftsmanship was displayed.

The kitchen was spectacular—a huge room with oak

counters and cupboards, a hardwood floor, and a glassed-in breakfast room in back.

"Well, Jill, do you think the place will do?" Tom asked after eyeing the kitchen.

"Oh, Tom," Jill said, throwing her arms around him. "Yes." She could relax. Everything was going to be just fine.

Chapter Two

FIRED, LAID OFF, PINK-SLIPPED, SHAFTED, TOM THOUGHT, it all meant the same thing. You were out of a job and out of control. Tom had built the emergency room at Sisters of Mercy Hospital in Brooklyn into one of the finest trauma centers in New York. The only problem was, it wasn't profitable. It was profitable, of course, to the people whose lives were saved, but not to the corporation that bought the hospital from the Sisters of Mercy.

Tom probably would have been invited to stay at the hospital in some capacity other than Chief of Emergency Medicine had he not been so vocal in his opposition to the closing of the emergency room. Although he was sorry that the emergency room had been closed, he was not sorry to have left the hospital.

For a start, he certainly would not miss the hospital politics, Tom thought, as he sat at the desk in his father's office waiting for Mrs. Fisher—his father's veteran nurse—to usher in the first patients of the day.

Tom drank the mug of coffee that Mrs. Fisher had given him and stared at the framed picture above the desk. It was a crayon drawing Tom had done in the first or second grade of a little boy standing next to a very big father with a fat sun shining over both of them. The picture was inscribed in childish lettering: To Dad from Tommy.

Tom had never meant to stay so long at the Sisters of Mercy Hospital. He had always intended to come back to California to work with his father. After medical school at NYU and an internship at Sisters of Mercy, Tom had thought he would stay on in the emergency room for a couple of years to get the kind of experience that was impossible to obtain in private practice in a small town.

He had worked two—and frequently three—twenty-four-hour shifts a week in the emergency room. Patients came one after the other. There were no names, not even faces—just limbs to be reassembled, bleeding to be stopped, hearts to be started again. Gunshot wounds. Stab wounds. The results of man versus car. Man versus bus. Man versus everything.

He had worked all day, then all night, and sometimes when he got off duty, he felt so good that instead of going to bed, he stayed up all that day too. Almost before he realized what was happening, he was made Chief of Emergency Medicine.

Although his work kept him extremely busy, he still found time to date a number of attractive women, but before Jill, nothing lasted. Women liked him. They were attracted to him. But they could never live with his schedule and he could never live with their resentment. Jill was so different from the others. She was so independent, so mature, so much fun. And she worked the same crazy hours he did, writing all night and taking off when she felt like it. Their schedules meshed as perfectly as their personalities, as perfectly as their bodies.

Tom moved from patient to patient, from meeting to meeting, and time slipped by. But, for the last year every time Tom had spoken to his father on the phone, Ben had asked his son when he was coming home.

"No pressure," the older doctor had said. "I just want to know if I should start looking for someone else. You know, I sure as hell would hate to see this practice sold to one of those new breed of guys who would use it as a stepping stone to owning a winery."

Tom had not wanted the practice to go to anyone else either, he thought as he looked around the comfortable office with its floor-to-ceiling bookshelves overstuffed with books and journals, the big old desk, the faded Norman Rockwell print on the wall, the artwork of Tom's youth, the worn couch where Ben took a nap every day after lunch without fail, the open windows that let the antiseptic smell out and the odor of the real world in.

Tom remembered coming to the office as a little boy with his father on Saturday mornings. It certainly must have been his mother's idea to give her a little free time, but Tom never saw it that way. He looked at it as going to work with his dad. Mrs. Fisher gave him orange juice and let him use her typewriter. Like the rest of the office, Mrs. Fisher hadn't changed much in all the years. She was still gruff, still hardworking, and still so caring. Good God, did she even have a first name? Ben had always called her Fisher. The kids called her Nurse Fisher. Everyone else, Tom included, called her Mrs. Fisher.

When Tom was nine years old, he had seen a baby born in this office. The mother had come in on a Saturday, unsure of what was happening. There was no time to get her to the hospital. Ben had called Tom into the examining room. He told Tom to stand back, to be quiet and to help if asked. Afterward, his father had given him his first cup of coffee.

Ben's coronary had occurred in the same month as the closing of the Mercy emergency room. Tom's decision to move back to Willowglen would have been completely effortless had it not been for Jill.

Jill had gone along with his decision, but he knew how hard it was for her to make the move. Jill had worked hard to build a secure life, with a good job and friends, after a grim girlhood overshadowed by her mother's insanity. Tom had not wanted to uproot Jill, but he felt he had no other choice. He believed that Jill would be happy in Willowglen, but if she were not, they would move. He would never want Jill to be unhappy.

Jill sat at her mother-in-law's kitchen table staring at a piece of toast. If I eat it, she thought, maybe it will make me feel better. Then again, maybe it will finish me off completely. She put her head in her hands and wondered what had ever made her want to get pregnant in the first place.

Everyone but Jill had bounced out of the house with a happy sense of purpose that morning. Tom had sailed off for his first day of seeing patients at the office. Peggy and Ben had breezed out for a trip to the A&P.

Bored with feeling sorry for herself, Jill took a determined bite of toast and conjured up an image of Dora's house fixed up the way she would like it. She had plenty to do. They would move into Dora's house on Saturday, and Jill would start working on the place right away.

Her nausea began to subside. She might actually enjoy being a country wife. Maybe she would even plant a garden. And, she would make the house a wonderful place for their child. She would have a little playground built at the side of the house and would never have to worry about cars or molesters or all those other urban dangers. It was a wonderful environment for a child—the pine trees, the clean air, all that space to run and play in. Little Katie or Charlie would have the kind of childhood that Jill knew only from watching *Father Knows Best* and *Leave It to Beaver* on television as a girl.

Her baby would have grandparents close by to dote on him, too. She suppressed a bitter thought of her own father living with that blonde in Florida. Jill had no right to not wish him a little happiness after all those years of trudging to work, coming home to a mother instead of a wife, trying to care for a daughter he did not understand, and visiting a wife every week who did not recognize him.

Jill might even come to enjoy Tom's parents if she could just learn to relax around them. Living at opposite ends of the country from his parents, Jill and Tom had spent very little time with them in the six years since their wedding. Certainly, Jill thought, not enough time with them to erase their memory of her wedding day. If Jill had not been so blindingly in love, she never would have risked having her mother brought from the institution to attend her wedding.

Jill was not the kind of woman who felt comfortable wearing flowers in her hair. She resisted at first when her friend began to weave baby's breath through Jill's luxurious hair the afternoon of the wedding. But the effect was so stunning that for once Jill had to admit that she was a very pretty woman, indeed.

Jill's wedding gown was an off-the-shoulder hand-embroidered long, white, cotton dress from Mexico. She had paid too much for it, but for once she did not care. With her friends fussing around her in the dressing room of the church, she felt like Elizabeth Taylor in *Father of the Bride*—a movie she had stayed up to watch on many a television late show.

"Jill," her father said, leaning in the door, "they are waiting for us."

"Let's forget the whole thing, Dad," Jill half joked.

"Too late, honey," he said, putting out his arm.

Jill had thought Tom's choice of the Beatles' "In My Life" for their wedding song was pretty corny. But Tom knew a nurse who sang beautifully, and since Tom invited the singer, Jill gave in on the song. Now, standing in the back of the church on the arm of her father in the late afternoon light, listening to the singer's rich and unaccompanied voice pealing forth, Jill found the beauty of the song and the moment almost too intense to bear.

The song ended, the bridal music began and the small procession ahead of Jill moved into the church. Jill's father touched her arm and, for the first time in their lives, father and daughter moved forward in perfect step with one another.

Jill looked from side to side smiling at her friends as she walked down the aisle. The pews were decorated with paper chains that children had made and the altar was a field of flowers.

Jill smiled at her mother—seated next to Jill's aunt in the first pew—hoping for some recognition. Her mother, wearing a shapeless purple dress, regarded Jill without expression.

The ceremony was traditional. Elizabeth, a college friend and an Episcopal priest, read from Corinthians that the greatest gift is love. Tom and Jill began their exchange of vows in steady, clear voices.

At "to have and to hold," Jill became aware that something was wrong. She heard a slight commotion behind her and saw a change in Elizabeth's expression. Jill's hands began to sweat.

"From this day forward, for better or for worse," Elizabeth read.

"From this day forward," Jill answered, feeling a prickly sensation in the back of her neck.

At first the sounds coming from behind her were just senseless noise. Then her mind grasped the words that the frantic woman was shouting. A fraction of a second later, she realized the shouting woman was her mother.

"That's not my daughter up there! The bride is not my daughter. She's an imposter!"

Jill whirled around to see her mother in lavender dress and corsage standing in the pew pointing at her, while a churchful of aghast people stared.

"Someone please help me," the agitated woman shouted. "The bride isn't my daughter. I am at the wrong wedding. Please someone take me to the right wedding."

Jill's mind went numb. The silence around her was long and horrible. Jill's father and aunt tried to escort her mother from the pew, but she resisted, grabbing on to the people around her and pleading: "Please, I have got to get to my daughter's wedding. Please take me to the right wedding."

Jill turned, put her flowers on the altar steps, then turned back, picked up her long skirt, and walked over to her mother.

"I'll help you get to your daughter's wedding," Jill said, taking her mother's arm.

Her mother's eyes, brimming with insanity, focused on

Jill. "Oh, thank you," she said. "I couldn't miss my daughter's wedding."

Tom joined Jill and the other family members as they walked the agitated woman out of the church.

Outside, Jill's aunt took her sister from her. Jill's father looked at her brokenheartedly and Jill patted him on the arm as if to say: We've been through worse, you and I. Jill stared at a small house across the street and wished she could disappear inside it.

Tom insisted that Jill look at him. He took her in his arms and told her she was the bravest, most wonderful woman he had ever known, and that he loved her more than ever. Then they went back inside the church and got married.

Tom's parents did not know what to say to Jill at the reception, and she could not look them in the eye. To make matters even more embarrassing for Jill—if that were possible—an unusually large number of the guests, no doubt as a result of the preceding tension, managed to get falling-down drunk at the reception.

Although Tom's parents never mentioned the wedding to her, she felt diminished in their eyes by the fiasco. She found it impossible to believe that after seeing such a public display of her family's situation, Tom's parents did not wish he had married another woman. It would be a relief to Jill to move into Dora's house.

The phone rang as Jill was trying to get the kitchen completely spotless before Ben and Peggy returned from the store. On the first ring, Jill knew intuitively that the call was the one she had been waiting for—the phone call that would give her the results of her amniocentesis, the test that would tell her whether her baby was normal or whether there was something hideously wrong.

Feeling her hands shake, Jill answered the phone. The caller identified herself as the receptionist of Jill's New York gynecologist and said the doctor would like to speak to Jill.

In the terrible void between hearing the receptionist's voice and the doctor's, Jill's life appeared before her as a collection of unhealthy choices. She did not jog. She was an exercise school dropout. She ate McDonald's cheeseburgers and glazed donuts. She drank, took too many aspirins, and swilled down coffee by the gallons. Had she done something that would hurt the baby in those first undetected weeks of her pregnancy? She should never have waited this long to have a baby. She was too old. Her system was falling apart.

"Jill, I have good news," the doctor said.

Jill sank back against the kitchen wall. Thank you, God, thank you.

"There are no abnormalities. Everything checks out okay. Would you like to know the baby's sex?"

"No. I mean yes. Yes, I would." Jill's heart danced. She was a winner.

"It's a boy," he said matter-of-factly.

Jill hung up feeling a hundred pounds lighter. She could have floated up to the ceiling and stayed there all day.

Tom and Jill celebrated all week. On Saturday they moved into Dora's house. It was the easiest move Jill had ever made. All they had to carry were their suitcases and a roaster pan full of baked ham and beans, compliments of Peggy. The rest of their belongings were on a moving truck careening recklessly—Jill imagined—across country.

Tom put down the suitcases on the veranda, opened

the front door, picked up a giggling Jill and carried her across the threshold.

Jill, held securely in her husband's arms, knowing her son was safe inside her, looked down the long hall with its elegant rooms off to each side and up the hand-carved staircase leading to those lovely rooms above and thought how crazy she was to have dreaded the move to Willowglen.

Chapter Three

JILL AWOKE BEFORE THE ALARM ON MONDAY MORNING, feeling like her old prepregnancy self. The nausea that had greeted her every morning of her pregnancy was gone, as was the ever-present exhaustion. She could not wait to get out of bed and start making the house her own.

Living with Tom in a cramped Manhattan apartment with temperamental plumbing, Jill had often fantasized about owning a wonderful house. In some fantasies, she got the house by writing a runaway bestseller. In other daydreams, the house was made possible by a winning sweepstakes entry. But never in her wildest dreams could she have envisioned inheriting a Greene and Greene mansion. She had to admit that the house considerably eased her unhappiness about having to leave New York.

Jill and Tom had not gotten around to doing any moving-in chores over the weekend. After two weeks with Tom's parents, having this enormous house all to themselves had seemed like a magical vacation—as if they were the only guests of a grand old resort.

The couple had explored every room in the house—

oohing and aahing at their good fortune. They walked hand in hand through the grounds and watched the sunset in each other's arms from the porch off their bedroom. They picnicked on the living room floor in front of a crackling fire and went to sleep by firelight in their bedroom. And, whatever resentment Jill had toward Tom because of the move to California had melted in a weekend of passion.

"How do I look?" Jill asked, posing theatrically in front of the house as Tom got in the rental car to leave for work on Monday morning. "Do you think this place is *me*?"

After Tom left, Jill returned to the kitchen for a second cup of decaffeinated coffee. After finishing the coffee, she lingered at the kitchen table awhile before realizing with a thud that she had no idea how to go about organizing such a big house. It would be useless to start in the kitchen, since none of her kitchen things had arrived. After rejecting the living room and other downstairs rooms as too intimidating a place to start, Jill headed upstairs to begin her work in the relative security of their bedroom.

Jill and Tom had chosen the first bedroom they had looked at for their own. Although all the bedrooms were lovely, this room had the advantage of adjoining the bathroom. In addition, the room had a northwest exposure, which would be good for sleeping late—Jill might as well take advantage of that in the five months left before the baby was born. The porch off the bedroom was perfect for afternoon sunbathing and evening sunset-watching. The most important factor in their selection of the bedroom, however, was that it was next to the little room where their baby would sleep—their little boy, Peter. She was leaning toward Peter today.

Tom's aunt Dora also must have considered this to be the best bedroom, Jill thought, as she turned into the lovely room. This had been Dora's bedroom, and it still contained her personal things.

Dora had slept in the single bed with the elegant inlaid-wood headboard that Jill was now using. Jill and Tom had tried sleeping together in the bed on Saturday night, but it had been so uncomfortable that Tom moved a second bed into the room on Sunday. Last night they had gone to sleep in their twin beds like a sensible married couple on a 1950s television show. Jill hoped that the king-size bed they had ordered from the Sealy outlet in Oakland would be delivered on time.

Jill made the beds so that she would have a smooth surface on which to sort Dora's clothes—and also, Jill thought, so that she would not be tempted to crawl back into bed before she got the job done. Finally, ready to face the task, Jill went to the closet and opened the door. The closet was the size of a small room and it was packed with racks and racks of Dora's clothes. Jill sighed. She was both awestruck at the sight of so many clothes in one woman's closet and overwhelmed by the enormity of the task ahead of her. She carried an armload of garments to the bed and was struck by how elegant and stylish Dora's clothes were. On top of the pile was an exquisite floor-length, slender, black evening gown. Jill picked up the gown and stared at the label—Givenchy, Paris. My God, Dora had bought this dress directly from the designer.

The gown was so classically styled that Jill had no idea how old it was. It could have been purchased in the last several years or it could have been thirty years old. Jill stared at the dress, trying to put it together with a seventy-two-year-old woman. How could she have possibly worn it?

Jill put the dress down carefully. The next item in the pile was a Chanel suit. No doubt, practically every woman over the age of twenty-five knew a Chanel suit when she saw one—the classically cut skirt, the collarless jacket, the leather piping. A suit like this would never go out of style.

Piled beneath the suit was a hand-tailored, burgundy silk blouse, and beneath that was a classic shirtwaist dress of emerald green silk. Jill's pulse quickened as she examined the clothes, and a delightful tingliness spread over her body. She ran her hands across the nubby wool of the Chanel suit and down the satin lining of the jacket. Being careful not to stain the fabric with the excited dampness of her hands, Jill brushed her fingers across the oriental silk of the burgundy blouse.

Feeling slightly flushed, she took off her sweater and her tee shirt with the logo of Haagen Dazs ice cream on it and put on the blouse. Although Jill was beginning to swell slightly from her pregnancy, she was still a slender woman. The blouse, however, was way too tight. Undaunted, she slipped off her jeans, removed the Chanel skirt from its hanger and slipped it over her head. That was as far as the skirt would go without a struggle. With a great deal of pulling and tugging, Jill managed to get the skirt bunched up around her waist, but the garment would go no further. Tom's seventy-two-year-old aunt had been built like a high-fashion model.

Jill tried to pull the long, narrow skirt back off. Somehow, as she was pulling the skirt over her head, she became trapped in the material. The waistband of the skirt had caught around her chest and the tapered narrow end of the skirt straightjacketed her arms above her head. As she tried to twist free, she became more entangled, the zipper of the skirt digging painfully into her flesh.

She felt as if she were going to suffocate, but that was absurd—no one ever suffocated trying to remove a too-small garment. She pulled and maneuvered. The skirt be-

came more twisted—the lining going one way and the skirt
another. She could not get enough air. *This is ludicrous,*
Jill kept telling herself as she felt progressively more entangled, more straightjacketed. She had somehow gotten
the back of the silk blouse over her head and the material
was now tight against her face like a plastic bag. Jill began
to panic. *Oh, no, please no. This is too absurd.*

Finally, the blouse ripped at the underarm seam, freeing
her to reach up and yank the material off her face and back
over her head. She took in great gulps of air. She was still
tangled in the garments, but at least she could breathe.
Then slowly, working like a contortionist, she managed to
rip enough seams to free herself from the clothes.

Jill's first sensation upon freeing herself was overwhelming relief, but then as she looked at the torn clothes
on the floor, she began to feel badly—and more than a
little stupid—for ruining them. Her mood subdued, she
put her tee shirt back on, then began carefully piling
Dora's clothes into the boxes she had gathered for the task.
As she worked, Jill noticed that Dora had no back-of-the-
closet outfits. Every garment that had belonged to Dora
Miles was of impeccable taste. All her clothes were classically styled, all bore the best labels, all were designed
for a tall, reed-thin woman who liked form-fitting clothes.
Any of the garments could have been worn comfortably
by a woman fifty years younger than Dora.

Jill worked efficiently until she came across a magnificent, royal blue Saint-Laurent evening gown. The gown
of raw silk almost seemed to beckon her to come inside.
She slipped off her tee shirt and carefully pulled the gown
over her head. Jill arranged the dress without attempting
to zip it, then studied her reflection in the mirror. She
looked smashing. The dress could easily be altered to fit
her, but where would she wear it? *My God, where had*

Dora worn it? And when? A strapless gown? Jill pictured Tom's parents and their homespun lives. She simply could not connect the Aunt Dora of these clothes to them or to this sleepy town or to the life of a woman in her seventies. Going through Dora's things was certainly proving to be more interesting than Jill would have ever imagined.

Jill put aside a few of the clothes for herself: a sequined jacket; a stunning oversize pullover that bore the label "Designed for Dora Miles by Antonia"; an English herringbone suit; a camel coat; and—after much deliberation—the Saint-Laurent gown. Jill would not want to offend Tom's father by grabbing too many of his sister's things for herself—especially since the clothes were going to charity.

After finishing the closet, Jill turned to Dora's bureaus. She was not the least bit tired. The picture of Dora that was emerging from sorting through her belongings was so intriguing that Jill found she was eager to delve further.

She attacked the bureaus with relish, filling box after box with form-fitting silk negligees and imported underwear. Dora's lingerie was so exquisite that the task of folding it and sorting it was pleasurable in itself. One bureau drawer contained only scarves. Although Jill almost never wore scarves, she found one long hand-painted scarf that was so beautiful she could not resist wrapping it around her neck. She put the jewelry, silver hairbrushes and other items of value into a box that would go to Tom's father.

At the bottom of the last drawer, under still more layers of lacy undergarments, Jill found a stack of yellowing envelopes tied together with a blue satin ribbon. She reached for the packet, her heartbeat picking up. Feeling both excited and a little ashamed of herself, she pulled a letter from the packet. To Jill's delight, the letter—handwritten on engraved stationery—was a love letter. It ended: *I wish you would reconsider my offer. Dora, you are the most desirable woman I have ever known.*

Jill looked at the postmark—1960. Dora was far from a young woman when the letter was written. Jill smiled. *Not bad, Dora. Not bad.*

Jill selected another letter at random. This one was postmarked 1932. It was from another man. Another man, some thirty years earlier, who found Dora Miles to be the most desirable woman in the world and who offered her everything. Jill had to admit to herself: She was impressed. She put the love letter back in its envelope and flipped through the other letters, stopping at one that carried the name of Maj. Benjamin Douglas in the top left-hand corner. The letter, dated 1943, was obviously written under wartime censorship. Tom's father was overseas but was not allowed to say exactly where he was. Jill scanned the letter, an eager eavesdropper to a far-off time when her father-in-law was a dashing young major.

Jill's eyes stopped dead in the middle of the page. Ben had written: "Oh, Dora, how I miss you! How I long to talk to you, to hear your laugh." Jill stopped reading. Ben had written to his *sister* that way? What about Peggy? Of course, she did not know what kind of letters he had written to his wife. But she did know that she felt distinctly uneasy. She admired Ben, as she supposed every one did. He was a man of integrity, of judiciousness, of apparent goodness. She did not want to know if there was anything—anything what?—about him. Jill put the letter back in the envelope, not wanting to continue her line of thinking. After all, what was so wrong with a man being close to his sister? Clearly, she was reading a letter from a more innocent time with sadly modern eyes.

Jill returned the letter to the packet and, with markedly less relish than before, pulled another from the pile. As she opened the letter—postmarked in 1940—a photo fluttered from inside onto her lap. Jill picked up the old photograph and looked at it. It was a picture of Dora—readily recognizable because of the vast number of photographs of her throughout the house—standing on the front lawn of her house holding an infant in her arms. Dora looked stunningly beautiful, wearing a simple dress with her dark hair pulled back tightly from her head. The infant, wearing an old-fashioned baby bonnet, smiled lopsidedly at the camera. Jill put the picture down and read the letter:

> Dear Dora,
>   My heart goes out to you in this, your hour of sorrow. What words can ease the pain you must feel at the loss of your baby boy, barely six months old. I weep with you. Your have my prayers and my deepest sympathy . . .

Jill reread the letter, stunned, her eyes stinging with tears. She had no idea. She did not know that Dora had lost a child. Without realizing that she was doing it, Jill placed a hand on her abdomen to check the safety of her own baby. The preciousness of the life inside her was overwhelming—so overwhelming that she could not bear the thought that babies can die.

Jill put the packet of letters into the box for Tom's father. She was quite tired and willing to rest.

That night, in the bed that had belonged to Dora Miles, Jill was racked by a vivid dream.

The room in her dream had a linoleum floor and an open window. There was a little girl in the room. She could not have been any older than two. Barely more than a baby. Her head, a mass of curls, bobbed as she played intently, lining up her dolls in a row of little doll chairs.

"Hat," the child said with a decided firmness of pronunciation as she arranged the bonnet of a doll. "Oh, nice! Nice hat."

Something outside the window caught the child's attention. "Oh, look, dolly! Bird," she said, pointing a dimpled arm toward the window. "See the bird."

Suddenly, the door burst open with a force that brought the occupants of the little room to a halt. The dolls' eyes widened in terror. A woman stood in the doorway. She was thin and tall, very tall, and she had no face.

The child froze. She knew. She knew why the lady had come. She glanced around desperately. There was no where to hide. Her dollies could not help her.

The very walls of the room undulated with fear. The little girl's heart began to hurl itself against her tiny chest.

"Please," the child pleaded, "please don't put me in *there*. I have been good."

The room spun as the toddler was jerked up by her small arm and yanked into that place. It was horrible and dark. The little girl pounded her tiny fists against the closet door, pleading, desperate to be let out. Finally, exhausted, she sank to the floor and in so doing realized that she could see through the crack at the bottom of the door. She could see part of the room. There was light and she could feel the air. She began to relax a little. Then she saw something coming toward her. It was a heavy blanket that was being stuffed against the bottom of the door. The blanket shut out all light and air.

Jill woke up drenched in sweat and gasping for breath. It was like before. Like the nightmares she had had before—the nightmares that had driven her to see Dr. Frank, the nightmares that Dr. Frank had driven away. They had been gone for ten years and now they were back.

Chapter Four

Jill, Jill
Jill the turd.
Your mom's a crazy
Looney Bird.

ONE OF THE MEAN OLDER BOYS STARTED THE CHANT. Then the other boys followed. Suddenly it seemed as if the whole playground had joined the chorus. Jill stood at the hopscotch court unable to move, blood pounding in her ears. Finally, hot tears clouding her vision, she ran through the jeering children and out of the playground. She raced home on instinct, the path completely obscured by her tears.

The phone was ringing when Jill got home. Her grandmother answered. It was the school, reporting that Jill had not returned to class after recess. Her grandmother stood, phone in hand, looking down at Jill. "I got sick," Jill murmured. "My stomach hurts."

Her grandmother put her to bed. Jill lay in the darkened bedroom, worrying that her teacher would hear about what happened on the playground and call her dad and tell him what happened. Jill would die if her dad found out what the kids had said. She would die of shame even if just her teacher heard about it. How could she face her teacher again?

But her dad! Her dad must not find out about today. Jill was so ashamed. Everything was all her fault. Her grandmother told her that her mother had never been sick until Jill was born. Jill had thought a lot about what she had done to make her mother sick. She figured out that she had been a bad baby, and a bad little girl, and that had made her mother sick.

Everything was all Jill's fault, but she couldn't bear for her father to know that.

The happiest Jill had ever been in her first eighteen years was when she left home for college. It was so good to get away and live with other girls—girls who had no idea of Jill's family history. It was wonderful, too, to date boys away from the watchful eyes of her grandmother.

Jill loved her dorm room. It was so airy. Her grandmother always kept the windows closed and the drapes drawn and the heat up at home. The overstuffed furniture that filled every room and all her grandmother's nicknacks had crowded in on Jill, making those airless rooms even hotter.

The world opened up for Jill that first year away, and it did not close in on her again until six years later. She was twenty-four and had just started working at Beckman Ink. She had never been happier. Then out of the blue she began to have terrible nightmares. No, nightmares was too mild a word to use to describe what happened to her. Those things were worse than nightmares. They were horrible, vivid, surreal experiences of being buried alive, locked up in dark and dangerous places, or being thrown into a foul pit of an insane asylum. As soon as she made an ally in any dream, the ally would metamorphose into an enemy. She would think that she had woken up from a terrible dream and then realize that she was still dreaming.

The next day she would be able to recall every detail of the dream. The horrifying images haunted her. Soon she was too terrified to sleep.

It made no sense. There was nothing that Jill could see in her life that would cause such dreams, especially that year. The dreams took a physical toll. She lost weight and more weight. Exhaustion remade her face. She was left without a single unjagged edge.

A number of her colleagues at Beckman Ink were seeing therapists that year, but—as Jill thought—her colleagues were sane. She felt that she could not dare inquire about getting help, because *she* would be locked up.

One day, wild from lack of sleep, Jill dozed at her desk. She immediately fell into a nightmare and then woke up screaming—to the astonishment of the only other person who happened to be in the office at the time. Unable to keep her secret any longer, Jill confided in her coworker—a woman Jill's own age. With the highest recommendation, the woman gave her the name of Dr. Lillian Frank.

Jill walked into Dr. Frank's cozy office, sat down in one of her green velvet chairs and responded to the sympathetic doctor by blurting out everything.

In the next few months, in that sunlit office, they went over and over the facts of Jill's life. Jill sat forward as she talked, her hands clenched in her lap. And, Dr. Frank's face—unable to remain expressionless—would register the pain of Jill's story.

They hammered away—doctor and patient—at the granite of Jill's burden, her guilt that she might have caused her mother's illness. They made strides, but the night-mares persisted. After Jill left, the psychiatrist would try to reason why the acute anxiety had manifested itself at this point in Jill's life, without an apparent trigger.

Think, Lillian Frank would say to Jill, *try to remember. Try to remember when you had that first dream. What day was it? What happened during that day?*

Jill could not remember. Her life seemed divided into before-the-dreams and since-the-dreams, but she still could not remember the last good day before the beginning of the bad ones.

Then one day her memory block crumbled, triggered perhaps by a word, a sound, a ray of light. She remembered. She had had the dream for the first time on the day after her birthday.

"How old," asked Dr. Frank, leaning forward in her chair, holding the missing piece to the puzzle in her hand, "was your mother when you were born?"

Twenty-four. On Jill's last birthday she had become the age her mother was when she gave birth to Jill—and the age her mother was when she began to go insane.

It was not surprising that this birthday was traumatic for Jill, the doctor explained, due to Jill's unconscious fear that what happened to her mother would happen to her. Moreover, the doctor said, Jill was now burdened by the additional guilt of having more years of sanity than her mother had been able to enjoy. Her nightmares were a manifestation of that fear and that guilt—fear that what had happened to her mother would happen to her and guilt that it had not.

An enormous burden had been lifted. There was an ex-planation for Jill's dreams that had to do with the world of reason. The disease was not incurable. The illness could be treated.

Jill had no more nightmares. Although she felt she could have ended her therapy right there, she continued to see Dr. Frank for three more years.

Jill sat alone in the living room of Dora's house, still shaken by the horrible dream of the night before. The nightmare was an isolated incident, she told herself, probably a result of her overactive pregnant hormones. But, what if the dream was not an isolated incident? What if the unbearable pattern of vivid nightmares that had driven her to see Dr. Frank was starting all over again?

No, that couldn't be it. She was overreacting to one bad dream. After all, she was pregnant. It was stressful moving, starting over in California. And, as happy as she was about the house, she had to admit that she was lonely. She missed Manhattan. It was so unearthly quiet here.

She would get busy, start the day, and not think any more about it. Jill got up from the overstuffed chair and put her exercise record for pregnant women on the stereo. A female voice pealed forth, sounding like a cross between a high school cheerleader and a marine drill instructor: "Knees, toes, tighten those rears. Careful now, no straining! Knees, toes, tighten those rears."

Jill was on the floor sweating through the leg lifts when she heard a noise over the sound of the record. She stopped exercising and listened, unable to make out what the sound was. She got up and turned down the volume on the stereo, the sweat from the workout glistening on her face. An animal? A cat? No, a baby. It sounded as if a baby were crying upstairs.

Jill walked out of the living room and into the hall. The noise was definitely coming from upstairs. She could swear it was a baby crying. Jill climbed the stairs slowly, stopping every few steps to listen.

The doors to all the upstairs rooms were open, except for the small room next to the master bedroom. Jill strode over to the doorway, took a deep breath and then pushed open the door with far more force than necessary. The room was empty except for Dora's sewing things, her hat boxes and other junk: the stuff they were going to get rid of this weekend so they could start turning the room into a nursery. Jill peered behind the boxes, but saw nothing.

The noise had stopped. Jill checked through the other rooms and the bathroom, but saw nothing out of place. She shrugged. *Hearing things. Two days alone and I'm already hearing things.* It probably was just a stray cat. They often sounded like babies.

Jill's stomach rumbled. To heck with the exercises. She had done enough for one day. She was starving. What was there to eat?

She took the back stairs to the kitchen—the straight, steep stairs without the architectural curves and fancy balusters, the stairs that many years ago had been for the servants. She negotiated the stairs carefully, holding on to the railing. A door at the bottom closed the staircase off from the kitchen.

Jill opened the door and nearly screamed. There was someone standing in her kitchen.

A startled girl of about fifteen stared back at Jill. A moment later, she said softly: "I came to call on you."

Jill's heart slowed to its normal beat. This was not Manhattan. This was the country. People actually dropped by here to visit newcomers.

"The door was open," the girl said timidly. "I knocked, but when you didn't answer, I came in calling for you. Dr. Douglas was my doctor."

Jill felt foolish. The noises she had been hearing must have come from this young girl.

"I'm terribly sorry," Jill said. "It's just that you startled me so."

The young girl nodded, her hands in the pockets of her cardigan sweater. She wore a simple, unstylish wool skirt that was too long for her and a sailor-type blouse under her sweater. She was a very pretty girl, though, Jill thought, with her light blue eyes and her straight blonde hair pulled into a pony tail.

"My name is Ellie Shaw," the girl said finally. "I live on Perris Street, in the house behind the drugstore. Dr. Douglas was my doctor from the time I was a baby."

"I am so glad you stopped by, but I'm afraid I'm kind of a mess," Jill said, looking down at her damp tee shirt and baggy sweatpants. "I was just doing some aerobics."

Ellie stared blankly at Jill. After a moment of awkward silence, Jill offered Ellie a seat on the sun porch. She joined her a few minutes later with a pitcher of milk and some Sara Lee coffee cake that Jill had been relieved to find in the refrigerator.

Uncertain of how to start a conversation with this very shy young girl, Jill asked her what perfume she was wearing.

"Evening in Paris," Ellie responded, seeming somewhat pleased at Jill's interest.

Jill smiled. What was the name of the perfume that all the girls had worn when she was Ellie's age? It smelled even worse than the stuff that Ellie was wearing. Intimate—that was it.

"You're having a baby, aren't you?" Ellie said, interrupting Jill's thoughts on perfume.

"Yes," Jill said, taking a quick glance at her stomach. "Does it show?"

Ellie nodded. "Do you want a boy or a girl?"

"I already know that it's going to be a boy."

"Oh, that's wonderful!" Ellie replied. "Sometimes people just have feelings about these things and the feelings are right."

Jill found Ellie's interpretation so charming that she did not want to correct her by offering the information that she had had amniocentesis. Ellie looked so sweet sitting in the morning sunlight that Jill had to resist reaching out to touch one of the blonde wisps of hair that floated against her face.

Ellie's shyness eased. She was full of a young girl's questions for Jill. Did Jill have a name picked out for the baby? Could she feel the baby inside her? Was she afraid?

Jill found herself pleased at the attention. Jill and Tom's concern over his father's health, the move from New York, and all the other changes of the last few months had overshadowed her happiness about being pregnant. As Jill answered Ellie's questions, her anxieties melted away, leaving only the excitement of having a baby.

When Ellie said she had to leave, Jill did not want her to go. She walked Ellie to the door and watched her ride off on a sturdy old bicycle. Then Jill turned back into the house, wishing she had thought to invite Ellie back.

The days improved. There were no other bad dreams. Jill and Tom bought two used cars—a late-model Olds for him and a blue Toyota for her. Jill splurged and hired an interior decorator from San Francisco. The decorator covered the living room sofas and chairs in a warm red fabric with a tiny floral design. She took down the overbearing picture of Dora from the niche over the fireplace and replaced it with a Japanese print. Jill bought some large ceramic ginger jars and placed them strategically around the room. The changes succeeded in making the room far more livable.

Jill and Tom finished clearing out most of Dora's personal things. They painted the baby's room yellow with white trim, and bought a crib, a changing table, a bureau, a toy chest and a rocking chair. Jill turned one of the spare bedrooms into an office for herself, setting up her desk and word processor beneath a window overlooking the front lawn.

Jill went to her new obstetrician, a bland professional who put her at ease. And, for the first time in her life, Jill forced herself to get plenty of exercise. She exercised to her record every morning and took a walk every afternoon.

Jill especially enjoyed walking in the downtown village. Although a few antique and country-trendy stores had opened to serve weekend tourists from the Bay Area, the little town of Willowglen essentially had not changed in forty years. In the center of town was the park with its bandstand, bronze cannon and willow trees. Next to the park was the combination historical society and public library, which was housed in an annex of the red brick fire department. Down the street, on the corner, stood the drugstore with its ornate Rexall sign. On the edge of downtown there was a gas station with skinny pumps and an ancient Coke machine.

One afternoon several weeks after Ellie's visit, Jill passed the young girl's house on one of her walks. On impulse, Jill decided to ring the bell. A round-faced Latin-looking woman answered the door. Jill introduced herself and explained that she was a friend of Ellie's. The woman, looking completely puzzled, replied, "Who did you say?" Jill repeated Ellie's name. The woman shook her head, saying there was no Ellie living there.

Jill stepped back and looked at the house. It *was* the house that Ellie had said was hers—directly behind the drugstore on Perris Street. Jill described Ellie to the woman, who listened attentively. Perhaps she lived next door. No, the woman replied, she could not think of anyone who looked like that. There were not even any high school kids living on the block.

Jill left, retracing her steps to the drugstore. Obviously, she had gotten confused somehow. Dime store? Could Ellie have said dime store, the house behind the dime store? Ellie had said Perris Street, she was certain of that, but where on Perris Street did she live? Jill fretted all the way back to the car. She hated losing phone numbers and getting addresses wrong. She hated not being able to contact someone she wanted to see. And she wanted to see Ellie again.

As Jill opened her car door, she realized that of course she had a way of finding out where Ellie lived. Tom's father was Ellie's doctor. She and Tom were going to dinner at his parents' house that evening—she could ask for Ellie's address then.

Ordinarily Peggy Douglas would never plan a dinner party on the spur of the moment. It took time to prepare for company—to check the specials at the Safeway, plan the menu, clean the house, pick the flowers, hang the guest towels, bake the pies, do up the bread.

But Ben had been feeling so much better lately. The color was back in his cheeks. He was sleeping less and eating more. Further, he was getting bored and restless and just plain tired of being treated like an invalid. So yesterday when, she and Ben had run into Ole Johnson at the hardware store—and Ben and Ole had been so glad to see each other—Peggy had just burst out and invited Ole and his wife for dinner tonight.

Too bad, Peggy had thought afterward, that you couldn't

invite the husband without the wife. Iris was a dried-up old prune of a busybody—head of the historical society. Lord, was she boring. So to sort of counterbalance Iris, Peggy also invited her good friend Lucille Banks, the former high school librarian, and the kids, Tommy and Jill. They all seemed glad to come, too.

Peggy got the rolls baked, the flowers picked, the house cleaned, the dinner made and her hair done all in one day. She was proud of herself. In fact, she felt great. Maybe she ought to do this spur-of-the-moment thing more often.

Tom helped himself to another serving of his mother's chicken and rice.

"My goodness, Jill, don't you ever feed my son?" Peggy good-naturedly jibed her daughter-in-law.

Jill glanced across the table at her husband. He really was eating as if he hadn't seen a square meal in weeks. "Tom can feed himself," she answered, realizing immediately that her response did not sound the way she had meant it to. Rather than flying out with the intended good humor, the remark landed on the table with a bitchy thud. Jill felt her cheeks redden while time slowed painfully. "One of your patients dropped by to see me, Ben," she said, moving quickly to change the subject.

Her father-in-law looked up, pleased.

Jill relaxed. She had moved gracefully from the impression she so feared that she might have given.

"A lovely young girl. Ellie Shaw."

Ben regarded Jill blankly. "Who?"

"Ellie Shaw. A cute little blonde. About fifteen."

Ben shook his head. "I can't place her."

"She said she lived on Perris Street behind the . . ."—Jill hesitated, remembering the wrong house—"the drugstore or the dime store."

Ben looked baffled.

"Shaw . . . Shaw," Ole said from his quiet end of the table, as if dusting off some odd bit of memory. "Wasn't that the name of the family on Perris Street who had that daughter who killed herself?"

"Dear," Ole's wife Iris said, as if addressing an old fool, "that was forty years ago." Dismissing her husband with a little flutter of the head, Iris Johnson suddenly brightened. "My goodness," she said in the direction of Lucille, "that was such a tradegy. That poor girl's mother! Do you remember that, Lucille?"

"I couldn't forget," the former high school librarian said with a palpable chill.

The lines in Ben's face seemed to deepen.

"I'll never forget the day they found her body," Iris said with relish. "I was getting my hair permed over at . . ."

"Honestly, Iris, that's ancient history," Peggy said, with undisguised irritation.

"Well!" Iris replied, obviously wounded. She picked up her fork and huffily returned to her dinner.

The ensuing silence was painful for Jill. All she had tried to do was make conversation, and look at the result: Her innocent remark had brought up something else; the conversation swerved in a different direction, careened out of control and now everyone was upset.

"Jill," Peggy said, seeming to sense Jill's misery, "I think it's wonderful that one of our young people came by to see you. You know, we"—Peggy made a small circle with her finger that seemed to include everyone at the table except Jill, Tom and Ben—"we still talk about the time in nineteen fifty-two when Mabel Fillmore's husband ran off with the high school cheerleader, but we don't know anything about today. Not even the names of the young people in town or what any of them are doing.''

''Can't get any young people to join the Elks,'' Ole added as he glanced hopefully in Tom's direction.

It's no wonder, Jill thought bitterly. She looked at Ben's ashen face and felt more tired than she could ever remember.

Chapter Five

TOM BEGAN TO APOLOGIZE AS SOON AS THEY DROVE AWAY. Except for the food, he admitted, it had been a pretty awful evening at his parents'—the atmosphere had been stifling, the conversation deadening.

"Every time I opened my mouth, I felt like I said something wrong," Jill said miserably. "I don't know what's wrong with me. I feel like I can't get anything right anymore—not people's names or where they live or anything."

"There's nothing wrong with you," Tom said, reaching across the seat to grab Jill's hand. "You're pregnant, that's all. Pregnant women just happen to be moody and forgetful. It goes with . . ."

"And that girl," Jill interrupted, ignoring Tom's assurances. "I was certain she told me her name was Ellie Shaw. But now I seem to have told your parents and their friends that I spent a morning chatting with a dead girl."

"Oh, Jill," Tom said, almost laughing, "so what if you got a name wrong? I do it all the time." He squeezed her hand. "Take it easy, will ya?"

Jill nodded. Tom was right. She was making too much of everything.

That night Jill dreamed that she was back at her elementary school being taunted by the mean boys again—except now the jeering children had been joined by Ellie Shaw and Iris Johnson. They all danced around Jill and pulled at her clothes, somehow forcing her to sink through the asphalt covering the playground. Down, down Jill went.

Jill awoke the next morning feeling drugged. She turned on the "Today" show while Tom was in the shower. A woman was telling the camera that her daughter committed suicide because she was terrified that she might kill her baby. Jill quickly turned the channel. A Viet Nam vet was holding his common-law wife and their five children hostage in a house in east Oakland. Jill snapped off the television.

Tom emerged from the shower glistening with good-morning cheer.

"You're so handsome," Jill said, her finger traveling around the curve of his bicep. "Stay home with me today. We'll stay in bed."

Tom laughed and kissed Jill on top of the head. He thought she was kidding.

Jill said good-by to Tom with a forced chipperness. No use acting like a cocker spaniel, she thought. Still, she could not remember a morning that being alone had made her feel so lonely. Turning the burner on full flame, she put on the teakettle, and then flipped on the radio. She was greeted with a fusillade of incomprehensible, grating music. Before she could turn the dial, the record ended and the disc jockey announced that the rock song he had just played was by the best-selling recording group in America. Jill had never heard of them. Nor had she heard of any of the groups or any of the records that the disc jockey said were coming up.

It had happened so fast. She was over the hill. The rock music that had been her music now belonged to people much younger. Heavens, she was old enough to be the mother of a teenager—and here she was having a baby. By the time her son was fifteen, she would be—oh, God, she would be fifty! Would he resent having a mother that old? Would she have the energy for a teenager when she was in her fifties? Oh, Lord, she hadn't thought of that one before.

Rotating the dial, Jill settled on a soothing "easy listening" station that she would have scoffed at a few years before. She made her tea and sipped it, wishing she had a job to go to like everyone else. Then she caught herself. She shook her head. What was wrong with her this morning? How many mornings of her work life—how many *Monday* mornings—had she wished she could stay home? Now that she could do anything she wanted with her days, she mourned her former rut.

On impulse she went to the phone and dialed the number of her old job. Her heartbeat quickened as she heard the phone ring on the other end. The phone was answered not by Marcie, the receptionist Jill knew, but by a young woman who responded to Jill's excited "Marcie?" with the news that Marcie no longer worked there. Then Marcie's replacement told Jill that the writers she had asked to speak to were all at lunch.

Marcie gone? Lunch? Jill thought, the thoughts bumping into each other. She hung up the phone, realizing that of course it was noon in New York. But Marcie gone? Suddenly her job seemed very remote. Her place had been taken by another person, just as Marcie's had. The job was moving along without her, moving along and away.

Jill hugged her arms to her chest. She wasn't going to mope around, wasting all this wonderful leisure time. She decided to bury herself in *Madame Bovary*. She had pulled the book from a shelf in Dora's library the day before and had spent a pleasant morning rereading the classic while curled up in a wicker chair on the porch off her bedroom.

She took her teacup and returned to the upstairs porch. *Madame Bovary*, however, was not on the little table next to the wicker chair where Jill had left it. She thought about the day before. She had definitely left the book face down on that little table—at least she was almost certain that she had.

She searched the sleeping porch, the bedroom and even the bathroom. She looked under the furniture, behind the bed, everywhere. Finally, after an hour's frustrating search, she found the book reshelved in the library. Had Tom turned suddenly tidy on her? Jill wondered, because she certainly had no recollection of putting the book away.

By this time, though, she no longer wanted to read. Her head was killing her. Would aspirin hurt the baby? She couldn't remember. Alcohol, yes. Cigarettes, yes. Coffee, possibly. But what about aspirin?

She ran her hands through her hair. What was wrong with her today?

She needed to get dressed and get out of the house. She went to her room, put on a pair of slacks, and then the fabulous hand-knit pullover that she had selected from among Dora's clothes. She had not worn the sweater before and she needed something to give her a lift.

Yes, she would go into town, walk around, maybe buy some lunch. She needed to be with people.

Jill had walked by the mechanical mannequins in the tailor shop window many times before. Tom had said the mannequins had been in the window for as long as he could remember and probably long before that. Today, however, the display caught her attention in a way that it never had previously. The mannequins must have been fifty years old, each connected by a thick lifeline to a socket in the rear wall of the display. They were dressed in turn-of-the-century garb: a father with slicked-down hair parted in the middle, a handlebar mustache and garters on his sleeves; a fat mother in an apron holding a rolling pin; a little girl with corkscrew curls and a little grey dog.

The heads of the mannequins moved from side to side while their enormous mechanical eyeballs rolled up and down. Their expressions fascinated Jill in a creepy side-show sort of way: see the mechanical family in their own little home, just twenty-five cents. Jill wanted to break away, but those mechanical eyes held on to her.

Finally the tailor came out of his shop. He said he had noticed her standing there for a long time and wondered if she wanted something. Jill gave him a weak smile. She started to say how interesting she thought his mannequins were, but then stopped herself. That wasn't the truth. His mannequins weren't interesting. They were odd. And, Jill realized, she was acting odd herself, very odd.

She told the tailor she was merely looking at his display, and then she turned and walked quickly away. She walked with her head down until she came to a cafe with a faded picture of a pastrami sandwich in the window. Maybe she needed something to eat. Maybe that was all that was wrong with her.

She went inside, sat at the counter, and ordered a mono-chromatic meal of grilled cheese on white bread, cottage cheese and milk. As she waited for her food, Jill had the sudden uncomfortable feeling that she was being watched. Glancing around cautiously, she saw that, sitting several empty seats away from her, a powerfully built, somewhat older man was quite openly staring at her.

Jill quickly turned away from his stare, her face hardening into the determined blankness of a woman accustomed to life in New York City.

"Forgive me, I realize I have been staring," the man said in a rich, almost theatrical voice. "It's your sweater. I did not think there was another one like it."

Jill glanced at her sweater and then at the speaker. He was a sun-creased, ruggedly attractive man who looked to be a virile sixty.

"I had it made for a friend," he continued. "From my own design. It's rather . . . rather shocking to see another one just like it. May I ask where you got it?"

Jill acknowledged the speaker with a pleasant smile. "Oh, I didn't buy it. It belonged to my husband's aunt. Oh, my goodness . . ." Jill stammered, her cheeks reddening as she grasped the possibility, "was your friend Dora Miles?"

He looked at Jill for a moment without speaking, his eyes deadly cold.

"I take it, then," he said slowly, the creases in his face seeming to deepen, "that I must prepare myself for the repeated shock of seeing her clothes on another woman."

His hostility was unexpected and jolting. Jill did not know what to say. She lowered her eyes, blood rushing to her cheeks. Before she could think of a response, the man got up and put two dollars next to his coffee cup.

"Forgive me if I have offended you," he said, bowing slightly. Then he left the restaurant.

Taking a deep breath, Jill turned to look straight ahead. She noted vaguely that her sandwich was sitting on the warming counter. The waitress, however, did not see the sandwich because she was staring intently at Jill.

Jill did not want the sandwich. She wanted only to escape this wretched cafe, go home, and get out of the sweater.

By the time Jill got home, she was so worn out she could think only of going to bed. She undressed, climbed into her still unmade bed, and pulled the covers tightly around her as the images from the morning whirled in her exhausted mind. Finally she felt herself drifting off.

Then her mother was in the room with her. Not the real mother she had known, empty-eyed and sick, but the fantasy mother who had made her childhood bearable. She was so happy to see her again. Jill lay on the bed while her mother fussed around her. Her mother picked up the pajamas Tom had left on the floor earlier that morning and hung them up. She opened the windows to let in some fresh air. She fluffed the pillows behind Jill's head and straightened the blankets covering her. Then she sat on the bed next to Jill, humming softly.

She put her cool hands on Jill's hot forehead and smoothed Jill's hair away from her face. Jill felt wonderful.

"I'm having a baby," Jill said. "Did you know that?"

Her mother smiled broadly.

"A boy, and I'm going to name him Peter. . . ." She hesitated; maybe her mother would want her to name the baby for Jill's father. Oh, God, her father! Did her mother know about Daddy and that woman in Florida? She had better not mention her father.

Her mother looked so good. Not at all like the last time Jill had seen her—all shriveled and full of tubes. Jill was so relieved that she hadn't really died.

She felt so secure. She didn't have to think; she didn't have to worry. Her mother would take care of everything.

Her mother continued to hum softly as her light fingers caressed Jill's face and hair.

Jill felt a slight cramp in her leg and she shook it out. There was a lot of noise coming from outside. She listened. It was the trash truck making its weekly pickup. They had to pay extra for the truck to come all the way up to the house. Wait a minute! She was no longer asleep. Although her eyes were still closed, she was most definitely awake.

The hand continued to caress her face. She was not dreaming. She was awake! She heard the men outside talking about the Giants game *and* she heard someone breathing beside her. Oh, God, no, this wasn't a dream. She was awake. Fingers continued to caress her face. A stranger was sitting on the edge of her bed touching her. Jill had had friends in New York—women who woke up to find— no, but not here, this couldn't be happening to her here. Oh, please no! She could hear the trash truck. It was driving away! She had to act. She could no longer lie still. She couldn't think. Her terror was overwhelming. Screaming, she grabbed hold of the hand and thrust it from her face. Still screaming, she opened her eyes. There was no one there. Nothing.

Gasping for breath, Jill looked around the room. There was nothing there. Nothing, but the lingering scent of perfume.

Chapter Six

NORMALLY, TOM LOVED THE DRIVE HOME FROM TOWN IN the evening over the narrow country blacktop that cut through the mountains toward the sea. The road, which led off the main highway a few miles north of town, wound along vineyards and sheep-grazing meadows, by modest ranch houses and elegant redwood homes, past private roads that cut further into the mountains to reach secluded houses like his own.

Trees, heavily and eerily laden with moss, surrounded and overhung the winding blacktop, creating a scene that even veterans of the passage found fantastic and enchanting. The route enveloped Tom in a profound sense of privacy, as if he were driving into some secret center of the world where only Jill and he existed.

On evenings when the full moon shining in the twilight added an iridescence to the moss-saturated trees, the fantastic effect was compounded. And Tom, reminded of Walt Disney films he had seen as a child, would half expect the trees to come to life and welcome him home with magic arms.

But tonight, the moon shining through the trees gave them a hideous cast, the curving blacktop was an impediment to his urgency, and the isolation of the route intensified his dread.

Ordinarily, Tom phoned Jill after lunch—to check in, to ask about the mail, to be refreshed by her voice. But today he hadn't had a moment's peace, what with patients stacked in the waiting room all day and two emergency sutures in the afternoon. By the time he had had an opportunity to call Jill, it was after five. The phone had rung and rung, and when Jill finally answered, Tom did not recognize her voice.

"What's wrong?" he gasped, fearing she had lost the baby.

Jill, barely able to speak, had answered that she had had an awful dream that she was not sure was a dream. She said the terror was unbearable and she could not make it go away. Yes, she had answered Tom, the baby was all right—but please just hurry home!

Every light in the house was on when Tom arrived. Both the stereo and the radio were playing loudly downstairs, and the sound of the television came from upstairs. Tom found Jill in front of the television in their bedroom staring at the six o'clock news.

"Thank God you're home," she said, turning off the set and falling into his arms.

"Are you all right, baby? Are you all right?" Tom whispered as he held her close to him.

"I don't know," Jill murmured. Breaking away from him, she sat on the bed.

"What happened?" he asked, sitting beside her, trying to sound calm.

Jill shook her head, as if trying to fathom what had happened herself. "I know it's not going to make much sense to you," she said softly. She told Tom about going to bed in the afternoon and dreaming her mother was in the room. Then she tried to convey to Tom the horror of realizing that she was not dreaming—that there really *was* someone in the room with her.

Tom's heartbeat quickened as he listened to Jill describe her experience, piece by graphic piece. He could feel her fear. Of course, the whole thing had been a dream, he told himself. Realistic nightmares were symptomatic of pregnancy; he knew that as a doctor. Yet, in a way that he could barely admit, Jill was scaring him.

"I got up," Jill was saying, "and your pajamas were hung up. *They were hung up, Tom.*"

"Jill, you know all this is a dream, don't you? That you hung up the pajamas yourself?"

"But that's just the point, Tom. I'm not sure."

"Of course it was a dream," he said, taking her in his arms. "Pregnant women are known for their spooky dreams. It's part of the heightened awareness of pregnancy—the hormonal changes—the natural anxiety that pregnant women have."

"I wish I could believe you," Jill said, pulling away. "It was so *real*, Tom. Oh, God, there must be something going wrong with my mind . . ."

"Jill, darling, there's *nothing* wrong with you. But I think maybe we should see your doctor tomorrow, talk all this over with him. I'll call him tonight."

Jill nodded. She had to find out.

Exhausted, Jill slept soundly that night, and when she awoke the next morning, the previous day seemed too nightmarishly unreal to have actually happened. She felt foolish for making such a fuss over a nightmare—and she knew it was just that, a nightmare—and foolish that Tom had disturbed her doctor at home over it. What had happened the day before, she decided as she showered, was that she had awakened frightened and then allowed the mood to overtake her completely. She shuddered, remembering the incident in the cafe. Who wouldn't have nightmares after an experience like that?

She felt a sudden flutter in her stomach, as if a butterfly were trapped inside. She clutched her abdomen with both hands. Could she have hurt the baby in some way by becoming so terrified? Was that why Tom was so insistent this morning that she keep the doctor's appointment he made?

Her doctor's office was located, as was the hospital where her baby would be born, in Santa Rosa, a city some twenty miles from their home. Dr. Sammons, her obstetrician, was so bland that between visits Jill could never remember what he looked like. But he had an air of competent professionalism that both Jill and her physician-husband found comforting.

Jill stared at the ceiling as Sammons examined her, anxiously wishing that the visit was over and that she was having breakfast in a charming cafe instead of lying on her back with her feet in stirrups. In the white-on-white world of the examining room, Jill felt remote from her terrified self of the previous day. Yet she could not completely push away the horror of the day before, nor her fears about what it all might mean.

After the examination, Jill dressed and then joined Tom in the obstetrician's personal office. "I feel so stupid," she whispered, as they took seats opposite Sammons's enormous desk.

Sammons walked briskly into the room and sat behind his desk. "Everything checks out," he said, scanning Jill's chart lying open on his desk. "As far as I can see, you are in perfect physical health."

Physical? Jill thought, growing alarmed.

The doctor told Jill that she could stand to gain a few pounds—information that would have ordinarily delighted her. Now, however, she leaned forward in her chair, wanting only to get to the point of her visit.

"I understand that you had quite a nightmare yesterday," Sammons said evenly, seeming to respond to Jill's anxious impatience.

Feeling nervous and speaking in a rush, Jill went quickly through the events of the previous day.

Sammons listened attentively. He appeared sympathetic, but unalarmed. Indeed, his expression seemed to indicate that there was a routine quality to Jill's story.

"This type of thing happens," he said when she had finished speaking. "Pregnancy is an intense time, probably the most intense time of a woman's life. Your hormonal level is dramatically increased and that *alone* is enough to play havoc with your emotions. And, dreams can be particularly vivid and disturbing during pregnancy. It is not at all uncommon for pregnant women to think that their dreams are real or to be confused about whether they are real. But, Jill, no matter how real a dream may seem—and I know yours seemed very real to you—they aren't real. So don't get carried away. Take it easy. Relax. You're doing just fine."

Tom squeezed Jill's knee, as if to say, "See, I told you, everything is okay."

Jill felt herself flooding with relief. She was fine. The baby was fine. These things happen.

Peggy chose a corner table in the soda fountain in the rear of the Rexall drugstore. At one time there had been a real soda fountain in the Rexall—a long marble counter that stretched across one side of the drugstore—but it had been torn out to make more shelf space. Then, about five years ago, the druggist had installed a makeshift soda counter and some tables and chairs in the back of the store. It wasn't as nice as the original fountain, of course, but Peggy still enjoyed coming here. It was a comfortable place for a woman to have something to eat by herself. And Peggy loved the smell of the Rexall—the combination of magazines, candy and cosmetics, nuts and ice cream, and new things in plastic. At odd hours the back of the Rexall was also a place where you could usually be left alone.

Peggy ordered a dish of chocolate ice cream for lunch, figuring that ice cream probably had fewer calories than a hamburger, even if you took the top half of the bun off. And besides, ice cream appealed to her more right now. She walked a few feet to the magazine rack, picked up the latest issue of the *National Enquirer*, and returned to her seat, paying for the tabloid along with the ice cream.

Peggy had been a girl in this drugstore. She had come here every day after school with her friends. Ben had brought her here for a Coke on their first date. Her friends had been surprised when Ben took an interest in her, and more than a little jealous. Of course, as jealous as some of them had been that the handsome Ben Douglas wanted to date plain little Peggy, they were nowhere near as jealous of the relationship as Ben's sister had been. Peggy shuddered at the memory of Dora Douglas Miles. Even as a girl, Dora had been awful. She had let Peggy know right away that she did not think Peggy was good enough for Ben, and she had done her best to keep them apart. She never let up either, even after she had married that rich congressman. Finally, after Ben and Peggy had been mar-

ried for several years, Peggy put her foot down. She refused
to ever see Dora again. If Ben wanted to see her, which
of course he did, he could do it by himself, which he did.

Peggy watched her ice cream soften in its little metal
dish and thought about how much it rankled her that the
kids were living in Dora's house. Peggy had never even
seen Dora's house and even now she didn't have the stomach to go over there. If Jill and Tom had *just* gotten a
place in town, then it wouldn't be such a big deal for them
to drop over. Peggy felt bad about the way her dinner party
had gone the night before last. Jill had seemed so unhappy
when she left. And no wonder! All that Ellie Shaw business. Such a common name. Anywhere else those kinds
of things wouldn't mean anything—someone having the
same name as a deceased person—but here everything is
something to go on about. She had said as much to Ben
after everyone left, but he had not answered her. He had
just sat there, staring into space, his face the color of ash.

Peggy looked at her watch. She should go home. Maybe
she could get Ben to nap. He hadn't slept more than a few
hours since—since the night of the dinner party. Last night
and the night before, Ben had left their bed to sit alone in
the living room. All night, both nights, she had heard him
stirring around.

All the years of long hours and emergency calls in the
middle of the night, of never getting enough rest, and now
with all the time in the world, Ben could not sleep.

Jill was so relieved by her visit to the obstetrician that
she felt almost euphoric for days afterward. Her relief took
the form of a zest for life—a gusto for fresh air, for music,
for lovemaking, and particularly for food. For the first
time in her adult life, she was not afraid of gaining weight.
In the two weeks since the doctor had told her she could

stand to gain a few pounds, her midsection had spread remarkably. She was five months pregnant and for the first time, she looked it. None of her clothes fit. She had resorted to dressing in a pair of sweatpants and one of Tom's old sweaters.

"For God's sake, Jill, buy some maternity clothes," Tom had said. He might be worried about losing his svelte and stylish wife, Jill thought, but I feel great. Still, she conceded to herself, her wardrobe did limit the places she could go.

The next day, she drove to Santa Rosa and went shopping. At a maternity shop decorated with oriental rugs and tasteful art, Jill was greeted warmly by a saleswoman about her own age. "Oh, do look around," the saleswoman cooed. "I have some lovely things for the geriatric mom." When Jill looked taken aback, the saleswoman responded pleasantly: "My dear, you're right in vogue. Most of my moms are geriatric moms. Everyone our age is having a baby. And besides, the younger ones can't afford my clothes."

Mildly pleased to be in vogue and thoroughly enchanted by the shop's clothes, Jill bought a well-cut melon-colored chemise, a red corduroy jumper, a blue-jean jumper, an elegant and expensive blue print jersey, several pairs of slacks, some jeans, and an assortment of tops. When the saleswoman rang up the items, the total came to eight hundred dollars. Jill was aghast. What would Tom say? Then she realized something: for the first time in her adult life, she was buying clothes with money that she had not earned herself.

"You're probably going to be pregnant only once in your life," the saleswoman said, responding to Jill's hesitation. "You might as well make the most of it."

Right, Jill thought, remembering that she had made the

move to California for Tom. If they had stayed in New York, she would still be at her old job. Jill pushed her Visa card across the counter.

After leaving the maternity shop, Jill meandered past a record store. She had not bought any records or discs in a long time. Several of her books on pregnancy suggested that the expectant mother spend some time each day exposing her unborn child to soothing music. Oh, why not, Jill thought, as she pictured her baby snapping his tiny fingers to the music while snuggled in her womb.

Jill went inside the store, selecting several classical releases and a collection of old Peter, Paul and Mary songs. Tom would probably tease her about buying the Peter, Paul and Mary, but so what? It seemed like good wholesome music for the baby.

When she got home, Jill hung up her new clothes and then went downstairs to play the records she had bought. Tom had hooked up their stereo in the library, a much cozier room than the living room. Jill, however, found she preferred using the stereo in the living room that had belonged to Tom's aunt. The older stereo did not seem as fragile as Tom's complex CD system. More importantly, it was easier to play her exercise record in the living room where she had more space to bounce around.

Jill unwrapped one of the records and took it over to the elegant stereo cabinet. There was a record already on the turntable. Surprised, Jill looked at the label. It was an old recording of Marlene Dietrich. Jill picked up the heavy record and examined it. It was at least forty years old. Wondering where it had come from, Jill unlatched the record storage cabinet below the turntable. It was full of Dora's neatly filed records. Jill had never thought to look in the cabinet before. She was quite casual about her own records, leaving the ones she played leaning against the stereo.

Tom must have discovered the old records and played one. But when could he have done that? The record had not been on the stereo yesterday when she played her exercise record. He must have played it last night. But when last night? Jill shrugged. It wasn't important.

Idly curious, Jill put the Marlene Dietrich record back on the turntable to listen to it. Then she collapsed into a deep, cushioned chair. The smoky German voice was mesmerizing. Jill shut her eyes. Suddenly, a vivid scene appeared before her closed eyes. As clearly as if she were watching a movie, Jill saw the living room filled with people. Languid women in long slinky dresses puffed on cigarettes in holders while slick-haired men in dinner clothes whispered in their ears. A butler crossed the room carrying a silver tray full of drinks in leaded glasses while a black man with rimless eyeglasses played the piano. The air was thick with smoke and bygone elegance.

Jill abruptly opened her eyes. The record had finished playing. She shook her head slightly, feeling vaguely uneasy. The image before her eyes seconds ago had been so vivid that she felt she would never forget it. She must have dozed off, although she did not feel like she had been sleeping.

She got up from the soft chair and took the record off the turntable. She would clear out Dora's old records— give them to someone who would really appreciate them. Yet, even as she thought this, Jill was aware of the truth: The fewer of Dora's possessions around, the less Jill would feel like a trespasser in this house.

The days passed uneventfully. Jill researched the region's history and fashioned the information into an article on the wine country, which she eventually sold to an automobile club magazine. She read a great deal. She slept later and found that she watched a little more television. She also jumped for the telephone when it rang and watched for the mail truck.

That afternoon, the mailman rang the bell. Jill eagerly answered the door. The mailman handed her a stack of envelopes and a package, about the size of a shoe box, addressed to her.

Jill tossed the envelopes on the hall table and examined the package. It was from her father in Florida. Wondering what the occasion was, Jill carried the box into the library to open it. She ripped through the brown wrapping, lifted the lid of the box, and found a note lying on top of tissue paper.

> Dear Jill,
> I have been sorting through some things and thought you might like to have the enclosed.
> > Love, Dad

That's it? That's all I get in the way of a note from him? Jill thought, as she removed the tissue-paper layering. She uncovered a pair of scuffed and ancient-looking baby shoes that she slowly realized must have been her own. Putting them aside, she dug to the bottom of the box to a pile of photographs. Why was her father sending her this stuff now? Probably his new wife didn't want any relics from the past messing up their shiny new condominium in Florida. Jill reprimanded herself. Maybe these photos were a gift, free and clear.

Slowly, and almost fearfully, Jill picked up the first photograph. It was a picture of her father—so very young, much younger than Jill was now—stiffly standing in his military uniform beside the running board of an old car.

Jill put the picture down and picked up the next one. A young woman, in a short skirt that showed off her shapely legs, stood with one foot on the running board of the same car. Looking sassy and on the freshly scrubbed side of sexy, the young woman confronted the camera directly with impish good humor. She was a knockout and oh, so familiar looking—so familiar looking because she looked just like Jill. Finally, Jill grasped the obvious. It was her mother. She brushed her fingertips across the image—over the pretty face, down the lines of the body, and back, again and again—studying the photo so intently that she felt she could dissolve into it. When at last she put the photo down, she picked up a yellow newspaper clipping from the box and learned that her mother had once been the all-city high school debating champion.

The next item in the pile was a gag photo of her parents that depicted her father as a musclebound bather holding Jill's mother as a mermaid in his arms. Jill remembered looking at this photo for hours as a very small child. Vaguely at first, and then much more clearly, she remembered the early childhood fantasy that was nurtured by the gag photo: Her mother was not at home with Jill because she was a mermaid visiting her castle in the sea.

There were a lot of pictures of Jill as a baby. Even as an infant, Jill thought, she looked worried.

The final photo was of the three of them. Her father, looking tired and drawn, held a two-year-old Jill; standing a world apart from husband and child, arms hanging limply at her sides, terribly thin in an ill-fitting dress, hair straight and lank, looking blankly ahead, was the mother Jill remembered—already old, already insane. The dates on the backs of the pictures indicated that a mere three and a half years separated the sassy young woman on the running board of the car from the decaying woman with the two-year-old child.

Jill shivered as afternoon fog pushed against the library windows. She put the photos and the baby shoes back into the box. Then standing on a chair, she placed the box on as high a library shelf as she could reach and shoved it far to the back.

At six months pregnant, Jill could no longer sleep through the night without having to get up to go to the bathroom. Damn, she thought as she forced herself to get out of bed, hating to wake up, hating the feel of the cold floor against her feet. She groped for her slippers and shoved them on. She did not need to turn on the light. She had the route from the bed to the bathroom memorized.

The heavy door to the bathroom was shut. Jill found the handle, pulled the door open, and then shut it behind her. A night light illuminated the huge room with a comforting low-level glow. Jill sat on the toilet, with the cold seat sending shivers through her. Why me? she thought. Why not Tom? Why was it that women *always* had to carry the babies? She flushed the toilet and started toward the sink. She had nearly reached the sink when she glanced into the mirror and froze in such terror that she was incapable of screaming.

Reflected in the mirror, in place of Jill, was another woman, another woman in Jill's nightgown, in the exact spot where Jill was standing. Jill shut her eyes, her heart hammering furiously. She was seeing things in the eerie light. She was still half asleep. She told herself all she had to do was look in the mirror again to see that everything was really fine.

Jill rubbed her eyes and then opened them. The stranger

in the mirror looked back at her. Jill moved her hand. The action was reflected in the mirror. Jill squinted, hoping desperately that her own face would come into focus. The face in the mirror squinted, but that face did not belong to Jill. Terror rooted Jill to the spot and a moment later it blotted out all consciousness.

When she came to, everything was very bright. Tom was leaning over her, his black doctor-bag open at her side. Jill did not know why she was lying on the floor. "You fainted," Tom said, ashen, touching the painful spot on the side of her head.

Jill wanted only to sleep, but Tom made her get dressed. "I just fainted," she protested on learning that they were going to the hospital.

"You *just* banged your head on a porcelain sink and fainted onto a hard tile floor," Tom said.

Her o.b. met them at the hospital. He poked and probed, as did another doctor, but except for the huge egg on the side of her forehead, there appeared to be nothing wrong.

It was not until after the exam, after getting dressed again, when Jill went into a rest room and looked in the mirror, that she remembered.

Chapter Seven

JILL STARED INTO THE SINK, UNABLE TO MOVE. SHE HAD to get a grip on herself. She could not stay in the ladies' room of the hospital clutching a sink forever. But she was terrified that if she lifted her head, she would see that other face in the mirror instead of her own. Her knees were weak. The fear made her short of breath. If she did not calm down, she might faint again.

Finally, without looking up, Jill turned from the sink and hurried out of the rest room into the hospital corridor. It was hot and stuffy. She took a deep breath and then wished that she had not. The hall smelled like some basement cafeteria doused in antiseptic and serving food steamed beyond recognition. The relentlessness of the hospital lighting made ordinary objects look alien and made strange objects, such as an intravenous hookup parked in the hall, look terrifying.

Tom was leaning against a counter at the far end of the hall talking to Jill's obstetrician, who was smoking a cigarette. Tom seemed relaxed. They belong here, Jill thought. Tom is a part of this place.

Tom smiled when he saw Jill. She did not smile back. He put his arm around her and asked her how she was. She murmured that she was fine. He suggested they grab a bite to eat in the hospital cafeteria. Jill shook her head. She wanted to get out of there.

It was light when they got outside. In front of the hospital, Jill observed a man helping a woman, hugely pregnant and obviously in pain, out of a car. In just three months, Jill thought, looking at the imposing building, she would be having her baby in that place.

When they got inside the car, Tom again asked Jill how she was. "Fine," Jill repeated.

"But you don't seem fine," Tom persisted.

Jill looked down. Tears fell from her face onto her blouse. She had to tell someone.

"Oh, baby, what is it?" Tom asked, putting his arms around her.

Jill stared through the windshield at the parking lot. "It's happening to me," she said finally, her voice barely audible. "Like my mother. It's starting."

Tom pulled her closer to him. "What do you mean?" he asked gently.

Jill looked at her lap. "In the bathroom at home . . ." She let the words trail off. Tom waited patiently for her to continue. Finally, she said it: "When I looked in the mirror, I saw someone else's face instead of my own."

"I don't understand," Tom said, genuinely bewildered.

Jill tried to make Tom understand what she had experienced. Confused, Tom interrupted her story with questions: Could someone else have been in the room? Where was Jill standing? Who was the person she thought she saw? What did the person look like? Young? Old?

Jill tried to answer. She could remember the experience

but not the face exactly. It was a woman. Young, Jill thought.

Tom became less confused as Jill talked, certain he understood what had happened. It was all quite obvious, he said: Jill, once again, had been dreaming.

"No, I couldn't have been," she replied. "I went to the bathroom. I saw the face. I fainted. You found me. It wasn't a dream. Don't you understand? Don't you see what is happening to me?"

"Honey, listen to me," Tom said softly. "I know what you are afraid of, but you are not your mother. You are not crazy. It is possible you were sleepwalking last night, but more likely you had the dream during the night. Then, when you got up and looked in the mirror, you remembered the dream. Now you think that it really happened—fainting is a very disorienting experience."

Jill wanted to believe him.

When they got back to the house, Tom showered and dressed for work. Jill knew he had to go back to the hospital—had to drive that distance again to make rounds. But he didn't mention it. He would not want to make Jill feel even worse.

Jill knew that she should go back to bed and get some sleep. But she was afraid of dreaming. She knew she should have some breakfast, but the smell of the hospital lingered in her mind and she could not eat. She should, at least, sit down, but she could not relax. She had to keep moving. She made some decaffeinated coffee and said good-by to Tom, assuring him that she felt fine. Then, coffee cup in hand, she began to pace: down the long front hall, into the dining room, past the stained-glass windows, into the butler's pantry, through the kitchen, back into the hall, through the living room, out into the hall again, up and down.

Finally, she sat down in the large nineteenth-century oak chair that graced the hall. She rubbed her hands back and forth across the tops of her thighs. She should eat. She should get some sleep. Above, the hall lamps—the beautiful Japanese-lantern lamps—swayed under the restless creaking of the floorboards.

Was someone up there?

No, that wasn't possible. Tom had just been upstairs.

The refrigerator motor started and Jill jumped. Calm down, she told herself. This old house was the safest place she had ever lived. Who could even find this house? A few months out of New York and already she had lost her nerve.

Jill glanced at the second-floor landing. She would go upstairs, check around, reassure her jangled nerves and then—and then, what?

Jill climbed the stairs slowly, listening for sounds. The house was quiet again. She looked into the back bedrooms—the rooms that she and Tom had been meaning to do something with, but hadn't gotten around to—and into the room she used for an office. There was nothing unusual. She looked into the nursery—nothing. She checked their bedroom and the sun porch. Her heart began pounding in the bathroom when she saw that the shower curtain was tightly drawn. She hesitated a moment and then flung the shower curtain aside to reveal an empty tub.

In the last bedroom, Jill sat down on Dora's faded blue chaise lounge and tried to put the morning in perspective. Tom was right. She *had* to have been dreaming when she saw the face in the mirror. She had been under a lot of stress lately. There was the baby, and all the changes in her life. She didn't have her job any more. Her nearest friend was three thousand miles away. Still, she had no reason to fall apart. She was stronger than that. She was not going to let her imagination continue to run wild. She would have a beautiful baby boy soon, and, by God, she was going to be a good mother to him.

Suddenly, Jill was aware of a noise—an indistinct sound coming from somewhere nearby. As she listened, every nerve in her body on alert, the indistinct sound clarified, as if she had fine-tuned a station on the radio.

Someone was crying.

I am hearing things, Jill thought miserably. She put her hand on her forehead, feeling for a fever.

The crying did not stop. Someone was sobbing, soft *wrenching* little sobs, like the sobs a child would make . . . or a baby.

Jill pushed herself up, went into the hall and listened. The sound was coming from the nursery. There had to be a logical explanation. Jill remembered hearing crying coming from that room once before. But there had been nothing in the nursery that day and there would be nothing in there now.

Then what was she hearing? It had to be in her own head. She pressed her hands over her ears. Everything was silent. She released her hands and heard crying. She put her hands over her ears again, this time for longer. She heard nothing and thought: This sound will be gone when I drop my hands. *I order this house to be quiet!* When she dropped her hands, the crying was even more wrenching than before. Jill couldn't just stand there. She had to find out what was going on.

She opened the nursery door. The room was empty, except for the furniture they had bought for the baby—a cradle, a mobile above the cradle, a changing table and a little white chest of drawers with red and yellow knobs. The crying had stopped.

Jill walked into the room. For a moment everything seemed normal. Then she noticed the cradle. Under the mobile, which hung perfectly still, the cradle rocked by itself—rhythmically, back and forth. Jill watched in stunned disbelief as the cradle swayed on its own. The windows were shut. There was no breeze. Back and forth the cradle rocked. And then Jill realized that the room was not quiet. The crying had merely given way to a very soft cooing.

Jill backed away from the cradle until she bumped into the baby's chest of drawers. Leaning against the chest for support, Jill stared hypnotically at the rocking cradle, all emotion frozen within her.

This is not happening. It is not real. This is all in my mind. My God . . .

Jill dropped her head in her hands. She *was* losing her mind. What was the use of denying it? She was no longer . . .

"No!" Jill screamed, as if there were someone there to hear her, a fierce anger breaking through her numbness. "Do you hear me? Damn it! I am not my mother. I will not give in!"

She ran from the room, hurried down the stairs, grabbed her purse from the kitchen table and raced out of the house, slamming the door behind her. She stopped outside to catch her breath. The sun was shining. It was a beautiful day. She listened. She did not hear voices. The trees did not dance. Everything was normal.

With no idea where she was going, Jill got into the car and headed out the long driveway. She turned on the car radio. She understood everything the announcer was saying. She navigated perfectly the long winding private road that led from their house. Expertly, she drove the car into town. If she were crazy, she could not do these things, Jill told herself.

She needed to be around people. She thought of going to Tom's office but dismissed the idea, not knowing what she would say to him.

Ben and Peggy! She had not seen her in-laws in a couple of weeks. Peggy was always urging her to drop by. Well, she would do just that.

Peggy did not seem at all surprised by Jill's unannounced visit. She welcomed her warmly, saying, "Ben and I were just having coffee. Come join us."

Ben was sitting at the kitchen table reading the *Wall Street Journal* through half-glasses. He, too, seemed delighted to see Jill. He told Jill that he had been thinking of doing some handiwork around her place, since he knew how busy Tom was and how much work any old house could use. Jill accepted the offer enthusiastically. She would love to have company during the daytime!

Peggy put a plate of homemade breads and sweet rolls in front of Jill, who was suddenly ravenous. As Jill made small talk with Peggy and Ben, she drank in the sunny normality of their kitchen—the floral-printed wallpaper, the ceramic-bear cookie jar, the little terrycloth toaster cover, the shopping list stuck with a magnet to the refrigerator door.

"You know," Peggy said to Jill, "I'm not at all surprised that you dropped by today, because I dreamt about visiting you last night."

Jill smiled between bites of banana bread and Ben shook his head as if after all these years of marriage he still could not fathom his wife's logic.

"I dreamt you were staying in a resort," Peggy continued without prompting. "It had a wide veranda, lovely lawns. Lots of people were strolling around. You and I sat talking in these big old wicker chairs on the lawn. So there you have it," Peggy said, patting Jill's knee. "I dreamt about you and here you are. You know," she suddenly sighed, "I have been blessed or cursed—I don't know which—with these prophetic dreams all my life."

Jill repressed the urge to say, "But you came to visit me in your dream, not the other way around." After all, she thought, why risk offending Peggy?

Suddenly, Jill was seized by a very clear memory—a memory that explained the dream. There had been a wide veranda and wicker chairs on the lawn in front of the place where they had kept her mother. Sometimes they had visited with her mother outside—sitting on the wicker lawn chairs. And then, in a flash, Jill saw herself seated in her mother's chair.

Peggy continued chatting about something or other as Ben nodded looking over his half-glasses. The human activity in the kitchen continued as before, except that Jill had stopped. She wasn't in the picture any more. She wasn't connected to this sunny kitchen. She wasn't connected to anything. She made an appropriate remark from time to time and neither Peggy nor Ben seemed to notice that there was anything wrong with her, but she was not there.

Her mouth tasted of ash. Coming here had been a mistake. She might break down in front of them. She had to get out of here. But where would she go? She fought back tears. She had to get a grip on herself.

Chapter Eight

JILL TRIED TO MAKE HER VOICE SOUND NORMAL. SHE TOLD Ben and Peggy that it had been lovely visiting with them, but she really must be going. She could not think clearly anymore. The weight pressing against her chest was enormous. She did not know where she would go or what she would do. She knew only that she did not want to break down in her in-laws' kitchen.

Peggy insisted that Jill take a bag of homemade chocolate chip cookies with her. Jill murmured a thank-you—her hands shaking as she accepted the gift—and hurried out the door.

In the short time she had been at Peggy and Ben's, the morning had turned ugly. The sun had been obscured by clouds, and a bitter chill had overtaken the air. Jill rushed to her car, started the engine and turned the heater on full blast. She drove to the main highway and headed south with no idea where she was going.

A massive dark cloud hung over the road, threatening to close Jill in its grip forever. She tried to think, but she could not. After a while, she was only aware of the white line on the highway and the cloud that followed her.

She drove for an hour until she had to stop for gas in Berkeley. After buying the gas, Jill drove aimlessly through the streets, finally parking—for no better reason than that there was a space available.

Jill found that she was in front of a shopping center, one of those very modern arcades that offer espresso bars and kitchen boutiques in place of McDonald's and Sears. Although it was a weekday, the arcade was filled with shoppers and coffee drinkers.

Jill mingled with the shoppers, trying to act like one of them. She moved from store and store, looking indifferently at shiny kitchen pots, framed posters, ceramic jars and pastel jogging suits. Finally she came upon a shop that she hoped would interest her. It was called The Best and the Brightest, and it contained toys and games for children. When Jill went inside, she was approached by a saleswoman who asked what she would like to see. Jill thought for a moment.

"I would like a little book with pictures of animals in it."

The saleswoman looked slightly appalled. "What type of reading program is your child on?"

"My baby isn't born yet," Jill said, wondering why the saleswoman could not see the obvious.

"I can see that," the saleswoman said. "What I meant was, what kind of prenatal program are you on?"

When Jill professed complete ignorance, the saleswoman brought out a tape cassette and a box of flash cards. In a tone that implied that Jill was already negligent in the education of her child, the woman explained a system that supposedly would have Jill's baby reading by the time he was a year old.

"With diligent effort on your part, there is no reason why your child could not become a genius," the saleswoman concluded.

Jill suddenly felt too tired to speak. What could she say to this woman anyway? How could she explain the odds that were already stacking themselves up against her baby like so many bricks in a genetic prison?

Jill's silence seemed to cause the saleswoman to lose some of her sure footing. "Perhaps," she said somewhat condescendingly, "you might find something that you would like at the little teddy bear shop two stores down."

"That sounds nice," Jill murmured, grateful both for the exit and the suggestion of what to do next.

The recommended store was called Theodore R. Bear and Company, and it sold nothing but teddy bears. Jill went inside. A saleswoman stood behind the counter talking to a young man about a teddy bear that he had brought in for restoration. The pair spoke in a solicitous tone that suggested the stuffed animal would be conscious of whatever procedure it was to undergo. To Jill's relief, they paid no attention to her.

Jill toured the shop looking at each toy animal individually. Stacked on shelves and arranged on tables were fat bears, thin bears, bears in yellow rain slickers, bears in jogging suits, bears wearing glasses, and bears that cost more than three hundred dollars. In the end, one bear stood out from the crowd. It was an old-fashioned naked bear with rounded ears, a fat tummy, and an expression that hinted ever so faintly of compassion. Jill picked up the bear and pressed it to her stomach.

Do you like him, son? Would you like to play with him while the other babies are learning to read?

The price was a mere thirteen dollars. That cinched it. Jill carried the bear to the sales counter. The saleswoman turned away from the young man, took the bear from Jill as gently as if it were a newborn, and then noting Jill's stomach, cooed: "Looks like our bear will be having a little brother or sister soon. I'm sure you'll make Teddy a wonderful mommy."

The inanity of the saleswoman's remark hit a nerve, and Jill was surprised to find herself suddenly angry. "For heaven's sake, it's just a stuffed toy," she snapped before she could stop herself. Here she was, Jill fumed inwardly, terrified that she would not be able to take care of her own son; then on top of that she had to listen to some saleslady coo about what kind of maternal relationship Jill was going to have with a teddy bear!

The saleswoman stiffened, then exchanged a look with the young man before making a lot of noise putting the bear in a paper bag.

Jill found herself feeling much better. She knew how to fight back, and by God she would. She would fight off whatever was trying to overtake her—whatever inherited gene was trying to destroy her mind. She would take them all on: her mother, who refused to stay well for her; Peggy and her damned dream; the saleswoman with her horrible reading program; all of them.

Suddenly famished, Jill stopped in a restaurant called the Sunflower and ordered lunch. The restaurant was full of people who sat alone at tables reading or writing in little notebooks. Jill picked up a discarded newspaper called the *Berkeley Express* from an empty table and glanced through it while waiting for lunch.

In the back of the newspaper, squeezed between an ad for a dating service and a shoe store, was one for a women's health care center in Berkeley that listed psychological counseling for new and expectant mothers among its services. Jill read the ad again and again, each time daring to feel more hopeful. Feeling shaky, she took the news-paper to a pay phone in the back of the restaurant and dialed the center. She was told that there had been a can-cellation and that a therapist could see her at three-thirty that afternoon. Jill was overcome with relief.

She phoned Tom and told him that she had gone to Berkeley to shop and that she was fine—just fine. Then she sat around the Sunflower reading the *Express* and drinking herbal tea until it was time for her appointment.

She found the center easily. It was bright, modern, and nicely furnished. The receptionist's questions about insur-ance and the rather high prices alleviated Jill's fears that the clinic might not be run by responsible professionals.

Two other women were seated in the waiting room—a pregnant woman and her companion. The companion had her arms around the pregnant woman, who seemed on the verge of tears. Jill overheard the companion telling the pregnant woman, "Look, this baby is as much mine as it is yours. And I'm telling you everything will be okay."

Jill wished that she could approach the pregnant woman to ask her if pregnancy was as bad for her as it was for Jill. Did this woman suffer terrors that made her doubt her own sanity? Was it possible that what was happening to Jill happened to other pregnant women?

The receptionist emerged to usher Jill into an office where she was greeted by a pleasant-looking middle-aged woman with brown hair that was trying to get loose from a bun on top of her head. The woman introduced herself as Dr. Theresa Hoffman and asked Jill to call her Terry. Then she asked Jill why she had come to see her.

Awkwardly and with much difficulty, Jill told the ther-apist about getting up the night before and seeing that face in the mirror in place of her own. The therapist remained expressionless, but Jill could tell by the alertness of her posture that she was following Jill's story with unusual interest.

Jill explained what had happened earlier in the day—hearing the crying, seeing the cradle rock by itself. Then she told her about the dreams that had seemed so real. Finally, she told the therapist about her mother and the years of therapy with Dr. Frank.

When Jill finished, Terry Hoffman sighed deeply, as if Jill's story had tired her in some profound way. Then, seeming to gather her energy, she spoke to Jill, choosing her words carefully.

"Jill, you are not crazy, but you do seem to be terrified that your pregnancy will undo you in the way that you seem to feel your mother's undid her. I think that may have been what the face in the mirror was about. You're terrified that motherhood will turn you into a different person, as it seemed to have done to your mother. So in the night—when you were closest to your unconscious mind—your fears manifested themselves. You looked in the mirror and saw what you were afraid of—that you had changed into a different person."

Terry Hoffman paused, regarding Jill carefully. "Are you following me?" When Jill nodded, the therapist said, "I don't usually talk to clients in such a straightforward manner in our early sessions, but you already have a good deal of experience with therapy."

The therapist poured paper cups of water for Jill and herself from a stainless steel pitcher on her desk. "Many women have unusual things happen to them while they are pregnant," she continued. "You see, a baby is an intruder in your life. It threatens to take your life over and change it in a way that you can't control. So it's natural to feel hostility toward the unborn child. But, you see, our conscious minds won't let us accept the fact that we feel hostility toward an innocent baby, so that hostility manifests or expresses itself in other ways—nightmares, perhaps, or even hallucinations. In your case, with your background, the difficulties you are having are understandable.''

Jill said she would be able to accept completely what the therapist was saying if it were not for her mother-in-law's prophetic dream. When Terry Hoffman looked surprised, Jill told her about the dream.

"Don't you see, Jill?" the doctor responded. "You are looking for confirmation of your worst fears. This was Peggy's dream, not yours. And even if it were your dream, so what? Dreams are symbols of the unconscious, not foretellers of the future.''

A chime went off somewhere in Terry Hoffman's office and Jill realized that her appointment was over. The therapist, however, continued to regard Jill thoughtfully.

"Jill, I recommend that you get more counseling,'' she said finally. "You are under a *great* deal of stress.''

"Yes, doctor—Terry—I would like to continue seeing you.''

"Oh, I'm afraid I couldn't see you on a continuing basis. I am here just to do crisis counseling and make referrals, and I'm not taking any new patients privately. Besides,'' she smiled, "I think Berkeley is rather far for you to have to go to see a therapist.'' Hoffman consulted a small black book and wrote a name and number on a card. "I am giving you the name of someone who I think is quite good,'' she said, handing the card to Jill. "She's on staff at Napa State Hospital and she has a private practice.''

A *state* hospital, Jill thought, her heart sinking. After what they had been through with her mother, she could not believe that anyone connected with a state hospital would be any good.

By the time she reached her car, however, Jill's disappointment over not being able to see Terry Hoffman again had been replaced by profound and almost giddy relief. The doctor did not think Jill was crazy. She did not think that Jill was embarked on a hopeless descent into madness. Indeed, she said that given Jill's background, her experiences were understandable. A well-trained, nononsense professional like Terry Hoffman certainly would have never let Jill walk out the door if she thought she couldn't function in the world!

At first, Jill fully intended to follow up on the referral she had been given. However, the days following her visit to Terry Hoffman went so smoothly, were so blissfully normal, that Jill slipped away from any idea of calling the therapist at Napa State. She was fine, so why dredge up the past? Understanding the reasons behind her anxiety attacks—and that's all those terrifying experiences were—had ended them. Any doubts that she might have got pushed further and further down.

A week after the visit to Terry Hoffman, Tom's father telephoned Jill to say that he was ready to start on the work he had offered to do around their house. Jill welcomed his company. She welcomed her own future—after all, there was no turning back.

Chapter Nine

JILL WATCHED WITH PLEASURE AS BEN'S STEADY hands—with their graceful, precise fingers—carved an elegant porch post from an ordinary slab of wood. The hands of a surgeon, Jill thought, like Tom's. It interested Jill to see the ways in which Tom was a mixture of his parents. His lanky good looks and scientific mind were so like his father's, but he had his mother's eyes and her straightforward charm.

Ben had come by nearly every morning for the past month. He seemed to love working on the old house. He had replaced the screens, mended innumerable door hinges, repaired all the household locks and latches, painted the front porch, and was now replacing the broken posts on the front porch with ones he was carving to match the originals.

Having Ben's company during the day had changed Jill's life. She was no longer lonely. Although Ben was not a particularly talkative man—they would often pass time together in comfortable silence—when Ben felt like talking, he shared bits of his life with such eloquence that Jill was transported inside the memory. Often when he completed a story of his younger years, Jill would feel the ache of nostalgia as keenly as if the memory had been her own.

Although Jill had always admired Ben, as everyone did, during these mornings in her late pregnancy she had grown to love him like a father.

"Where did you learn to carve wood like that?" Jill asked as she watched Ben work from her vantage point on the front porch swing.

"My father," Ben said without looking up from his work. "He was a carpenter—a craftsman, really."

Jill was surprised. She told Ben she thought his father had been a banker.

"My stepfather was the banker. My natural father was a carpenter and," Ben said matter-of-factly, "a drunk."

Jill experienced the electric anticipation of a young person about to be granted access to the secret regions of a revered older person.

"He was a gentle drunk," Ben said, continuing to sculpt the wood, "the kind who would go to sleep quietly on a street corner. My mother, however, was not so gentle. She did not treat me badly, but she was horrible to my sister Dora."

Jill was surprised. She could not even imagine the glamorous Dora as a child, much less a sadly deprived child.

Ben stopped talking, completely absorbed in his work. Jill waited patiently, hoping Ben would continue with his story. When he did not, she leaned forward and gently urged him to tell her more.

When his father could no longer work, Ben said, his mother took a job as a bookkeeper with one of the largest wineries in the Sonoma Valley. Then she divorced him. It was quite a scandal for a small town. Apparently it was

one thing to have the town drunk for a husband and quite
another to divorce him because of it.

The situation was particularly hard on Dora. The little
girl desperately wanted to be accepted by the other children, but they treated her cruelly. The children teased Ben,
too, but Dora was always there to protect him. "She was
like a shield between me and the outside world," Ben told
Jill. "I would have done anything for her."

Ben told a chilling story about his mother's insensitivity
to Dora—a story that Jill, of all people, could empathize
with. One Easter, when the family was still together, Ben's
mother insisted they all attend church despite the fact that
Ben's father was drunk. Dora, knowing the ridicule she
was sure to face, pleaded to stay home. Her mother would
not permit it. In church, their father did the best he could,
but he hiccuped and sang too loudly. Dora's classmates
across the aisle snickered. Humiliated, Dora tried to leave
the pew, but her mother held her there, gripping her wrist
so tightly that it bruised.

When Ben and Dora were eleven and thirteen years
old, however, everything changed. Their mother remar-
ried and they moved twenty miles from Sonoma—where
they had always lived—to Willowglen. Their stepfather
was a respected man in the community and he loved his
new family.

Ben's life as a boy proceeded much as before, but
Dora's life was turned around and made wonderful. She
lived in a clean house where she was not ashamed to bring
her friends. She had pretty clothes. Most important of all,
she was accepted. Indeed, she was the most beautiful and
popular girl in town.

"There was a part of Dora, though, that was always
afraid that some of the old bad life might seep through the

hills from Sonoma and destroy her new life,'' Ben said. ''But it never did.''

Jill wanted to know more.

Ben said there wasn't much more. Dora married a wealthy, much older man. He died when Dora was still young, and she devoted the rest of her life to community service.

Later that morning, Jill came across Ben looking at a photograph of himself with his arms around Dora.

''I remember the day that picture was taken like it was yesterday,'' Ben said, showing Jill the photograph. ''I was home from my first year in college. I hadn't seen Dora in six months and we had so much to talk about.'' Then Ben shook his head and said, ''Jill, it all goes by so fast. One day you are running around with your whole life ahead of you and the next day you are an old duffer who can't believe how fast it all has gone by.''

Jill wanted to tell Ben how much he had come to mean to her, that she had decided to name her baby after him, but she felt awkward and tongue-tied. Then, Ben was on his way out the door, and the moment was gone.

Chapter Ten

USUALLY JILL WAS VERY DISAPPOINTED WHEN TOM COULD not make it home for dinner. But today when he phoned at five o'clock to say he was on the way to the hospital to assist in an emergency surgery, Jill felt relieved. It had been a long day—she had visited the obstetrician, gone shopping and cleaned the house—and she did not feel like cooking dinner.

Jill thought she would take a nice long shower, then heat a can of Campbell's Soup-for-One and eat it in front of the TV while watching the evening news. After the news she would climb into bed and read her paperback biography of Elizabeth Taylor without having to endure Tom's teasing about her choice of reading material.

Jill climbed into the tub—not an easy task for a woman seven months pregnant. Before turning on the shower, she checked to make sure the shower curtain was tightly drawn. She was far too bulky to be able to wipe up water from the bathroom floor.

Jill looked at her enormous belly under the spray. The water missed her legs entirely, running straight off her stomach to the tub floor. Would her body ever return to the way it was before? Where would all that flesh go after the baby was born? Would it just hang there like sagging elephant skin? The baby was kicking her so actively that he made her belly jump. It looked as if someone were poking a finger from inside a tightly inflated balloon. Just two months to go. Two months! It seemed like she would be this way forever.

Jill jerked her head to one side, suddenly aware of sounds coming from the bedroom. Footsteps. Tom? Was Tom home? No, it couldn't possibly be Tom. He was in surgery right now.

Her heart gave a sudden pounding thud as she heard what seemed to be the closet door being opened and shut. My God. There was someone in the bedroom. Had she left the front door unlocked? Think. Yes, she had! Oh, God, she had!

Jill moved away from the shower spray to hear more clearly. She was not imagining anything. Those were footsteps. Someone was walking around in her bedroom.

Maybe it was Tom. Maybe the surgery was cancelled. But Tom would never go this long without poking his head in the door to say he was home. Besides, even if the surgery were cancelled, he still could not get home this quickly.

To her horror, Jill remembered that the door between the bedroom and the bathroom was ajar. Whoever was in the house must know that someone was in the shower. *Please just take what you want and leave.*

Jill huddled against the shower wall, away from the spray, the pounding of her heart cutting short her breath.

The bathroom door creaked as it was pushed further ajar. Jill shut her eyes. Then she heard the footsteps miraculously turn away from the bathroom door, go through the bedroom and down the hall away from her.

Jill waited on adrenaline alert, listening for sounds of the intruder. Why hadn't she locked the front door? She was being robbed, she was sure of that. But she couldn't hear anything more. Was he gone? Or was he waiting for her?

She was shivering from fear and cold. How long had she waited without hearing anything? Ten minutes? Five? One minute? Was he outside the bathroom door this very minute waiting for her?

Jill waited until she could stand it no longer. He had to have left. Slowly and carefully she got out of the shower, leaving the water running. She grabbed a huge yellow towel from the rack—ridiculously remembering that she and Tom had stolen the towel from an overpriced Hilton hotel—and wrapped it around her.

Peering through the semi-open door into her bedroom, she could see no one. But she could see the telephone. The telephone with its magnificent fifty-foot cord. She tiptoed across the bedroom floor, picking up the phone as gingerly as if it were an ancient Greek vase. Carefully, she pulled the phone back into the bathroom with her, shut the door to the bedroom as quietly as possible and locked it. Then she went to the bathroom door which led to the hall and locked it.

She lifted the receiver. To Jill the dial tone sounded loud enough to be heard throughout the house. Her hands shook so badly that she could barely get the dial to make the circle up from zero. When the operator answered, Jill at first could not talk. Then, in a voice that she did not recognize as her own, she asked for the police. The operator put her on hold. It seemed like an eternity before she was finally connected to the police. She had to go through another switchboard before she finally got an officer on the line. Somehow Jill managed to get her voice to work; somehow she managed to tell the officer that intruders were in her house; somehow she managed to gasp *"Please hurry."* The officer took her name and address, and said that the police would be there in fifteen minutes.

Fifteen minutes! There was nothing for her to do but wait. She wedged herself into the far corner of the bathroom and, since she had no clock, she began to count silently: One thousand one. One thousand two. At ten thousand sixty, she started over. All her concentration, her entire being was focused on counting.

Her body suddenly convulsed with the recognition of footsteps on the stairs. He hadn't left. He was coming back for her. The footsteps grew louder. If only she had a gun. A gun? She had never used one in her life.

Jill looked at the door leading to the hall and watched in horror as the door handle turned against the lock.

She shoved her fist against her mouth to keep from screaming and bit hard into the flesh. The footsteps moved away from the hall door and around into the bedroom. Jill turned her eyes to the door leading to the bedroom and watched as that knob turned against its lock.

She was being circled like a helpless wounded bird, all thumping heart, while some cat took its time—a cat who would play with a bird until it died of fright.

A sharp pain shot through her abdomen. Jill grabbed hold of the sink to keep from falling. I can't be having the baby! No, not now. It can't be. Jill could barely breathe. She needed air. The bathroom walls seemed to be contracting toward her. She had to get out of there. She had to lie down.

Jill moved a few steps toward the bathroom door and then watched helplessly as the unscrewed doorknob came flying into the center of the bathroom. It would be only a matter of seconds before the door would be completely open.

In unreasoning terror, Jill climbed back into the bathtub. She closed the shower curtain, crouched against the wet tile wall away from the spraying water and waited. Minutes passed—a seeming eternity. The shower spray turned from warm to icy cold. Oh God, how much longer? Her heart was exploding, pounding blood into her ears. Her mind went blank.

Suddenly, she heard footsteps approaching her from the hall again. See the little birdy. See her heart burst.

He was making much more noise now. He was done playing. Jill covered her ears. Tom, Tom, why aren't you here?

The door burst open. Jill saw his silhouette through the shower curtain. He was standing in front of her, a gun in his hand.

So it is to be a gun. At least a gun and not a knife.

Jill shut her eyes and heard the shower curtain being ripped aside. It sounded like the tearing of her own flesh.

"Ma'am, are you all right?"

The voice was flat and even. Jill opened her eyes slowly. It took her a second to realize that it was a policeman who stood before her. Another policeman stood in the doorway. They had broken down the door between the hall and the bathroom.

The police officers helped her out of the bathtub and into the bedroom. Jill sat on the corner of the bed holding the yellow Hilton towel tightly around her. She told the police what happened. One officer searched the house while the other stayed with her. He asked if she needed to see a doctor. When Jill shook her head, he questioned her further about what had happened.

The second officer returned to the bedroom about fifteen minutes later. In a tone of voice that implied he doubted Jill's story, the officer reported that he had found no sign of disturbance.

No sign of disturbance? Jill wanted to say. How hard did you look? But she kept quiet.

The other officer pointed to the doorknob from the door to the bedroom that was lying in the middle of the bathroom floor. "There, that's a sign of disturbance," he said with an annoyance that made Jill like him.

The second officer nodded curtly and left the room saying he would dust for prints. Jill shivered, then looked down at her towel-wrapped body. For the first time since the police had arrived, Jill was conscious of the fact that she was not dressed. Before she could say anything, the officer with her said he would wait outside while she dressed.

Jill got dressed and brushed her hair. Being dressed made her feel less vulnerable and more in control. The police would find whoever had broken into her house and put him away.

She let the officer back in her room. He asked her a few more questions and told her to make a careful search of the house. "Take your time. If there are missing items, we want to make sure every single one is reported." He gave her some forms to return to the police station when she discovered whatever might be missing.

The second officer came back into the room with the bathroom doorknob in a plastic bag. Without ever looking at Jill, he told his partner that there appeared to be only one set of prints on the door handle. "Probably hers," he said. "The doorknob looks like it came off by itself. The pins were rusted clear through."

He took a sample of Jill's fingerprints, while the first

officer—seeming to dismiss what his partner had just said—told Jill: "I don't want to alarm you, but the intruder may come back. He may not have had enough time to do anything—or he may have only been checking out the situation."

He believes me, Jill thought almost gratefully.

"We would prefer not to leave you alone," the officer continued. "Is there anyone you can call to stay with you?"

Jill nodded, relieved at the suggestion. She certainly did not want to be alone. She telephoned her father-in-law and told him what had happened. Ben said that he would leave immediately.

Jill made coffee for the officers. They did not leave until Ben arrived.

As soon as Ben and Jill were alone, Jill threw her arms around her father-in-law and buried her face in the rough wool of his sweater. He held her in a fatherly way for a long time.

Then he went through the house checking the lock on every door and window with Jill close by his side. She could see how worried he was about her safety, and she understood that Ben—like Tom—expressed his fear in anger. He railed under his breath about windows that did not seem secure enough and about inadequate police patrolling. Finally, he said, "Jill, I don't know why we didn't think of this before, but tomorrow we are going to buy you a big guard dog—a well-trained Shepherd or a Doberman."

The idea made both of them relax. It was a perfect solution.

"Meanwhile, what we need is a great, roaring fire,"

Ben said as they walked arm in arm into the huge living room. Jill happily agreed, saying she would make them something to eat while he built the fire.

Jill went into the kitchen, turning on every possible light in the dark room—even the little light above the stove. She bustled around the kitchen, taking the kind of intense pleasure in ordinary activity that sometimes follows trauma. She selected from the refrigerator carefully. Everything looked so bright and tempting in the calm order of plastic containers. She felt the wood of the carving board as she sliced the cheese. She read the instructions on the cocoa can and measured the powder carefully into the pan of milk—instead of her usual method of tossing ingredients casually together.

Jill put everything on a tray—bread, cheese, apples, grapes, cookies, two mugs of hot cocoa. Balancing the tray carefully, she carried it out of the kitchen, down the hall and into the living room. Ben stood with his back to her, facing the fire he had built.

"Oh, Ben, it looks just magnificent," Jill said as she crossed the room toward him.

Ben turned around to face Jill, but when he saw her he looked startled. He shook his head and rubbed his eyes.

"Ben, what's wrong?" Jill asked, walking further into the room.

"What do you want?" Ben asked. His voice was shaking.

With a sickening lunge of her stomach, Jill saw that Ben was terrified. His face had completely drained of blood and his body seemed immobilized with fright.

At once Jill understood. He was behind her. The intruder was behind her with his gun or his knife or his accomplices. In a moment he would speak. He would say what he wanted of them. He hadn't gone away. He had only been hiding. It was like a nightmare, but it was real. She wasn't going to wake up. It was really happening.

Jill's arms went limp. The heavy tray fell to the floor and Jill felt the sticky burning of hot chocolate splashing against her legs. She stood for a moment without moving and then she could wait no longer. She had to see him—had to stare him in the eye. She turned around.

There was no one there.

For a moment, she thought she might be dreaming. She shook her head. She could see clearly behind her into the hall and across to the dining room. There was no one there.

She turned back to face her father-in-law. He stood rigid with fear, his eyes locked on her face.

"Ben, my God, what is wrong?" Jill implored. She went toward him, and, as she did, he backed away from her.

"Your heart, Ben. Is it your heart?" She reached out her arm to touch him, to try and help him, and when she did, he screamed in a horror so visceral that Jill began to shake in fear.

"Ben, I don't know what is wrong. I don't know how to help you," Jill said, tears splashing down her cheeks, her heart pounding frantically. This can't be happening, she thought desperately.

Ben stared at her with hollow-eyed terror—as if *she* were the intruder, as if *she* were going to harm him.

Why didn't he recognize her?

She had to help him. She had to do something. She reached out toward him with both arms. Ben jerked away from her as if she were a wild animal on the attack, his arms flying protectively in front of him.

"Ben, Ben," Jill pleaded.

Suddenly he was clutching at his chest. Before Jill could react, his knees buckled. Jill rushed to support his fall. She went to the floor with him, cradling him in her arms. He died a moment later, his eyes open wide in terror.

Chapter Eleven

THEY BURIED BEN DOUGLAS IN THE RAIN, A SOFT PERSIS-
tent rain that fell from a heartwrenchingly grey sky. Following Ben's wishes, there was no funeral. A man of
science, Ben had no use in life—or in death—for what he
had called the emotional claptrap of religious ceremony.

Still, Peggy felt, a man—her husband—should not be
laid to rest without the comfort of a few words. So, she
had arranged for a brief graveside service.

The family made no announcement of the burial time.
Yet, long before the simple ceremony, the small-town
cemetery had begun filling with people. Friends clustered
around the gravesite murmuring that they could not believe Ben was gone. Ben's patients came too, but they
stood away from the gravesite so as not to bother the family.

The minister who presided was Ben's age and they had
fished together. Although the minister tried to speak
evenly, the pain of the loss of another old friend broke his
voice.

Tom, for the first time in his adult life, wept openly.

His father had been larger than life; his father could do everything; and his father had died without letting Tom in on the secret of his strength. Now Tom was in the front line. There was no one to turn to and everyone was turning to him. He was thirty-six years old and he felt like a boy. His father had died retaining all of his stature for himself.

Peggy, however, did not cry. She would have plenty of time for that later—alone, night after night, in the bed that she had shared with Ben Douglas for forty-five years.

You carry on, Peggy told herself. You *do*. She had, in some way, been prepared for this since Ben had complained of those first chest pains a year before. Yet nothing had prepared her for the monumental emptiness of waking up without him.

Jill did not cry either. She was numb, in so much pain that she could not even feel her pain. She had killed Ben. She was sure of that. That one policeman had been right: There was no one in her house that day. She had only *thought* there was someone in the house. She had called Ben, worrying him terribly. He had raced out of the house, probably leaving in the middle of dinner. He had driven all that way with his heart pounding, each hammer of fear tearing at the weak tissue of his heart. All that worry over Jill for nothing, and it had killed him. That look on his face when he died—it was an accusation.

Tom would find out some day what had really happened and he would leave her. But that didn't matter. Jill would deserve that and more.

Jill could not make out the words the minister was saying. She had not understood anything anyone had said to her all morning. But what did it matter? She was a hostage in a bad dream and she was never going to wake up, because this is what her life had become. She tried to remember her life before—their apartment in New York, her job, going places in taxicabs, having lunch with her friends. But remembering the way her life had been before didn't help anything. It was a different life—as severed from her as Ben was from the body they were putting in the ground.

Ben. Ben was in that stupid shiny box they were lowering into the ground. She had done that to him.

She wanted to go with him, find him, and beg his forgiveness for a thousand years. But she could not, because she had to think about her baby. She had to get him safely into the world. She didn't deserve to mother him, but she had to make sure that he would be born.

The mourners returned to Peggy's house after the burial. In perfect control of her emotions, Peggy greeted the visitors, chatting pleasantly with each one. Friends and neighbors arrived with covered dishes of food. Somehow these homemade pies, casseroles, and loaves of bread in their covered containers comforted Peggy in a way that words could not. She took each woman's dish and carried it to the dining room, lingering a moment to arrange it carefully on the table.

Clusters of people stood talking and eating and drinking throughout the house. Ole Johnson and a group of Ben's other old friends—men who had grown up with Ben, worked with him, hunted and fished with him—took over a corner of the living room where Peggy had set up a bar. Tom stood with these men and they told him stories— stories that began, "Did your dad ever tell you about the time we . . . ?" The stories took place on the high school football field, or during the war, or on fishing trips. All had happened a long time ago. As the men had more to drink, they began telling the stories over again, changing a detail here and there.

Tom listened to each story with an intensity that he did not quite understand. Was he planning to remember the stories so that he could tell them to his own son someday? Or was he trying to piece together from bits of old stories a clearer understanding of who his father had been?

While the men drank and reminisced, the women congregated in the kitchen to wash dishes and to talk. As soon as a plate or a glass was put down somewhere in the house, it would be whisked into the kitchen, washed, dried, and put back on the dining room sideboard to be used again. Sometimes people used three or four clean dishes, because they could not find a plate or a glass that they had only seconds before put down. But all of this dishwashing was fine with the women in the kitchen. It made them feel useful.

Jill was one of the group of dish dryers. She dried each plate methodically, running the towel across each surface again and again.

As they worked, the women spoke to Jill about having babies. They did not seem to notice that Jill did not speak in return. When one of the older women got too deeply into a story of blood and pain, one of the younger women would stop her, saying: "Oh, come off it, you'll scare Jill. It's not like that anymore, anyway." Then the younger woman would tell her own story, like how she had fallen in love with her obstetrician, told him so during the delivery, and then in total embarrassment had to change doctors. There were stories about children who had been lost for hours in shopping malls and husbands who had no understanding of how long it took stitches to heal.

As far as Jill was concerned, all the stories were interchangeable. They all had to do with blood and loss and pain. No story was less gentle than another.

* * *

Late in the evening, after everyone had left, Jill, Peggy and Tom relaxed together in the living room. Peggy allowed herself a drink for the first time that day. Tom, who had lost track of all he had drunk, had yet another scotch on the rocks.

Peggy and Tom talked about practical matters having to do with the will, the medical practice and other such things, while Jill listened. Then Peggy began talking about Ben's clothes and his books and whether Tom could use any of them. Suddenly, for the first time that day, she began to cry. Tom put his arms around her and held her while Jill touched Peggy's knee.

Peggy allowed herself to cry for a moment. Then she got a Kleenex from her pocket, dried her eyes, went to the kitchen and returned carrying plates of leftovers.

Finally, very late in the night, they went to bed: Peggy alone to the room she had shared with Ben, Jill and Tom to the guest room. Tom pulled out the couch that opened into a bed, and suddenly the toll of the day—the strain and the grief, and the drinking that had been used to ease the strain and the grief—hit him. He collapsed on the bed with his clothes still on, out cold.

Peggy, though, alone in her room, could not sleep. Neither could Jill.

Chapter Twelve

THE DAYS FOLLOWING BEN'S BURIAL WERE ACHINGLY long, the hours and minutes thickened by such a numbing heaviness that they seemed barely capable of passing at all.

Tom spent as much time as he could helping his mother complete the unfinished business of Ben's life. Peggy found a comforting sense of purpose in the work and great solace in her son's company. Although she had lost her husband, Peggy told herself, she was nevertheless a fortunate woman. Her son had come home, and soon she would have a grandchild.

Tom, however, could find no thoughts to comfort him. His burdens—the understandable needs of his mother, the increasing demands of his patients, the weight of his father's affairs—bore down oppressively on him. Exhaustion etched his face, weighted his limbs and deadened his mind.

Everything would have been bearable, though, had he not been so desperately worried about Jill. She seemed to be blaming herself for his father's death. Even worse, she was terrifyingly unable to express her grief or her guilt.

She was locked inside herself and he could not reach her. No matter what approach he tried, he could not get Jill to talk about what was going on inside her.

The baby kicked Jill constantly, as if, Jill thought, he were afraid that she might forget about him. In fact, it seemed to Jill that she had forgotten everything else—how to feel, what life was like before—everything but her baby's well-being. Although she no longer cared about eating, she ate for the baby. She got out of bed only because she thought she must move around for the baby's sake. She kept alive for the baby.

At night, Tom pleaded with her to tell him about her feelings. She didn't know how to tell him that she didn't feel anything anymore. People felt things. She wasn't a person anymore—just a container that held a baby.

Two weeks after Ben's death, Jill had an odd dream. She was standing on Main Street in the dream when she saw Ben leaning against a black 1930s sedan. She was so happy to see him that she ran to him. As she got closer, she saw that he was young—younger even than Tom was now. The sunlight was brilliant and Ben—in white pleated slacks with his strong arms folded across his chest—was heartbreaking in his youth and his good looks.

Ben smiled when he saw Jill and motioned her closer. Then, looking her directly in the eye, he said, "Be careful, kid." Before Jill had a chance to ask him what he meant, he walked away.

Jill's heart began to race. She had not told him.

"Ben, I'm sorry," she called after him. "Wait, please. I am so sorry."

But he did not hear her. He was gone.

It took Jill a long time to realize that Tom was holding

her, that the dream had ended and her wrenching sobs were real. She tried to tell Tom about the dream, but she was crying so hard that she could not.

Tom wanted to cry himself—not in grief, but in relief. At last the wall of pain that imprisoned Jill was crumbling.

Finally able to express her grief, Jill spent the better part of the following days crying. Slowly, Jill felt herself pulling out of the deepest sadness she could remember.

One afternoon, a week after the dream, Jill noticed that the house had become hot and stuffy. She drew back the curtains that had remained closed since Ben's death and saw that the weather had turned sunny and warm.

She opened the heavy double doors leading from the hall to the back porch. Shielding her eyes against the sun, she ventured onto the porch and out into the garden. She was amazed to see that the garden was alive with flowers. Neither Tom nor she had done anything to the garden other than to water it. They had never even gotten around to hiring a gardener. Yet, despite the lack of attention, their garden was in luxurious bloom.

Jill went into the house and came out carrying scissors and a basket. She snipped yellow and peach-colored roses, daisies and daffodils, irises and bluebells—all in faultless bloom—and put them into her basket. Then she went inside and searched until she found the perfect vase—an enormous glass bowl that had belonged to Dora.

Jill spent an hour arranging the flowers in a magnificent bouquet. Then she gave careful consideration to finding the most desirable spot to show off her creation. She finally settled on the dining room table.

When Tom called, he was delighted by how much better Jill sounded. She told him about the garden and her flower arranging. Her simple story elated him. It meant she really was pulling out of her depression.

"What do you say I try to get out of here early, stop by the store, pick up a couple of steaks and a bottle of wine, and you and I have a little candlelight dinner?" Tom asked expectantly.

"That would be wonderful," Jill replied. "Just wonderful.

For the first time since Ben's death, Jill felt happy. She took a shower, fixed her hair, put on her prettiest maternity dress, applied some makeup and even dabbed on a little perfume.

When Tom got home and saw Jill, he burst into an ear-to-ear grin. "You look so beautiful," he said to her, kissing her face, her hair.

"Come see my flower arrangement," she said, grabbing him by the hand. "I don't want to sound immodest, but I think you're going to be really impressed by my newfound talent."

She led him to the dining room. Then, demurely standing aside, she let him enter the room ahead of her.

Tom stood with his back to her for a moment without saying a word. When he turned around, Jill was astonished to see that he looked pale and drawn.

"I don't get it," he said simply.

Jill's eyes began to sting. "Don't you like it?" she said, deeply disappointed by his reaction.

"Is this a joke?"

"Is *what* a joke?" she replied, as she walked into the room to see what could possibly be the matter.

She stopped dead in her tracks, not believing the evidence before her eyes. The elegant vase she had placed on the table just a few hours before now contained a huge arrangement of dead flowers reeking the sickly odor of decay.

"I don't understand," Jill stammered. "I just picked them a few hours ago. It's not possible! How could they have died this quickly?"

"I don't know," Tom said, staring at the fetid arrangement, as if transfixed. As Jill regarded him desperately, he reached out his hand and touched what was left of a daisy.

"Was there . . . could there have been anything in the vase," he asked haltingly, "before you put the flowers in? I mean, some cleaning solution or . . ." His voice trailed off. He looked at the windows. Then his eyes traveled from the windows to the vase and back, as his mind frantically groped for some equation of sunlight and chemical that would explain the decomposing mess in front of them.

"No, no, nothing," she answered. She could feel herself shaking. *"Oh, Tom, what is going on?"*

Tom turned to look at Jill, his eyes searching her face.

"My God, Tom! You don't think *I* did this?" She was almost yelling. "Do you? *Do you?"*

Tom shook himself ever so slightly, as if he were trying to wake from a dream. Then he pulled Jill into his arms and buried his face in her hair.

"Of course not," he said. The truth was he did not know what to think.

Chapter Thirteen

SEVERAL DAYS AFTER THE BIZARRE INCIDENT WITH THE flowers, Tom and Jill began taking Lamaze classes. They practiced their breathing exercises at home with a stopwatch. They bought a car seat for the baby, a Snuggli carrier, and a baby swing that their childbirth teacher had recommended. Jill washed the baby's clothes in Dreft detergent and put them away in his bureau.

Indeed, everything the couple did that week had the air of logic, of normalcy, but it was just that, Jill thought—air. Although Tom was valiantly resisting the idea, their lives were no longer normal and had not been for a long time.

In Tom's determination to find out what could have possibly happened to her flowers, he had gone as far as seeking the advice of a UC–Berkeley botanist. But, Jill knew that neither Tom nor anyone else would be able to find a scientific explanation for what had happened to those flowers. No one, other than herself, had seen how fresh they were when she put them in the vase. Nothing could decompose that fast. She could not delude herself, and she did not know how much longer Tom would be able to delude himself.

Still, she was extremely touched by his determination to find a rational theory for what had happened. She could see how hard he was struggling to avoid the only possible explanation for those flowers: that she had done it herself, arranged a bunch of dead flowers in yet another moment of madness. And, she feared that when Tom stopped trying so hard, he would have to come to that conclusion.

Except that she hadn't done it. Those flowers *were* fresh and beautiful when she picked them that afternoon. She could not possibly have been so far from reality that she saw decay as vibrancy, that she smelled rot as fragrance, and that dead leaves felt alive and supple to her touch. It simply could not have happened. Oh, God, could it?

Jill hugged her abdomen. Thank God, the baby kicking inside her was a boy, a boy to break the link, end the awful cycle from mother to daughter.

She needed to rest. Her constant state of agitation could not be good for the baby. She lay on her bed—on her left side, as the doctor had ordered—placing pillows beneath her legs, beneath her belly, behind her back. But despite the array of pillows she could not get comfortable. The unusually warm weather for June added to her misery. At least, she had only three more weeks until the baby came. Three weeks. It seemed like a lifetime.

What was the use of lying here if she could not sleep? She would only think, and she did not want to think anymore. She pushed herself to a sitting position and got off the bed. She could watch television, but there was never anything tolerable on in the afternoon. She would go downstairs, pick out a new book to read.

As she reached the bottom of the stairs, she noticed a slight burning odor. Instinctively, she hurried to the kitchen to check the stove, but found nothing amiss. Turning back into the hall, she followed the vague scent down the corridor toward the living room.

For a millisecond, Jill was not sure what was out of place in the hallway. When it hit her, the realization was accompanied by a surge of adrenaline that jolted her like an electric current. The doors to the living room were closed! The heavy sliding doors—so heavy that Tom and Jill *never* shut them—were closed tightly in front of her.

Jill's mind raced. Had Tom? No, of course not; she was alone in the house and the sliding doors had been open earlier. As Jill stood transfixed in front of the closed doors, she slowly became aware that she could hear sounds coming from within the living room. Music. Solemn, heavy music. An organ was playing. A dirge . . .

Jill put her hands over her ears.

This is not happening. This is not real. This is a dream. There is nothing in that room. Nothing!

With frantic resolve, Jill grabbed the handle and tried to slide open the door. It would not budge. Using both hands, she was able to part the doors just far enough to peer into the room. There was nothing to see. The room was dark.

The deathly music was louder now, louder and more insistent. It pounded into her brain. She had to get inside that room. She had to stop that music.

Straining, putting all her strength into the effort, she managed to part the sliding doors far enough to squeeze through to the other side. The drapes had been drawn against the living room windows. The enormous room was oppressively warm and dark—dark, except for the eerie glow of candles flickering in the distance.

Jill stood absolutely still, her back against the doors, her eyes fixed on the far end of the room. There, in the candlelit shadows, a long black coffin lay on top of a draped platform.

Jill's heart pounded in her chest. It wasn't real. It was all a bad dream. She had to be dreaming. But, oh, God, why didn't she wake up?

Of course she knew what was in the coffin. *She* was in the coffin. In order to awake from this awful dream, she would have to go to the coffin, lift the lid, look inside.

Pushing against her dread, determined to force what *had* to be a dream to resolution, Jill crossed the room.

I will look inside. I will see myself, pale, unreal, dead. Then I will be awakened by my own screams.

The casket lay in front of her. The wood was dark and polished, so polished that she saw her own terrified reflection in it. She reached out her hand and felt the smooth wood, felt the cold brass handles.

See, it's not so bad. You can do it.

Her chest tight, barely able to breathe, she groped for the latch. All she had to do was look inside.

She released the coffin latch, lifted the lid and held it open. She looked straight ahead, staring at the white satin lining of the coffin lid for so long that its quilted pattern swam up in front of her eyes.

Now! Do it now and get it over with. Look!

She dropped her eyes. The face that stared back at her, grotesque and bloated, with open, unseeing eyes, was not her own. The face on the decomposing body belonged to her beloved Ben.

Jill screamed, again and again, her heart pounding as if it might explode. But she did not wake up. She felt herself starting to faint, felt the prickle in her head, the rushing in her ears, the nausea. She welcomed the loss of consciousness—but it was not to come. She remained standing, staring at what was once Ben. He lay there in front of her, his hands clasped on his chest—his beautiful, elegant hands now looking as if they were about to burst.

Jill let go of the casket lid. It slammed with a clamor that echoed in her skull. Holding her hands to her ears, she turned around and screamed once more. In front of her, directly in front of her, blocking her way, stood a black-veiled figure, draped in mourning clothes.

"Who are you?" Jill demanded, dropping her hands from her ears, screaming into the darkness of the veil.

The veil rustled slightly, but the figure did not move.

"What do you want from me?" Jill screamed desperately.

The figure did not move.

Hesitating no longer, Jill darted around the figure and, moving as fast as her pregnancy would allow, crossed the room and shoved her way through the sliding doors and into the hall. Her purse was on the hall table where she always left it. Without pausing to think, Jill grabbed her purse and ran outside to her car.

Frantically, she searched for her keys in her purse. When they did not turn up immediately, she dumped the purse upside down, emptying the contents on the hood of the car. She picked up the keys and, leaving everything else where it was, unlocked the car, got in, and started the engine. The contents of her purse flew off the hood as she raced down the hill without ever looking back.

As she navigated the winding road that led from their house onto the main highway, Jill tried to think. She knew she had to calm down. Her heart was pounding at an alarming rate. She rolled down the window and let the fresh air blow over her. Where was she going? Breathing in great gulps, she turned onto the highway leading into town. She would go to Tom's office. Tom would . . . Tom would what? What would she tell him? If she told him what had just happened—exactly as it happened—he would never believe her. No one would believe her. But she could take him to the house and show him . . . Oh, God, not to be alone in this any longer!

Jill braked for a red light at the intersection just north of town. Her eyes traveled to the Safeway parking lot. She watched the shoppers loading their cars. She saw them with their brown bags of groceries and with their plastic bags of groceries and knew—knew absolutely—that Tom would find nothing at home.

She could not tell Tom. After all, how much more could he take from her—how much before he gave up completely?

Ben's decomposing face swam up in front of her. Jill shuddered violently. It wasn't real. How could it have been real? Except that it had seemed as real as the light turning green in front of her.

Jill drove past Tom's office and past the town. Of course, she had been hallucinating. There was no other explanation. She had to figure out what to do next. She had to calm down, get in control before she saw anyone. But she did not want to be alone. She needed help.

Then she remembered Terry Hoffman. Jill was having a breakdown; Terry Hoffman was a psychologist. She had helped Jill before. Jill would go to her office, tell her what had happened, and Terry Hoffman would make sense of it.

Jill pulled onto the highway leading south into Berkeley and Oakland. Terry Hoffman would help her. She shut everything out of her mind—except finding her way to the Women's Clinic and Terry Hoffman.

She got caught in traffic on I-80 outside Berkeley. Once inside the city, however, she easily found her way to the clinic where three months before she had met with Terry

Hoffman. Jill pulled into a parking space right in front of the building, got out of the car, and climbed the few short steps to the front door of the clinic.

The glass door was locked. Jill could not believe it. She pulled on the door a second time. The clinic *had* to be open. Someone *had* to be inside. She pounded on the door with her fists until they ached. Finally, she noticed the time on the clock above the vacant reception desk—7:05 P.M. Daylight saving time and the brilliant June sun had conspired to make it seem much earlier. No one was inside. They had all gone home.

Jill sat on the steps, fighting back tears. She had to think. She had to keep control. If Terry Hoffman was listed in the telephone directory, Jill could call her at home.

Jill pulled herself up slowly and walked a half block to a telephone booth. To her immeasurable relief, she found both an intact telephone book and a listing for Theresa Hoffman. It was not until she picked up the receiver to make the call, however, that she realized she had no purse and no money.

Jill occasionally tossed odd change into the console of her car. Now she walked back to the car, praying to find a quarter among the pennies.

She found fifty-two cents among the crumpled gasoline charge slips, hairpins and loose sticks of gum. Then she returned to the phone booth and dialed Terry Hoffman's number. She got the doctor's answering service and was told that the doctor would call her back.

"I can't wait. It's an emergency," Jill pleaded.

The operator sighed and then asked Jill to hold the line. She held on for what seemed like a very long time. Just when she was certain that she had been disconnected, Terry Hoffman's voice came on the line.

Jill explained who she was and then said: "I *have* to see you, Dr. Hoffman. It can't wait."

Terry Hoffman was silent for a long moment. Finally she said that she had group therapy in her office from eight o'clock to nine-thirty. Then somewhat hesitantly she added that she could see Jill at nine-thirty, but didn't Jill think that was rather late?

Jill assured her that nine-thirty was fine. The doctor asked Jill what she would do until then.

"Have dinner somewhere," Jill lied. Even if she had had some money with her, she felt too queasy and full of heartburn to eat.

Terry Hoffman gave Jill directions to her office, which was about five miles away. Jill then called Tom. She reached him at the office after getting no answer at home. "Where are you?" he demanded, sounding anxious. "I've been calling home for two hours with no answer."

Jill took a deep breath and explained that she was in Berkeley and would be seeing Terry Hoffman, the psychologist, later that evening.

Tom was concerned and full of questions. Jill tried to sound nonchalant. The psychologist had an opening at nine-thirty and Jill had decided to take the appointment. It would do her good to talk to someone about how she had been feeling. She had come to Berkeley early because she felt like getting out of the house.

Tom said he was worried about her driving all the way home so late at night. Jill suggested meeting him at his mother's house, so they could drive the difficult part of the way home together. Tom took Terry Hoffman's phone number and then hesitantly hung up.

Jill felt relieved. Now all she had to do was find a place to wait out the two hours until her appointment. She got into the car and followed Terry Hoffman's directions to her office. When she reached the office, she drove past it, cruising aimlessly through traffic. A few blocks from the doctor's office, she chanced upon the brightly lit public library. She could easily kill a few hours in there.

As she pulled into a parking space, she noticed that her gas tank was nearly empty. On top of everything else, Jill thought with a shudder, she would have to borrow the money for gas from Terry Hoffman.

The library was open until nine o'clock. Never before had a downtown public library looked so good to Jill. After visiting the rest room, Jill made her way to the large periodical reading room. She pulled a *McCall's* magazine in a plastic cover from a magazine shelf and found a seat in the breeze of the large floor fan, which was circulating warm air through the room.

Across the table from Jill, a derelict read the *Wall Street Journal*. Next to him a young man with a pale, pimply complexion was intently studying the Bible. An old woman at the end of the table was furtively tearing coupons from the library's copy of the daily newspaper.

The detritus of society, Jill thought, surveying her tablemates. And I fit in perfectly—a hugely pregnant woman who sees and hears what is not there.

She tried to read an article titled, "Fitting Your New Baby Into Your Dual Career Lifestyle," but she could not concentrate on it. She traded the *McCall's* for a *New Yorker* and read a very long piece about sharks. The article engaged her attention, even though she did not feel very well. Her back hurt and there was a dull ache in the floor of her pelvis.

At least the time passed quickly. At a quarter to nine, Jill got up to replace the *New Yorker* with another magazine. As she stood in front of the shelf, trying to find another magazine that would interest her, she was seized with a contraction so sudden and severe that she had to grab onto the shelf for support. Jill tried to count the seconds to take her mind off the pain, but she could not concentrate on counting. The pain was like nothing she had ever experienced. Vaguely she was aware that warm water was gushing down her leg.

She felt a hand lightly touching her back.

"Are you all right?" a soft feminine voice asked.

Jill shook her head. The pain was too intense to allow her to speak. Finally, the contraction subsided and Jill turned around to face one of the librarians, a small, copper-haired young woman.

"My baby isn't due for another three weeks . . ."

The librarian waited for Jill to say something else, but Jill's mind was a blank. She heard the announcement that the library was closing in five minutes, then was seized by another contraction more severe than the first. Jill turned her back to the librarian and placed her head on her arms against the shelves. This time she was able to do her breathing exercises. They helped slightly, although not as much as the childbirth preparation class had led her to believe.

When the contraction subsided, Jill turned around to face the librarian, who had been joined by another librarian, an attractively dressed middle-aged woman. Except for the three of them, the room was empty.

Feeling wet, Jill glanced downward. She was standing in a pool of pinkish-red water.

"We'll call an ambulance," the older woman said.

"No, no, not an ambulance." Jill could not stand the thought of being put in an ambulance. "If you could just get me a taxi."

"I could drop you off at the emergency room," the young librarian offered. "I go by there on my way home."

Jill nodded gratefully at the young woman. The older librarian obviously did not approve of the idea, but when she tried to voice her objection, the younger librarian said, with surprising sharpness, "It will be all right, Virginia."

The young librarian maneuvered Jill outside and into a car. While driving, the young woman spoke to Jill in a soft, monotonous way, but her conversation floated by Jill without penetrating. Although Jill nodded occasionally out of politeness, all her concentration was focused on one concern: Had something gone wrong with her baby?

The county hospital was enormous—ten times the size of the modern suburban hospital where Jill had planned to have her baby. The librarian pulled into a parking space designated for emergencies and helped Jill inside.

The emergency room swarmed with people. Old women lay on the waiting-room benches. Mothers held yellow-complected, limp children in their arms. A man vomited into a wastepaper basket; another held a handkerchief over a bleeding arm.

When Tom had been head of the Sisters of Mercy Emergency Room, Jill had occasionally gone there to see him for one reason or another—but that was different. Then she was a well person who walked quickly past the human misery around her. Now she was a part of the misery, and she could not look away.

Jill and the librarian made their way to the front desk, where a nurse seemed to be performing her own version of triage. "Take a number," another nurse said in English and then in Spanish to the people crowded around the desk. But the first nurse did not seem to be following a system of numbers. In a few moments she picked Jill out of the crowd and Jill explained her symptoms.

"Hospital insurance?" the nurse asked.

"Yes."

"Name of the company and your number."

Jill hesitated.

"The number on your card," the nurse said.

"I have a card; but not with me. It's Blue Cross or Blue Shield."

The nurse asked for forty-five dollars. Jill explained that she did not have any money with her, but that she could indeed pay for the hospital services.

"Take a seat. We'll call you," the nurse said.

Jill looked over at the librarian, whose pale complexion had drained to a stark white.

"I'm afraid I need to leave," the librarian said, her voice high and anxious. "I'm feeling quite faint." Before Jill could think of what to say, the librarian had squeezed her hand and scurried out of the emergency room.

Feeling completely abandoned, Jill took a seat opposite a Hispanic woman who looked at least as pregnant as she did. The woman was surrounded by family. Her husband sat next to her holding a toddler on his lap. A small girl leaned against her mother's legs and stared up at Jill with huge brown eyes. An older woman sat on the other side of the pregnant woman holding her hand. An older man hovered nearby. Jill fought back the loneliness that was washing over her in waves. She wanted to call Tom, but she was afraid if she got up to look for a telephone she would miss her name being called. She was angry at herself for not thinking to ask the librarian to call Tom.

She wanted to cry. Instead she used the big clock on the wall to time her contractions. They were not as severe as the first ones. They came about four minutes apart and lasted about a minute. Water continued to leak out of her.

She was kept waiting only fifteen minutes. When her name was called, she was ushered into an examining room. She was told to keep her dress on but to take her panties and sandals off. The nurse helped her up onto the examining table and placed her feet into stirrups. Then a man in blue surgical clothes, who did not look old enough to be a doctor, came in the room. Without saying anything to Jill, the man inserted two rubber-gloved fingers into her vagina.

"Five," he said to the nurse. "Send her upstairs."

Before Jill could say anything, he left the room.

"Is everything all right?" Jill frantically asked the nurse. "He didn't say if everything was all right." Her words came out in a rush. "The baby is early. He was supposed to be born at St. Luke's in Santa Rosa. My doctor is Dr. Sammons. Who is going to call him? I need to reach my husband . . ."

"First, we'll go upstairs to O.B.," the nurse responded pleasantly. "The resident on duty will call your doctor. Everything seems to be fine with your baby. If there is any doubt, they'll hook you up to a fetal monitor."

"I would feel so much better if I could just call my husband right away," Jill said as the nurse helped her off the examining table.

"Upstairs," the nurse repeated. "You have plenty of time. There is plenty of time for your husband to get here."

Jill started to object, but her objection was cut off by a particularly fierce contraction. She leaned against the wall. The pain was horrible, but it took her mind off everything else—and in an odd way, Jill found relief in the pain.

"Pant, pant," the nurse said, as she made exaggerated panting noises like an exuberant exercise instructor on a morning television program.

When Jill's contraction subsided, the nurse led her out of the examining room to where an orderly—wearing the same surgical blues as the doctor who examined Jill—waited with a wheelchair.

My God, Jill thought, you can't tell the doctors from the orderlies in this place. Was that man who examined me even a doctor?

"Okay, we are going for a ride," the orderly said when Jill was seated in the wheelchair. He spoke as if Jill were a child on her way to a tonsillectomy.

The orderly pushed Jill into a huge elevator crowded with people, then wheeled her out on the tenth floor. The O.B. floor seemed only slightly less chaotic to Jill than the emergency room. People were crowded around the reception desk, elevators were opening and shutting, the loudspeaker was blaring. The orderly parked Jill and left without explaining what was going to happen next. Two men in lab coats, who did not seem old enough to be out of college, walked past.

"What a night!" one of them was saying.

"Must have been a bad night for TV nine months ago," Jill heard the other one say.

Nobody seemed to be paying any attention to Jill. She got up from the wheelchair, walked to the far end of the admitting desk and asked a woman in white if she could use the telephone.

"I'm sorry, you'll have to use the pay phone at the end of the hall," the nurse replied.

As if Jill were a tourist in a country where she did not speak the language, Jill said slowly and carefully: "I'm afraid I don't have any change."

Wordlessly, the nurse opened a drawer, fished through some paper clips, found a quarter, and handed it to Jill.

Holding the coin tightly in her hand, Jill made her way to the phone booth at the end of the hall. Just as she was about to enter the booth, another nurse caught up with her.

"What are you doing down here?" she demanded. "You should not have left your wheelchair."

"Look, I'm just going to call . . ." A contraction cut off Jill's sentence. Jill held on to the side of the phone booth.

"This is why we can't have women in labor strolling around the hospital," the nurse said softly. "Once you are admitted on this floor, you can make all the calls you want."

When Jill's contraction ended, the nurse took her by the waist and led her down the hall, around a corner, through another hall, and then into a hall where Jill was horrified to see four women in labor lying moaning on gurneys in the corridor. Jill could hear women screaming further in the distance. The nurse led Jill into an examining room.

"I'm sorry we haven't got a room for you just yet," the nurse said as she helped Jill out of her dress and into a hospital smock. "After the doctor examines you, we'll put you on a gurney and then into the first available labor room. I promise you won't have to wait long. It's just that it's a very busy night."

After Jill had changed into the smock, the nurse said, "Your jewelry. Let me have your jewelry for safekeeping."

It took Jill a moment to realize that she was wearing jewelry. The few things that she wore were like part of her. Then, slowly, Jill handed over her wedding ring, the small diamond ring that had been her mother's engagement ring, and the gold earrings Tom had given her on their first wedding anniversary. The nurse put the items in a manila envelope.

Jill tried to hide the fact that she was going to cry. The

loss of her jewelry was too much to bear. She felt as if the last vestiges of her identity had been stripped away. Now she was truly no one.

The nurse helped Jill onto the examining table and then left her alone in the room. Tears splashed down Jill's face. Where was her husband, her bag with her things in it, her doctor, her hospital, her life, her self? Her tears became sobs.

A county hospital! This was not the way having her baby was supposed to be. Nothing was the way it was supposed to be any more!

"Ohhh, what's the matter in here?"

Jill looked up to see that a dark-complected doctor, who spoke in the soft, lilting accent of India, had come into the room. Jill took a deep breath and then described the unexpected onset of her labor and her general predicament.

The doctor shook his head sympathetically.

"I will personally call your doctor and your husband, and see that you get the best care possible," he said.

Then he took Jill's medical history and asked her a number of questions about her labor. He seemed concerned about its rapid and early onset.

"Did anything unusual happen to you today or yesterday?" he asked. "Anything particularly stressful? Did you fall?"

Jill was jolted by the sudden image of Ben's bloated body inside the casket in her living room.

The doctor noticed the jolt and waited for Jill to explain.

"I had a nightmare this afternoon when I was napping," Jill said, recoiling at the memory. "A very vivid, almost real nightmare . . ." She completed the sentence in her mind: *so real that I ran screaming from the house,* so real that the pain of labor seems dreamlike in comparison.

The doctor listened without offering comment. Then he examined Jill thoroughly and gently. After the examination, he sat on a little stool next to Jill.

"You are having a faster labor than most first-time mothers, but that is not a problem. I would say we are looking at about four more hours until you deliver. That is plenty of time for your husband to get here and for us to confer with your doctor. The baby appears to be fine— as soon as we get you into a labor room we will hook you up to a fetal monitor just to be sure."

The doctor spoke carefully, giving each word a practiced uniformity in emphasis. "I am, however, a little concerned about you. You are showing signs of considerable stress. Your blood pressure is quite high. I am going to give you something to bring down your blood pressure and to relax you. I want you to relax and not worry. This may not be as comfortable as the hospital you were supposed to deliver in, but I can assure you we will care for you just as well."

The doctor ordered an injection for Jill, patted her arm, and left, telling her again not to worry. A few minutes later the nurse came, gave Jill the injection, and left the room, informing her that an orderly would soon bring a gurney for her.

With great difficulty, Jill got off the table, used the bathroom, and then picked up the quarter from the little table where she had placed it. She trusted the doctor to call Tom as he said he would, but she would feel better knowing absolutely that Tom was on his way.

She padded out of the room in her hospital slippers and turned in the direction that she thought led to the phone booth, following the path that she remembered. She wound up, however, in a corridor that looked just like the one with the telephone booth, except that it lacked the phone booth. She turned into another hallway and realized that she was completely lost.

She knew the drug she had been given was taking effect, because she felt confused in a floating sort of way. Walking, however, seemed to ease her contractions.

Suddenly Jill was confronted by a nurse who demanded to know why she was wandering around the halls. Jill tried to explain, but the nurse did not seem to pay attention. She grabbed Jill firmly by the waist and led her through a pair of swinging doors down another hall to where an empty gurney stood—all the while reciting to Jill why hospital regulations did not permit her to walk around alone.

The nurse helped Jill onto the gurney, instructing her to lie on her side.

"You'll be more comfortable on your side," the nurse explained as she put a pillow behind Jill's back. "Now," she added, "you stay right here. I'll get your chart and find out where you are supposed to be."

Jill was going to ask the nurse to call Tom, but before she had a chance to say anything a loudspeaker at the end of the hall blared, "Code Blue," followed by several names.

"Ohhh, I'm supposed to be getting off in five minutes," the nurse moaned as she rushed away. Jill knew that a Code Blue meant a critical emergency, but she did not want to think about the possibilities for critical emergencies in the O.B. ward.

At least, Jill thought, the corridor in which she was parked was quiet. Unlike the frantic activity she had seen elsewhere in the hospital, this corridor was completely calm. Before she got onto the gurney she noted that the doors leading off the hall were all closed and that the desk at the end of the hall was empty. She was the only person in the hall.

Her contractions were worse lying on the gurney than they had been—closer together and more insistent Still, she realized that she felt better lying on her side than she would on her back.

She felt drowsy between the contractions—no doubt because of the shot she had been given. Sometimes a contraction caught her off guard and then it was really horrible.

She had nothing to look at except the double doors of the elevator opposite her. They never opened.

Jill wondered when someone would come back for her. Still, if she had to wait on a gurney in the hall, she would rather be here than in that other hall with those women who were screaming for their mothers.

She had no idea how much time had passed. She counted during her contractions, but could not keep track of the time between them. Sometimes it felt like there was no time between them. No one ever told her it was going to hurt like this—*not like this*. Sweat poured from her face.

How long had she been left alone? Where was the doctor who promised her such good treatment? Why hadn't someone come? Should she try to get off the gurney and find someone?

Jill called out for a nurse, but her voice was dry and weak. Had they forgotten her? How could they forget a patient? What if her baby started to come? Just as she was gathering the breath to call out again, the doors behind her swung open. To her profound relief, Jill saw the white skirt of a nurse's uniform. Before Jill could maneuver her head around to see the rest of the person, the gurney started to move.

"Oh," Jill sighed deeply, as the nurse pushed the gurney across the hall to the elevator. "I thought I had been forgotten."

The nurse jabbed the elevator button and then quickly returned to her spot behind the gurney. Wordlessly, she pushed Jill into the elevator.

Jill put her hand on her stomach and said silently to her baby: We are on our way to a real room at last, my son. Daddy will be here any minute, and everything is going to be just fine.

After a slow start, the elevator lurched slowly down— and down.

"Say," Jill said pleasantly, "aren't all the labor rooms on the tenth floor?"

The nurse, who persisted in standing behind Jill's head where she could not see her, did not answer.

The elevator continued to descend.

"Where are the delivery rooms?" Jill asked. "The labor and the delivery rooms are near each other, aren't they?"

The nurse did not answer.

Jill craned her head to see where the elevator was headed. It had passed the first floor and was descending to B.1. Finally, the elevator stopped. The doors opened onto a deserted hallway.

This can't be right, Jill thought, as panic merged with the pain of labor.

Jill cleared her throat. Her mouth was so dry that it was difficult for her to speak.

"I think perhaps there has been a mistake," she said in a politely logical manner. "I don't think I'm supposed to be down here."

The nurse did not respond. She pushed Jill out of the elevator and down an empty hallway.

Oh, no, this isn't right. This is not right at all!

"Stop!" Jill demanded as she tried to raise herself up on the gurney. Then, as she was gathering the breath to cry out again, she was seized by a contraction so strong that it pushed the breath from her lungs. The pain was unbearable. Jill tried to pant. She tried to control her fear to make the pain bearable.

She was pushed into a cold, dark room.

Another contraction hit immediately after the previous one, then another and another pounded her down. The pain was insufferable and Jill was overcome with an uncontrollable urge to bear down.

A nurse would not bring her to the wrong place, Jill reasoned through her pain. She was in a hospital. There were lots of people around, professional people, medical people.

The lights came on so suddenly that Jill's eyes shut reflexively against the glare. When she opened her eyes, the first thing she noticed was the cement floor. It was crisscrossed with gutters.

Her urge to push was no longer controllable.

"The baby is coming; I can feel it," she called out to the nurse, who seemed to be opening and shutting drawers and moving gurneys around in a part of the room Jill could not see.

Her legs began to shake as her body was seized by a fierce nausea. She leaned over the side of the gurney and began to vomit violently. When the spasms subsided she wondered vaguely if the gutters were in the floor because women got sick in the delivery room. But that didn't make any sense. Why wasn't the nurse helping her? And where was the doctor?

She was freezing. It was so cold in this room.

"Get the doctor!" Jill screamed at the nurse as soon as her strength would permit her.

There was no response. Jill was certain, however, that there were other women in the room because she could hear the nurse moving gurneys.

"What kind of nurse are you?" Jill called out as she struggled onto her back from her side. She forced herself up on her elbows. It was then that she saw the slablike chrome tables. They had sinks on one end and scales hanging over them.

"Why have you brought me here?" Jill screamed. *"What is going . . ."*

An icy hand clamped over Jill's mouth. The nurse, her face covered by a surgical mask, peered down at Jill. Her eyes were deadly cold, maniacal.

Jill stared back, barely breathing, her body shaking out of control.

After a moment, the nurse lifted her hand from Jill's mouth and began roughly shoving her from the gurney onto the metal table. In unendurable pain, her mind frozen in terror, Jill did not resist. When the nurse was done shoving Jill onto the table, she pushed the gurney away.

Thrusting her head up, Jill saw that there was a woman lying on the table next to hers. Fighting against her pain, Jill lifted her head higher to see the woman more clearly.

But the person on the slab next to hers was not a woman. It was a man, naked and blue-skinned, with a hideous Y-shaped incision running down his body, and very obviously dead.

Crying out, Jill tried to push herself into a sitting position.

The nurse pushed Jill's shoulders back onto the slab and glared down at her.

"No, no, no," Jill whimpered, helpless, her body banging against the metal slab. "You're not here. You're not real. This isn't happening!"

The nurse walked to the other end of the slab. Pushing Jill's legs apart, she looked between them and then shook her head.

"What is it?" Jill cried before another contraction made speech impossible.

The nurse began rattling drawers, pulling out instruments and lining them up on the table.

This isn't happening. No! None of this real. This is all a hallucination, Jill thought desperately. Like before. It's some sort of horribly real dream. It's the shot they gave me. The drug is giving me this nightmare.

Except that this could not be a nightmare. The pain was too real. No longer seeming to have an origin, the pain enveloped her completely, stretching minutes and seconds into a time frame that was no longer comprehensible.

The nurse appeared above the mound of Jill's stomach. Wordlessly, she grabbed Jill's hospital gown and pulled it over her belly, leaving Jill naked and exposed.

Jill tried to scream, but she could get out only a feeble cry. Her heart was hammering so furiously that each massive beat seemed to reverberate on the metal table beneath her.

"No, no, no," she whimpered. "Oh, God, please no!"

Then in one bone-chilling gesture, the nurse traced a finger from Jill's breastbone down the length of her rounded belly to her groin.

Jill's mind exploded with the awareness of what the nurse was going to do to her. Struggling desperately, she tried to maneuver herself into a sitting position.

With one hand, the nurse pushed Jill back on the slab and held her there. With the other hand, she groped for something. Then her arm rose above Jill and Jill saw it, saw the scalpel, saw it gleaming. She saw it coming toward her, coming at her, coming at her baby. With desperate, frantic strength, Jill slammed her fist into the soft underside of the nurse's wrist. The nurse's fingers opened reflexively and the scalpel went flying.

There was a silence in which neither Jill nor her attacker moved.

Then, inexplicably, the nurse turned, grabbed the gurney that Jill had been pushed into the room on and left with it.

Jill tried to think. She was soaking wet. The baby was moving further down the birth canal. Her mind, her whole body was focused on one impulse—to push him out. But she dared not.

Please don't let my baby die!

"Help me!" she managed to scream between enormous peaks of pain.

There was no break in the contractions now—no break in the mind-numbing pain. She could feel the baby's head pushing against her. Screaming, she tried desperately to hold him back. But she had no choice. Her body was out of control.

She felt herself ripping.

The door swung open. Jill turned her head and saw a young man in blue work clothes staring at her aghast.

"What are you doing here?" he demanded. "No one is supposed to be down here at this time of night."

"Help me, please. I'm having my baby."

"I can't do that. I don't know anything about that. I'll get a doctor."

"No!" Jill screamed. "There is no time. You have to help me."

The man, looking very frightened, walked over to Jill. She directed him to the other end of the slab.

"Oh, Jesus, lady!"

"Please just catch him."

In one enormous gush the baby was in the world. The janitor looked at him a moment in disbelief and then placed the crying infant on his mother's stomach. Jill's eyes met the young man's. Tears of gratitude splashed down her face.

The young man took off his shirt and wrapped it around the infant. Then he went to the phone, dialed, and shouted, "Code Blue, the morgue" into the receiver.

Chapter Fourteen

JILL AWOKE SLOWLY FROM A DEEP, DEATHLIKE SLEEP. When she first opened her eyes, she did not know where she was.

"Jill?" Tom said softly when she stirred. He was sitting on a chair next to her bed and he looked horrible. His face was ashen and lined. He had not shaved.

Of course, she realized, she was in the hospital. Her hands flew to her stomach—the realization of where she was and the gesture were so close together as to be nearly simultaneous. The baby was no longer inside her.

"The baby," Jill said frantically. "Is the baby all right?"

Tell me the baby's not dead. Please tell me he's not dead.

"The baby is fine," Tom said, reaching for Jill's hand. "Just fine." His voice sounded odd—as if his mouth and throat were very dry. "How do you feel? Do you know where you are?"

Jill ignored the questions. Her mind was too busy trying to recall what had happened. The reading room of the

library suddenly came into focus. She remembered the
pain, her water breaking, leaning against the shelves, the
two librarians. But why on earth was she at that library?
She tried to work her way back from that point, but her
memory insisted on rushing forward. The images flew into
her mind. She remembered riding to the hospital with the
librarian, the emergency room, trying to phone Tom, the
Indian doctor examining her, getting the injection. But then
what? Her mind hit a blank wall. Had she been unconscious?

"Did they deliver the baby by caesarean?"

"You don't remember?"

Jill shook her head. Tom must have been up all night.
She did not remember ever seeing him look that bad.

"When can I see the baby? When are they going to
bring him to me? They know I am going to breast-feed
him, don't they?"

Tom dropped his gaze from Jill's face. His hesitation
caused her stomach to plunge.

My God, he's a Down's baby. The test was wrong. He's
not going to be all right. Something went wrong at the
delivery. That's why I don't remember it.

"Tell me what's wrong with the baby," Jill said, her
tone of voice demanding a straight answer. She braced
herself.

"There's nothing wrong with the baby, except that he
is a little underweight. He is in the special-care nursery.
You can see him just as soon as we make sure you are up
to it."

"*Up to it?* What are you talking about?" She wanted
to add: And just who is this *we* you are talking about?

"It's really nothing," Tom said, taking her hand between both of his. "We just want to check you over, run
a few tests. It's not that unusual . . ."

Not that unusual, bull! Tom was lying to her. She had heard doctor doubletalk before, but never from her own husband! What was going on? She began to feel panicky. Why was Tom acting this way? It was like some sort of awful dream . . .

Jill's body went rigid with the sudden image of a grotesque nurse wheeling her down a deserted hallway. She shook her head to rid it of the horrifying image. A dream, it was just a piece of a bad dream.

"I don't understand why I have to be examined before I can see my baby," Jill said, focusing her concentration away from the shadowy nightmare and onto the present. "And what about my milk? Is the baby too little for me to nurse? I don't understand."

Tom took a deep breath, then replied slowly and gently: "They think a formula will be best for the baby."

Jill pushed herself into a sitting position, her eyes on fire.

"Listen to me, Jill," Tom said gently but firmly. "Before we talk about breast-feeding, I have to know what you remember about the baby's birth. Tell me everything."

"I was at the downtown library in Oakland . . ." Oh, God, why was I there? ". . . and my water broke." With mounting anxiety, Jill summarized the events from that point to the examination by the Indian doctor. Again her mind hit a blank wall after the injection, except that she remembered some hanging scales. Could they have been in the delivery room—to weigh the babies?

"That's all I can remember. Do you know what happened after that, Tom?"

Tom lowered his eyes. His hands were shaking.

"What happened, Tom?" Jill said, throwing the weight

of all their years together behind the demand. "Tell me what's going on."

"Apparently," Tom said, his voice barely audible, "you wandered away from the examining room down to the basement. Lost and disoriented and in an advanced state of labor, you wandered into pathology, lay down on a slab and . . ."

"Stop!" Jill screamed as the vile images tore into her brain—the gutters, the hanging scales, the dead bodies, the scalpel above her belly—images that came not from some horrible nightmare, but from reality! She began to gasp for air and to retch. Tom reached for a pan and held her as her body convulsed and she vomited violently. When it was over, she collapsed against the pillow.

"How could it have happened?" she asked through uncontrollable sobs. "Why would someone do that to me?"

"Do what?" Tom whispered.

"I didn't wander into the morgue. I was pushed in there!"

Tom looked at her, his expression a mixture of confusion and horror. "*Someone* took you down there?"

"Yes!" Why don't you know that? Why doesn't anyone know that?

"Who, Jill? Who took you down there?"

"I don't know. A nurse. Some nurse. And Tom, she tried . . . she was going to cut my baby out!"

"*What?*" Tom screamed.

Jill put her hands over her face to shut out Tom's horror and then she burst into sobs.

Tom grabbed Jill in his arms. Even through her own sobs, she could feel him shaking. "I'll get whoever did this to you," he whispered, the words coming in a painful rush.

He let go of Jill and picked up the telephone.

"One of your nurses *took* my wife to the morgue!" he said, almost yelling, when he got ahold of the person he wanted. "Get the police."

"That was Paul Vance, the head administrator in this excuse of a hospital," Tom told her in a strained, but even voice after he hung up. Jill could tell that Tom was struggling to calm himself, fighting to be in control. "He's coming down here."

Jill nodded. She was so tired. None of this seemed real. If only they would let her sleep, she felt half certain that she would wake up in her own bed at home—or perhaps, she thought weakly, she would just find herself in the midst of another nightmare. Nightmares within nightmares within nightmares.

Jill heard a loud knock on the door and realized that she had been dozing. For a moment, she didn't know where she was, and then she knew quite clearly. There would be no reprieve . . .

A tall, blandly clean-cut man who looked to be about forty-five entered the room. Jill thought vaguely that he looked like scores of men she had seen—men who were in charge of banks or insurance offices or just plain in charge.

"The police are on their way," he said quietly to Tom.

Tom nodded and then tersely introduced Jill to Paul Vance.

"Can you tell me what happened, Mrs. Douglas?" Vance asked. He looked pale and shaken.

Trying to control her emotions, Jill told Vance what had happened to her from the time she was left alone on the gurney in the hall. As she recounted what she now remembered quite clearly, the administrator seemed to become more sure of himself. Vance began questioning Jill, gently pressing her to give some of the same information again and again.

No, she could not describe the nurse. No, she could not describe her uniform. No, she could not say how tall she was. No, she could not guess her age.

"Vance, don't you see that this person had her face covered up?" Tom interrupted. "Don't you see that she did not want Jill to be able to describe her?"

"Mrs. Douglas, have you ever experienced any adverse reactions to medication?" Vance asked, ignoring Tom's questions and abruptly changing the subject. "Any side effects like dizziness, vomiting, fever, rash, hallucinations?"

"No, nothing ever."

"I know you are probably very tired," he said soothingly, "but could we back up? Could you tell me how you happened to arrive at this hospital—so far from your house— without your husband knowing, and without your purse?"

Ben's death-distorted face swam in front of her eyes.

"Yes?"

Jill realized that she had shuddered. Vance continued to look at her expectantly.

"I had to leave my house very quickly."

"Why?"

"There was someone there. I mean, I thought there was someone there."

"I don't understand."

"I had a dream that I thought was real and I got very frightened . . ."

With stunning objectivity, Jill heard her own words, heard how they must have sounded. She paused and tried to recoup. It was too late. She saw Vance look at Tom and knew unmistakably what his look meant. She saw Tom's

face slacken and his body—which moments before had
been rigid with rage—slump.

The terrible silence was broken by a pantsuited nurse
who had come to check on Jill. Vance patted Jill on the
shoulder and muttered: "You rest and let us take care of
everything." Then he indicated to Tom that he wanted to
speak to him out of the room and the two of them walked
out.

A few minutes later, after the nurse had finished with
Jill and gone, Tom returned. He looked beaten, destroyed.
He sat on Jill's bed, looking at her as if he did not know
what to say. Finally, apropos of nothing, he said, "I found
your purse in the driveway and I think I got everything
back into it."

Before Jill could react, Tom covered his face in his hands
and began to cry. Then he grabbed Jill in his arms. "It's
going to be all right," he whispered. "We'll make you
well."

Later that morning, Jill was examined by the hospital's
Chief of Obstetrics, then by her own obstetrician, and then
by a neurologist who ordered a series of tests. Then in the
afternoon a psychiatrist came to Jill's room.

His name was Dr. Shapiro. He was a trim, little man
with wild eyebrows, and Jill did not like him. She did not
like his air of studied casualness or the cliched way he
held the tips of his fingers together as he listened to her
talk.

She wanted to order him out of her room, but she did
not act on the desire. Nor did she show him the dislike
she felt. Through the examinations of this long day, Jill
had come to see perfectly her true position. She was like
a traveler without documents being detained in a country
in which she had no rights. They could do anything they

wanted to her here. They could lock her up for years. They could give her drugs . . . Drugs! Of course, that was why they were not going to let her breast-feed her baby. They were planning to give her drugs.

No one believed her. That was obvious. Not even Tom could believe her anymore. In a way, she did not blame them. Ben could not possibly have been in a coffin in her living room and yet she had seen him there—seen that woman. If all that had been some sort of psychotic hallucination, then how could she be so sure the birth had happened the way she remembered it? How could she be sure of anything?

She felt certain that she was slipping into psychosis and it terrified her. But no matter what, she would not let this psychiatrist and the others know her fears. From this point on, she had to be careful, very, very careful. In the midst of all the evidence to the contrary, she had to appear sane. She was not going to let them lock her up. She was not going to let them take her baby from her.

Jill answered the psychiatrist's questions, using the most precise English at her command. She repeated the story of her labor up to the point of the injection. Then she equivocated. She said that everything after that had become hazy to her. Since no one believed her account of the birth, sticking to her story might only make things worse for herself. She told the psychiatrist that she now thought the account of the birth she had given earlier might have actually been a nightmare.

She tried to take the edge of horror off everything she said. She prayed she sounded reasonable.

Jill told Dr. Shapiro about her childhood, her mother's insanity, her own three years of therapy with Dr. Frank, her happy marriage to Tom, the stress of the move from New York, her fondness for Ben and her grief over his recent fatal heart attack in her presence. The interview lasted two hours.

After Dr. Shapiro left, they finally let Jill see her baby. A nurse pushed her in a wheelchair to the special-care nursery. There, through the awful distance of a pane of glass, Jill saw her infant son for the first time since he had ceased to be connected to her body. He was an impossibly tiny baby, with red wrinkled skin and a tuft of blondish-brown hair. Jill tapped her fingers against the glass.

Benjamin, my little Benjamin, please forgive me.

Later that afternoon, Tom met with Dr. Shapiro in one of the hospital's drab consulting rooms. Although Tom was the husband of a patient, Shapiro—following the accepted code of behavior among physicians—spoke to him in the language of colleagues. The pain of one and the empathy of the other could only be discerned in the weary tone that punctuated the sentences of their professional language.

"Essentially, Jill has found the perfect punishment for her Oedipal guilt that her birth caused her mother's insanity," Shapiro told Tom. "That punishment, of course, is that her child's birth would in turn cause her own insanity and death."

But, Shapiro continued, he believed that her conflict would have remained dormant had Tom's father not died. At a time when Jill was particularly vulnerable—she was, after all, pregnant, in a strange place, and away from her old friends—she found a substitute father/mother in Tom's father. However, he suffered a fatal heart attack, after Jill—who was frightened about intruders in the house—had summoned him. In her mind, Shapiro maintained, Jill had once again killed a parent. The belief that she was responsible for her substitute father's death rekindled the guilt that she had caused her mother's death. Then, under the extreme stress of going into labor unexpectedly and finding herself alone in a foreboding hospital—and with the strong possibility that she had an adverse reaction to the meperidine she had been given—her defenses broke.

"In this state, I think Jill may have unconsciously sought out the morgue for her delivery as a way of acting out her punishment without actually having to die."

Tom shook his head. Freudians had always been hard for him to swallow, but this was *his* wife, *his* Jill being trivialized by their theories.

Seeming to sense Tom's thoughts, Shapiro leaned forward and said: "Tom, you asked for my analysis of what happened to your wife and I gave it to you."

Shapiro went on to say that Jill appeared to be acting quite rational now and as long as she received psychotherapy, he saw no reason to prevent her from going home—that is, he cautioned, as long as someone remains with her at all times.

Throughout that week, a team of hospital administrators investigated the events surrounding the birth of the Douglas child. Two nurses described separate occasions on which they had found Jill wandering, lost and disoriented, through the hospital. It was noted that Jill had arrived at the hospital in a distraught state without so much as a wallet with her. Absolutely no evidence was found indicating that anyone had taken Jill into the morgue.

The investigation would finally determine that Jill Douglas, heavily drugged, in an extremely confused and disoriented state, wandered down to the basement by herself—possibly in an attempt to leave the hospital. Then, thoroughly lost and disoriented, and needing a place to rest, the patient wandered into the morgue.

An ad hoc committee of doctors, nurses, administrators and support staff was formed to determine ways the hospital could improve patient supervision despite the understaffed and overcrowded conditions.

Chapter Fifteen

PEGGY AWOKE WITH A START, HER HEART POUNDING FROM a chilling nightmare. Still in the nightmare's grip, she reached out for the warm comfort of her husband's sleeping body. Her hand brushed against empty sheets and she combed the darkness to find where he lay. Not finding him, she lifted herself on one elbow and strained to see in the darkness. The space beside her was empty. She called out to him and, in so doing, fully woke up.

The pain and the enormity of the empty space beside her wrenched her insides. She had to act quickly before her grief overwhelmed her. With a massive and determined effort, she got out of bed and turned on the light. The time was barely five A.M., but she had to get up, had to put distance between herself and that moment of resounding anguish when she realized that he was not there, was not anywhere.

Peggy reached for the worn corduroy robe on the chair beside her bed. Over the years Ben, and even Tom, had given her many pretty robes. She wore them on Christmas morning, on vacation, and when she had house guests. But for real life, she had been putting on the same corduroy robe for more years than she could remember.

Turning on the lights along the way, Peggy went into the kitchen and pulled a can of coffee from the shelf. She filled the percolator three-quarters with water and then measured six teaspoons of coffee into the basket. She could not drink more than two cups and she certainly did not like to waste, but for all the mornings of her marriage—for more than forty years—she had measured six teaspoons of coffee into the pot. She could not bear the sadness of making less.

She took a loaf of bread from the refrigerator and put a slice into the toaster. One thing no one ever tells you about being a widow, Peggy thought, was how damnably long it takes to finish a loaf of bread.

The smell of percolating coffee and toasting bread made Peggy feel better. She had made it through the pain of another morning, made it through yet another shock of waking up and finding Ben not there.

She buttered the toast, then sprinkled onto it a teaspoon of the cinnamon-sugar mixture that she kept in a little cut-glass bowl on the counter. She took the toast and a cup of coffee and sat down at the kitchen table.

A car pulled up in front of the house. She heard the thud of the newspaper hitting the driveway and the roar of the car driving away. Not even in Willowglen, not even in their little town, did a boy on a bicycle deliver the newspaper anymore.

Now safely out of bed and with a cup of coffee between her hands, Peggy could think about her nightmare. In the dream, she had been alone in her barely lighted living room when the ghost of Dora Miles suddenly walked into the room. Although terrified, Peggy was also angry. She demanded to know what Dora was doing in her house. Dora had replied, "I am bringing you something of Jill's."

Then she noticed that Dora was carrying a cloth-wrapped object in her hands. The thing inside the cloth was pulsating, beating, and Peggy knew that it was Jill's heart. Dora came toward her, reaching out her hands to give her Jill's quivering heart. Peggy recoiled in a horror so acute that pains shot through her own heart. Dora continued to walk toward her, smiling. An instant later, Peggy was awake and reaching for Ben.

Peggy drew her robe tighter around her and took several comforting sips of coffee. Because her dreams so often foretold a piece of the future, her nightmares had the power to frighten her long into the daylight. But surely, Peggy told herself, this absurd dream meant nothing—that is, nothing beyond what she already knew: that she was terribly worried about Jill and that she would have to go at last to the home of Dora Miles.

Tom had not answered any of Peggy's questions about Jill and the baby to her satisfaction. He had told her that the baby had come unexpectedly while Jill was in Oakland on some errand or another, that the birth had been difficult, that Jill's doctor had wanted her to have no visitors, but that both Jill and the baby were fine. They were coming home from the hospital today and Tom had asked Peggy to stay with them for a while.

She knew that Tom was keeping something from her. Ever since Tom had been about six years old, he had followed the less-told-to-Mom-the-better school of thought. A lot of men were like that—keeping most things to themselves. She knew there had been a lot that Ben had never told her, although she was now sure that most of it had to do with his sister, Dora.

When Ben was a young and fabulously handsome doc-

tor, with most of the women in town concocting illnesses
to see him, and Peggy was a tired young mother—up to
her elbows in diapers and unable to lose the weight she
had gained in her pregnancy—she had worried that in the
part of Ben's life he was not telling her about he was with
another woman. But as the years went by, she realized that
the only people who really mattered to him were she and
Tom and, of course, Dora. Maybe he was above all the
attention he got, maybe he was oblivious to it. More than
likely, she and Tom and Dora—and being a doctor—took
up all his time.

Peggy had never even set foot in Dora's house. Even
after Dora had died and Peggy's own son lived in the
house, she could not stand the thought of visiting there—
the thought of seeing Dora in some detail of household
design, in some piece of leftover furniture.

Of course, when Tom asked her for help, she could not
turn him down for some petty reason. Still she felt uneasy.
Not only would she be going to Dora's house, but she did
not know how Jill felt about her coming. Jill had been so
withdrawn since Ben died that it was hard to know what
she thought. Peggy did not want Jill to think that she was
some pushy mother-in-law intent on taking charge of the
new baby.

Tom had said that they would be arriving at Peggy's
house from the hospital about noon. He had told his mother
not to bother making lunch for them.

Of course, Peggy was going to bother to make lunch.

She was completely ready by eleven A.M. She had lunch
made—sandwiches, fruit salad, iced tea and cookies—and
the table set. She was all packed for her stay with Tom
and Jill. She was bringing two suitcases—one for her
clothes and the other for her baking things. Peggy's idea
of helping Jill included stocking her freezer with enough

casseroles and baked goods so that Jill would not have to
cook for six months. Peggy had no idea of what kinds of
pans Jill had in her kitchen. Moreover, while she certainly
did not want to offend Jill, she needed her own pans to
cook properly.

Peggy spent the next hour checking and rechecking how
she looked in the mirror, how the table looked, and running to the window every time she heard a car.

Promptly at noon, Tom pulled into the driveway. Peggy
rushed outside, arriving at the car as Tom was helping Jill
out with the baby. Jill smiled at Peggy and, without saying
anything, pulled the blanket away from the baby. Peggy's
heart raced. It was like looking at Tom for the first time
all over again—a tiny, lean baby with the longest legs and
the prettiest face. And, once again, Peggy's heart flooded
with love.

After lunch, when Tom had left the room for a few
minutes, Peggy leaned over to Jill and asked her if she
really wanted her to come home with them.

Jill nodded emphatically and squeezed Peggy's hand.
Peggy saw that there were tears in her eyes.

Jill rode in the back seat with the baby while Peggy sat
in the front nervously looking out the window. Peggy was
as anxious as if she were on her way to a reunion with her
worst enemy. You're being a silly old fool, she told herself
again and again.

The drive up the winding private road that led to Dora's
house seemed interminable. Just like Dora to make going
to her house an event, Peggy thought. Finally the house
appeared at the top of the hill. The house was just the sort
of grandiose statement that Peggy would have expected
from Dora Miles.

Peggy actually had some idea of what the house would

look like from a photo story that had appeared on Dora and her house in the Sunday magazine section of a newspaper sometime in the fifties. Peggy had glanced at the article when it originally appeared, then found that Ben had kept it when she went through some of his things after his death.

Still the magazine pictures had not prepared her for how close the place was to being a mansion. All the elaborate woodwork and stained glass was overwhelming—and foreboding.

Tom held the baby while Jill showed Peggy around.

"I thought I would have done more with the house by now," Jill said softly. "More to make it our own, but somehow . . ."

Her voice trailed off and Peggy wanted to take Jill in her arms, tell her that everything was going to be all right, but she had a feeling that it wasn't true. Peggy did not *know* that anything was wrong. She had only a feeling. But it blew through her insides and chilled her to the bone.

The baby was a wailer. He cried day and night, and his wails could be heard throughout the huge house. Benjamin would often cry for two to three interminable hours at a stretch, red-faced, kicking, squirming, screaming. Tom diagnosed colic. They consulted the pediatrician. They changed formulas. They tried a pacifier. They walked the floor with him. Nothing seemed to work.

Sometimes it seemed as if there were no difference between night and day in the household. Since no one could sleep during one of Benjamin's crying periods, three o'clock in the morning could seem like midday with the house lit, the television going, and the teakettle boiling.

Jill was exhausted, more exhausted than she had ever thought it was possible to be. Yet, in a way, the disintegration of the household was a relief to her. All focus was on the baby and the moment: Could they get him to sleep? Did he take enough of his bottle? Did he need to be changed? All experience outside the moment-to-moment care of the baby receded—even the horror of his birth.

Although the baby's incessant demands absorbed Jill completely, they also frightened her. She was afraid that the baby had been harmed in some way by the traumas of her pregnancy and his birth. Tom did his best to reassure her, but Jill could not stop worrying.

One afternoon, after the baby had finally fallen asleep following two hours of kicking and screaming, Jill turned to Peggy with her fears.

"Of course, he's alright," Peggy assured. It wasn't the baby that Peggy was worried about. New babies turned households upside down—a fact most parents mercifully forgot. *She* had forgotten, until this experience brought it all back to her. But, there was something more than a new baby going on here.

"What's wrong, Jill?" Peggy asked, reaching across the kitchen table to take the younger woman's hand. "Please tell me what's really wrong."

"Tom hasn't told you?"

"No," Peggy answered softly.

Jill dropped her eyes and took a deep breath. "I had a really hard time with the baby's birth. Oh, Peggy, I was . . . I went crazy for a while. I had hallucinations, wild hallucinations. But, it's not like what happened to my mother. How my mother was. I'm fine now. Like I always was. Still, we are on eggshells, and I worry about the baby, that somehow . . ."

"Oh, you poor child!" Peggy said, grabbing Jill in her arms.

Grateful, Jill returned the embrace, holding on tightly.

Almost imperceptibly, Peggy shuddered. Even this room—the heart of the house—she thought as she held Jill in the kitchen, is cold, cold even in the heat of summer, cold even in embrace. This house was not good for Jill. It was not good for any of them.

Even in death, Dora Miles was hurting her still.

The worst really did seem behind Jill. Despite her exhaustion, there were no signs of illness or instability. No bad dreams, no hallucinations, nothing out of the ordinary. The baby made eye contact with her and once—she was sure of it—he smiled.

Jill appreciated Peggy's help and she genuinely enjoyed her company, despite Peggy's not very subtle criticisms of their house.

One afternoon, when the two women were relaxing on the wide front porch as the baby napped inside, Jill asked her mother-in-law why she so disliked Dora Miles.

"Because there was nothing to like about her, nothing," Peggy said.

Jill looked at Peggy, waiting patiently for her to elaborate.

"Dora never wanted Ben to marry me," Peggy said finally. "I don't think she wanted Ben to marry anyone. She showed how she felt by ignoring me. Before I finally refused to see her ever again, when we would all be together, she would act as if I were not there. I went through entire evenings, entire holiday meals, where Dora never once spoke to me. She would dominate the conversation, glittering, sparkling for Ben, as if I were invisible. Oh, on occasion she would ask me to get up and get something. The most hurtful part was that Ben never noticed.

"Dora never had any interest in Tom either," Peggy continued softly. "I don't think she saw him more than

once or twice in his life. She never even sent him a birthday card. Can you imagine that?''

Jill shook her head.

''You know, the difficult part about Dora was that other
people did not see her as I did. She was the pacesetter for
this whole county. She had elegant, stylish friends. She
was supposedly selfless when it came to charitable causes.
She married a rich man and she donated his money to
everything. And . . . no matter what she did, how vain or
selfish the act, she seemed to believe that she was always
right, always above reproach.''

Peggy stopped talking. It felt good to have someone
listen to her about Dora Miles, but she did not want to
overdo it. She didn't want to come across like some old
crab.

She scanned Jill's expression. There was nothing but
sympathy in her young face.

Chapter Sixteen

AFTER JILL HAD BEEN HOME FROM THE HOSPITAL FOR TWO weeks, Tom hired a highly recommended housekeeper. Although Jill agreed with Tom that his mother was looking tired, she was not eager for Peggy to leave. For her part, Peggy—as much as she enjoyed being with her family—needed to get away from Dora's house to get a handle on the shapeless fear that was growing inside her.

Peggy returned home on Sunday. Mrs. Sanchez, the housekeeper, arrived at eight o'clock the following morning.

Mrs. Sanchez spoke very little English, and Jill almost no Spanish. Jill, who had never had any household help before—and, indeed, had never even pictured herself as the type of person who would have household help—was at a loss as to how they should proceed. Mrs. Sanchez, who seemed faintly amused by Jill's discomfort, knew exactly what to do though. Once Jill was able to grasp that *aspiradora* was the Spanish word for vacuum cleaner, Mrs. Sanchez went to work on the enormous house, the earphones of a small radio plugged securely into her ears.

Jill was relieved that Mrs. Sanchez went her own way, essentially ignoring her. Jill had the security of another adult in the house while being nearly free of the disruption of another person's presence.

Mrs. Sanchez had had four children, and she handled Benjamin in a relaxed, surehanded way that Jill admired. Although Jill cared for the baby almost exclusively, she felt comfortable leaving him with Mrs. Sanchez for trips to the store and appointments with her psychiatrist.

Jill saw Dr. Shapiro twice a week. His office was in north Oakland, nearly an hour's drive, but Tom had so much confidence in Dr. Shapiro that he thought the psychiatrist was worth the trip. Jill did not care about the drive, but she hated having to see the psychiatrist. She wanted to put the horrible experience of Benjamin's birth and the insanity preceding it behind her. Moreover, she did not really like Dr. Shapiro. She did not like going over the same material of her childhood again and again while he nodded and said "hmm." Unlike her sessions with Dr. Frank in New York, where Jill had felt that she and the psychiatrist were partners in a discovery, her sessions with Dr. Shapiro had all the equality of a gynecological examination. She was the naked and exposed female. He was the fully clothed physician.

Six weeks after the baby was born, the nearest general practitioner to Tom—the physician with whom Tom traded relief coverage—died of a heart attack while jogging. Now, until another physician could be found to take over that doctor's practice, Tom had the work of two doctors. He worked weekdays from early morning until late in the evening, all day on Saturday, and a half day on Sunday.

Worn down, Tom eventually caught a cold and passed it to Jill. And, as careful as they tried to be, they could not prevent Benjamin from catching it.

Benjamin, never an easy baby, grew even fussier with a cold. Jill was as exhausted as Tom. Their conversations in the evening dwindled to a rundown of the baby's bodily functions.

Because he was sick, the baby could take only a little milk at each feeding. An hour later, he would wake up wailing with hunger. During the night, Jill would feed him, then go back to sleep, only to wake up some time later not remembering that she had returned the baby to his crib. Panic-stricken, she would be certain that he had fallen on the floor or that she had rolled over on top of him.

During the day, she would feed him and put him down to sleep. Then, as soon as she sat down to rest, she would hear him crying. She would get up and go to him, only to find him sleeping. She would leave the room and hear him crying again.

On one particularly difficult afternoon, as Jill paced the floor of the nursery with the crying baby, she suddenly heard strains of Beethoven's Fifth Symphony being pounded out on the piano downstairs. Jill was surprised. She had no idea that Mrs. Sanchez played the piano. The poor woman must have been trying to drown out the baby's wailing.

"See what you have done, Benjamin," Jill said gently to the baby. "You have driven Mrs. Sanchez to pounding on the piano."

Jill walked out of the nursery with the baby and was astonished to see Mrs. Sanchez down the hall mopping the bathroom floor. Mrs. Sanchez did not notice Jill until she arrived at the doorway. Then Mrs. Sanchez smiled and pulled the radio earphones from her ears.

"Piano?" Jill said, knowing even as she tried to make herself understood that Mrs. Sanchez could not have possibly been playing the piano downstairs just seconds before.

"¿*Qué pasa?*" Mrs. Sanchez asked, looking at Jill with concern.

"Tired," Jill said. "I guess I'm just tired."

The housekeeper nodded. Using her hands, she told Jill to go lie down while she watched the baby.

Jill went to her room, shut the door and got into bed. She was asleep immediately, except that she could hear Benjamin crying—no, screaming. He was screaming in the next room. Jill got out of bed and went into the nursery. She was so tired though, so very exhausted, that she had to sit down. She collapsed into the rocking chair. The baby continued to scream. She would get him in a minute. She just needed to rest one more minute.

Mrs. Sanchez came into the nursery. "I'll quiet him down," she said in perfect English. Then she picked up a pillow and put it firmly over his head. After a few seconds the baby stopped crying. Jill continued to rock. The quiet was so nice. The silence was so peaceful.

Jill began to feel uneasy. There was something wrong with what Mrs. Sanchez was doing. The baby might suffocate. My God, you can't put a pillow over a baby's face! Jill had to do something. She had to stop Mrs. Sanchez. But she did not have the strength to get out of the rocking chair. Her legs would not function. She could not get out of the chair! Her heart began to pound. She had to do something! Her baby was in danger. She had to save her baby. She began to scream.

Jill awoke screaming. She had bolted into a sitting position and was upright in her bed screaming. Still shaking, she got out of bed to look for Benjamin and Mrs. Sanchez. She found them in the kitchen. Benjamin was reclining in his plastic infant chair quietly watching Mrs. Sanchez clean the stove.

Mrs. Sanchez turned around, looking surprised to see Jill.

''No sleep?'' she asked.

''No,'' Jill said. Sometimes it was better not to sleep.

Two weeks later, Jill received a telephone call from a former coworker, Judy Miller. She was in San Francisco on business and asked Jill to join her for dinner.

Jill had never paid much attention to Judy Miller when they worked together. She remembered her as a rather mousy and not particularly talented drudge whose main topic of conversation was her husband. Yet, like a lonely traveler who is delighted to have the company of someone who would never interest her at home, Jill felt excited about the prospect of seeing Judy. She would have gossip—news of the old gang. More importantly, Jill had not had a night out on her own in longer than she could remember.

Jill went through her entire wardrobe looking for the right outfit to wear. She was pleased that she could fit into her pre-pregnancy clothes and displeased that she did not have the time to buy something new. Jill selected a still-stylish skirt, a blouse, a sweater to wear over the blouse, a tweed blazer and boots. The outfit was casual, yet appropriate for dinner, a good blend of California and New York—perfect, Jill thought. She realized that she did not want anyone from her former life to know that she had slipped from what she once had been.

Jill met Judy at Tadich's Grill in San Francisco. She did not recognize her former coworker. Judy had undergone a metamorphosis; the lanky hair had been permed, the lackluster corduroy skirts and turtlenecks had been exchanged for an expensive-looking dress-for-success suit and a dramatic silk blouse, her face had been remade with makeup brushes.

"Judy, you look fabulous," Jill gushed.

"Judith. I know it's hard at first, but I would like you to call me Judith."

Jill nodded, taken aback, and Judith gave Jill a breathless rundown of her life in the last year. She had decided she was going nowhere at her former job at Beckman Ink. Moreover, she decided that her marriage was holding her back. She looked everywhere for a better job, pounded on every conceivable door. Finally, she talked her way into a position at ABC Television, researching documentaries.

She left her husband and got an apartment in Manhattan. One of the first stories she researched had to do with women who became athletes in their thirties and forties. She thought it would be a great idea for a book. She approached a publisher. He loved the idea. She got a five-figure advance to do *The Over Forty Guide to Total Feminine Fitness*. She was spending a lot of time on the West Coast to research her book. Indeed, she laughed, she was practically bicoastal.

A book—Jill could not believe it. Everyone who worked at Beckman Ink was going to write a book someday. But, she could not believe that Judy—Judith—someone she had always considered inferior, had written a book, even a stupid book, and gotten a glamorous job as well.

And what had she done in the same period? She had slipped into being a housewife, a crazy housewife at that. She wanted to rise above her jealousy and feel happy for Judy, but she could not. She felt miserable.

Driving home alone through the starry night after dinner, Jill was able to distance herself from her jealousy. After all, she had a beautiful son. Her marriage to Tom, although a little strained lately, was still good. Her emotional breakdown had been a result of her pregnancy, not a result of leaving New York and her job. If she had gotten pregnant in New York, the same thing might have happened. But the most important thing was that she was much, much better now. Even Dr. Shapiro assured her of that.

Besides, if Judy/Judith could turn her life around like that, there was no telling what Jill could do.

Except for the porch light, the house was completely dark when Jill arrived at eleven-thirty. She entered the house carefully and took off her shoes before going upstairs so as not to wake Tom or the baby. She tiptoed down the hall, stopping to peek inside Benjamin's room. It was dark and peaceful. Not wanting to risk waking the baby, she turned and tiptoed into her own room. Being careful not to wake Tom, Jill walked softly across the room without turning on the lights.

Tom would enjoy hearing about Judy/Judith in the morning, Jill thought as she undressed in the pitch dark. Tom had always enjoyed her stories. He had such an intelligent way of listening, his eyes dancing in appreciation of the absurdity underlying what he was being told. He had such a nice sense of humor too, so wry, so understated. She loved the way he smiled, the way his whole face brightened. He had such a marvelous face—and such a wonderful body. And, his body felt so good against hers.

Jill was flushed with the sudden recognition of how much she wanted him. It had been so long since she had really desired him, really thought of something else besides caring for the baby. She took off the nightgown she had just put on. She would slide into bed next to him, kiss him awake—slowly, gently, her hands roaming across his firm body.

She stood by the bed a moment watching the rise and fall of his breathing under the blankets. Then she climbed into bed and in one motion slid her body around his. Jill's body recoiled before her mind could comprehend that the person in bed next to her was not Tom. Before that hideous thought could register in her mind, he was on top of her, pinning her down, blowing foul-smelling breath in her face.

Jill struggled to free herself, kicking him, pushing up at him with her legs and arms. She twisted her hands around to dig her fingernails into his hands, and all the while she screamed, barely pausing for breath between the cries. Then a vile hand came down over her mouth. She bit down on it, hard—the flesh tasting like rancid meat. He jerked his hand from her teeth and reached across to the side of her head for a—my God, he was reaching for a pillow. He was going to put it over her face.

Jill's upper body jerked a few degrees away from him, her arms reaching out to the bedside table. Her hand touched her water glass. Without thinking—there was no time for words to form in her mind—acting on an instinct older than civilization, Jill grabbed hold of the glass and smashed it against his temple. He jerked sideways toward the center of the bed, freeing Jill's upper body for a moment.

She reached toward the bedside table again. This time her hands fastened on the lamp. Grabbing it firmly by the metal neck, she pulled it toward her. And, in a moment that contained no reasoning, no thinking, no comprehension, only the will to live, Jill smashed the ceramic base of the lamp squarely down on his head. Jill could not see what she was doing in the dark, but she could hear. The sound of the lamp smashing against his skull was deafening.

As if charged by an electric current, his body jerked away from hers, jerked again and then went limp. Jill bolted from the bed and stood over it, the room spinning. She stared down at the body on the bed, her chest heaving, watching—waiting for the body to move.

Contradictory fears flew at her. She did not want him to really be dead. She could not bear the thought that she might have killed a human being. But she was also terrified that at any minute he might jump off the bed and lunge for her. She did not take her eyes off the barely discernible heap on the bed for what seemed like an eternity. Her neck felt as if it had a noose around it, cutting off her air. She was shaking. She could not stand it any longer. She had to know. Slowly, she let one of her hands drop onto the body. Her hand landed on a cold, fleshy mound with a small protrusion in the center. Jill jerked her hand away and, to her horror, the body on the bed convulsed and threw an arm toward her. Horrified, but unable to look away, Jill watched the fingers clench inward like a claw. The fingernails were long and tapered like a woman's.

Jill's hand flew to her breast. It had been a breast that she had touched on the body. It was a woman. She had killed a woman. A noise like rushing water filled her ears and her whole body shook. Vaguely, she was aware of a somewhat familiar sound emanating from somewhere on the floor. A few seconds later, she realized that it was the telephone receiver lying off the hook on the floor. She must have knocked it off the table when she grabbed the lamp. Shaking, Jill followed the noise, picked up the phone and dialed the operator.

"I have killed someone," she said. "I have killed an

intruder in my home.'' When she hung up, she did not remember whether she had given her name or her address. She was so cold. Her body was wet and sticky. Making her way to the pile of clothes she had worn earlier, she slipped her arms into her blazer.

Suddenly her mind was jolted by a new horror. Where was Tom? Had he been killed? Was he lying somewhere dead in the house? *And the baby?*

Jill ran next door into the baby's room. She could negotiate her way perfectly through the dark room to the baby's crib; she had done it a million times. She reached the crib and looked into it. The baby was not there. Frantically, she searched the crib for him with her hands. He was not there.

''No!'' Jill screamed as she ran to the light switch. When she turned on the light, she had to close her eyes for a second. When she opened them, she began to scream. Benjamin's little sheet was smeared with blood.

Jill jammed her fists against her mouth and began to rock her body back and forth sobbing. Eventually, she was aware that there were sirens and flashing lights outside the house.

Jill did not remember leaving the baby's room. The next thing she was aware of after hearing the sirens was that she was opening the door for the police. She pointed upstairs, and when she did so, she realized for the first time that her hands and arms were covered with blood. She glanced down at herself and saw that blood was smeared over her entire body. Three of the policemen bolted upstairs. The fourth took her by the arm and sat her down in the hall chair.

Jill pulled her blazer down to cover the tops of her thighs. The policeman asked if she would like to wait to talk until a female officer was present. Jill shook her head.

"My husband and my baby are missing," she stammered.

The policeman nodded grimly. He asked her to tell him what happened. She tried to tell him. In some faraway part of Jill's mind she was aware that she was not talking clearly, but she was helpless to do anything about it. As she tried to get her story out, she was aware that the police were walking throughout the upstairs. She wondered what they were looking for.

After a period of time, the length of which Jill was unable to judge, one of the policemen who had been upstairs came down to question her. He asked her what her assailant looked like. Jill told him that it was dark and she could not see, but she did not understand why he asked the question. She wanted to say, "You know what he looks like, you just saw him," but she could not express the thought.

An ambulance had arrived outside. A paramedic came in carrying a little bag and rushed over to Jill. He asked her where she was hurt. She said nowhere. He shined a light in her eyes, then began to bandage her wrist. She was aware that the police were now looking through the downstairs. What were they looking for?

"My baby, my husband!" Jill cried out. Where were they? Why weren't the police doing more?

One of the officers came over to her.

"We are trying to reach your husband now," he said.

Jill looked at him, uncomprehending.

"Your husband left a note taped to your bathroom mirror," the officer said. "The note said he had to leave on an emergency call and that he would drop your baby at his mother's on the way."

Jill grabbed the policeman's arm. "My baby?"

"Your baby is safe," he said.

Jill looked up to see Tom pushing his way past the uniformed people toward her. Jill began to cry. He was safe. He was safe.

Tom ran over to her and crouched down beside her. His face was distorted with fear. "Jill, Jill," he said, surrounding her with his arms.

"There was someone in the room," she said. "In our bed. He tried to . . . she tried to . . . I don't know. I hit him . . . her with the lamp."

"Where are you hurt?" Tom asked, lifting her arms gently, looking at her bandaged wrist, his face ghastly white.

The paramedic moved closer to them. "Surface lacerations, doctor," he said.

A police officer walked over and put a hand on Tom's shoulder. "May I speak with you privately a moment, doctor?"

Tom nodded. He took Jill's face in his hand and told her that he would be right back. Then he followed the police officer to the far end of the hall.

Tom was not sure what had happened. He had been told by his service that there was an emergency at home, but they had not known what it was. He had driven home as fast as he could in a state of terrible anxiety, and when he got home and saw Jill, he felt as if someone had ripped a hole through his insides. He had not been there to protect her.

"Did you get him?" Tom asked, trying to control the terrible rage that was overcoming him.

The police officer hesitated.

"Tell me, damn it! Did you get him?"

"Doctor, please calm down and listen," the policeman responded in an aggravatingly calm tone of voice. "There is *no* perpetrator."

At first Tom could not grasp the meaning of what the officer was saying.

The policeman continued: "There was no one upstairs, no sign of a break-in, no evidence of anyone except your wife having been in her bed. Evidently, she smashed the lamp against the bed's headboard and cut herself in the process. Her wounds are self-inflicted."

Time stopped. Tom looked down the hall. He saw the milling police officers, the paramedic filling out a form on a clipboard, the stained-glass window above the door illuminated by the flashing lights of the patrol cars outside. And he saw Jill, his beloved wife, sitting in the hall chair, half-naked, covered in her own blood, staring into space.

Chapter Seventeen

IT WAS ONE A.M. BY THE TIME THE POLICE AND PARAMEDics left the Douglas house. Tom detected a certain embarrassment for him from the departing officers, but he felt only numb panic. He drew a bath for Jill, pouring in some bubbling soap so that she would be spared the sight of blood-tinged water. Then he helped her into the tub. She was like a large doll—vacant, pliable, staring.

Tom left her soaking and went into the bedroom. In a glance, he saw what the police had seen—a broken lamp on the bed, some blood from Jill's cuts on the sheets. There was no sign of a bashed-in head, no evidence of an intruder.

Tom picked up the phone and called Jill's psychiatrist. Then he heard, he realized later, what his own patients must hear waking him in the night—first coughing, then a faintly exasperated hello. Tom explained what had happened as succinctly and unemotionally as possible. Then he listened to a version of the advice that he himself must have given a thousand times in the night: Give her a sedative, take one yourself, meet me at the office first thing in the morning.

Tom helped Jill out of the bath and into a nightgown. He gave her a sleeping pill and took one himself. Jill asked about the baby, and he assured her that the baby would be fine with Peggy for the night.

Tom took Jill into the guest room, where they both climbed into the same twin bed. Jill fell asleep almost immediately in his arms. But Tom, despite the sedative he had taken, could not sleep. The evidence of Jill's mental illness overwhelmed him. After tonight, there could be no more denial, no more pretending that everything was under control, that it would all be alright. Tom had lost the center of his life and he was numb with grief.

Jill awoke the next morning in a state of profound detachment. She was aware of where she was, aware of what had happened the night before, but she felt as if it had happened to someone else. Her own feelings were blank.

She did as Tom told her. He said get dressed, and she got dressed. He said try to eat, and she tried to eat. In fact, unless she was given a direct command, she did not move. Even slight movements took an energy and a will that she did not have.

In the car with Tom, she thought at first that they were going to the police station to do whatever it was that the police had crime victims do. Had she not been so numb, she would have felt surprise when she learned that they were on their way to Dr. Shapiro's.

When they arrived, she sat alone in the waiting room while Tom talked to the psychiatrist in the inner office. After a short time, Dr. Shapiro opened the door and asked her to join them. Jill noticed that he looked worried.

Jill sat on the couch next to Tom and for a few moments

nobody said a word. Slowly, Jill's mind grasped the situation. She had been through a horrible ordeal, and they wanted her to talk about it. They wanted to help her through the bad feelings they assumed she had. But there was a wall between her feelings and what had happened. Talking about last night wouldn't change anything.

Finally, Dr. Shapiro leaned forward. "Tell me about last night," he said gently.

"I would rather not talk about it," Jill said softly.

"I can understand that. But won't you please try?"

Jill stared at her lap for a long while and then without looking up, she forced herself to reconstruct the events of the night before. Her voice was dull and thick but even.

When she finished, she looked up and saw that Dr. Shapiro lacked his usual neutral expression. He looked devastated.

"Can I go now?" Jill asked.

She saw Tom glance at Dr. Shapiro. It made her angry. She wanted to say, "*You* can stay if you want to." Tom was acting as if *she* were the crazy one, not the person who broke into their house and tried to . . .

"What did this person—your attacker—look like?"

Dr. Shapiro's question startled her. It reminded her of the policeman's question the night before: "Tell me, what did your assailant look like?" Jill's stomach began to tighten.

"I don't know," she answered. "It was dark."

Jill turned to face Tom. She asked him if he had seen the body. Could he describe it?

Tom averted his eyes from her face. His reaction was like a light being turned on in a dark room for Jill. She had been sitting in the hall the whole time the police were in the house and she never saw them remove the body. No one had been led out of the house on a stretcher or in handcuffs.

Jill felt short of breath. She turned to Tom and desperately asked him to tell her exactly what had happened. What did the police tell him? Who had attacked her? Was the person still alive?

Tom looked helplessly at Dr. Shapiro. Jill's heart pounded and the room seemed to close in on her. No, it *had* to have been real!

"No! You can't tell me it didn't happen!" Jill cried out desperately.

There was a horrible silence, and then Jill collapsed against the couch, sobbing. Tom tried to put his arms around her, but Jill pulled away.

Finally, Dr. Shapiro said, "It was a nightmare, Jill—a nightmare that you thought was real."

Jill continued to sob.

"I think you must know that it wasn't real," Dr. Shapiro said softly.

Jill shook her head. It was hideous, and now they were telling her that it didn't even happen. Now they were telling her that last night was only the beginning of a different kind of horror.

"Jill," Dr. Shapiro said, "I'm going to start you on some medication—something to even you out, so that you can stay at home. And you will come here every day, and we will try to get to the bottom of this."

Jill did not want to take Dr. Shapiro's pills, but she did not have a choice. Dr. Shapiro's words—*something to even you out, so that you can stay at home*—played again and again in her mind. Translation: Take your pills, or we'll lock you up. Besides, there was Tom, asking, checking, hounding: Did you take your medication? Remember to take your pill. Here's some orange juice to take with your pill.

Benjamin was her only solace. He was the only person in her life who responded to her as if there were nothing wrong with her.

She went dutifully to Dr. Shapiro's office every day. At first he tried to get her to recall everything that had happened during the day preceding her nightmare. She went over and over her dinner with Judy/Judith, the drive home, the mundane events of earlier in the day. After four or five sessions of this, Jill thought she understood what Dr. Shapiro was trying to do. He was trying to jar some recognition on her part of when she had gotten into bed and fallen asleep.

Finally several sessions later, Jill told the psychiatrist: "I have tried, Dr. Shapiro. I have tried and I still cannot believe it was a dream. I mean, I know it must have been, but the evening is all one continuous thread of reality to me."

"All right," Dr. Shapiro said thoughtfully, "let's *assume* for a moment that it was not a dream—that it actually occurred. Let's examine that."

Jill nodded.

"You *say*," the psychiatrist said slowly, "that there was a man waiting for you in your bed, that he attacked you and that you killed him. But later when you examined the body, it was female. How could that be?"

"It was dark," Jill said. "I couldn't see. I *assumed* it was a man attacking me. I mean, why would a woman? Later, when I felt the breast, I realized it had been a woman all along. My assailant did not change sex in the middle of the incident, if that's what you are getting at."

The psychiatrist considered what Jill said.

"All right," he responded. "But why would a woman

have been hiding in your bed? Why would a woman have leapt on top of you and pinned you down?''

"She was trying to kill me.''

"But why was she trying to kill you? Why would some woman want to kill you?''

Jill was quite agitated. "Because she was crazy, Dr. Shapiro. *Because she was crazy.*''

Now it was Shapiro's turn to be agitated. The psychiatrist leaned toward Jill. His manner was urgent, intense.

"Who tried to kill you because she was crazy, Jill. Who?''

"The woman in my bed, that's who!'' Jill's voice was uncharacteristically shrill.

The psychiatrist settled back in his chair. His mind was working very fast, but he did not want in any way to appear excited.

"You know,'' he said finally, "I am thinking about the dream you had in which Mrs. Sanchez tried to suffocate your baby with a pillow.''

Jill was surprised at the change of topic. The psychiatrist asked her what she thought the dream meant. Jill considered it a moment. She had had enough therapy in her life to interpret a dream, and her interpretation of this dream made her feel very guilty.

"I think the dream means,'' Jill said slowly, "that a part of me could not stand one more minute of my child's screaming. But, since I would never harm my child, my subconscious let Mrs. Sanchez do it.''

The psychiatrist nodded. "An obvious interpretation of the dream of a harassed new mother. But, that is not what I think your dream means. Because you see, Jill, if you can be Mrs. Sanchez in the dream, you can also be the baby who is being suffocated.''

Jill looked at him, unsure of what he was getting at.

"In your horrendous nightmare last week," he said, "a woman tried to hold a pillow over your face. In the dream we were just talking about, a woman tried to hold a pillow over Benjamin's face—and here Benjamin could represent you."

The psychiatrist hesitated. He knew he was taking a risk, but he felt that Jill was close to seeing what he saw.

"And," he continued, "in your old, recurring nightmare—the one that prompted you to seek psychiatric help in New York—in that dream a child is thrown into a suffocating closet by a woman."

"What are you getting at?" Jill asked coolly, although she was beginning to guess.

"What do *you* think it means?"

"I think you are suggesting that my mother might have tried to suffocate me," Jill said, grasping how perfectly his evidence pointed to that conclusion. "You are suggesting that in the period when I was very small, before my mother was institutionalized, that she tried to kill me."

The psychiatrist said that he did not know, but that he thought it was a possibility.

Jill felt as if she were being pushed deeper into her chair by a ponderous weight. Dr. Shapiro looked worried, and Jill guessed that he was concerned that his theory had overwhelmed her. But after all she had been through, Jill was not devastated by the thought of what her insane mother might or might not have done to her. Rather, Jill was oppressed by a sudden vision of endless days and years in Dr. Shapiro's office, of pills exchanged for other pills, of Tom forever watching her every move as he grew ever more haggard. She had become a psychiatric specimen, never again to be treated like a normal adult.

Chapter Eighteen

THE FALL STARTED EARLY, BRINGING DAY AFTER DAY OF grey skies. Jill thought that the weather matched her life perfectly. The pills that Dr. Shapiro made her take dulled her senses and flattened her emotions to such an extent that all moments in her life became equal, all experience was filtered through the same deadening haze. The pills robbed her of her energy. Taking care of the baby, getting to Dr. Shapiro's every day, and cooking dinner took everything she had.

Occasionally, she would take Benjamin with her to a nearby town to eat lunch at McDonald's—a McDonald's that was designed without arches to fit tastefully into the quaint village. There, Jill would watch the young mothers—women much younger than she—talk in artificial, nursery-school-teacher tones to their small children.

"I promise, I'll never talk to you that way," Jill whispered to Benjamin. Yet, Jill felt comfortable in the company of these women. They would never look askance at a mismatched outfit, a makeupless face or an unstyled hairdo hanging over the eyes.

In the evening, Jill and Tom were both so tired that they barely communicated. Although neither of them spoke of it, there was a definite rift between them. Jill knew that Tom felt overwhelmed by the burden of her illness, but that he would never admit it. Jill, for her part, could not help thinking that only a year ago—before the move that Tom wanted to make, the move for Tom's career and Tom's parents—her life had been immeasurably better.

Mrs. Sanchez had called Jill this morning not feeling well, so Jill left the baby with Peggy while she went to the psychiatrist. Jill felt that Dr. Shapiro expected more of a change in her behavior after what he considered to be the big breakthrough regarding her mother. But Jill had nothing new to say, no progress to report.

Driving back from the psychiatrist's to pick up Benjamin, Jill dreaded that Peggy might ask her to stay for coffee. Jill had pulled back from Peggy, getting off the phone quickly when she called, refusing her invitations. Ashamed of what Peggy might think of her, Jill had not been able to deal with her well-intentioned questions. She did not know how much or how little Tom had told his mother about her condition, and she just did not feel like facing her—or anyone—now.

Peggy greeted Jill warmly with the news that Benjamin had just fallen asleep and that she had a fresh pot of coffee brewing for them. Jill tried to demur, but Peggy insisted. After all, she said, they so seldom got to see each other anymore.

Resigned, Jill sat at the kitchen table. Peggy put a plate of homemade breads on the table, poured them each a cup of coffee and sat next to Jill. The women sipped their coffee in silence for a few moments and then Peggy put her hand on Jill's knee.

"Jill, what's going on?"

Jill stared at her cup. Tom obviously hadn't told her. But what was the point of lying? Anyone could see that there was something really wrong with her.

"I have had a mental breakdown," she said without looking up. "I told you about the craziness when the baby was born. We thought it was all over. But it's not. I've gotten worse, much, much worse. I am sure that Tom didn't tell you because he didn't want to worry you—not so soon after Ben. But I didn't want you to know either . . . I didn't want you to think less of me. That's why I have been avoiding you."

"Oh, my dear Jill!" Peggy cried, circling Jill in her arms.

"You have been seeing a psychiatrist, then?" Peggy asked when their embrace had ended.

"Every day."

Peggy nodded slowly, as if she were trying to piece together something. She asked more questions, specific questions: What kind of mental breakdown? What exactly were the symptoms? What had caused it?

Jill answered Peggy's questions openly and honestly.

"When did it all start?"

"My childhood, I suppose. Although it might be inherited."

"No, the hallucinations. When did they start?"

"When I was about four months pregnant."

"Here? When you were staying here with us?"

"No, after we moved into our house."

"Dora's house!" Peggy slapped her hand against the table. "Of course. It's all starting to make sense."

Jill had no idea what Peggy was talking about.

"You know, Jill, I read that sometimes when people hear voices or see things that aren't there, they aren't crazy. They are really having a psychic experience. They are picking up a conversation or an image from the past or the future.''

Jill stared at Peggy incredulously. The older woman continued speaking, her words coming out in an excited rush.

"In fact, there is even a psychologist in Berkeley who specializes in helping people find out if their problems are a result of some psychic experience." With evident excitement, Peggy rose from her chair. "I'm going to go find you that article!"

Jill was flabbergasted. She certainly had not expected this turn of events over a cup of coffee with Peggy.

Peggy returned with a copy of the *National Enquirer*. When Jill saw the newspaper, she burst out laughing.

"Oh Peggy, you can't be serious!"

Peggy looked as if she had been slapped. Jill, to make up for hurting Peggy, picked up the article and read it. The article was a summary of a talk given by Colleen Murphy, Ph.D., which claimed that certain episodes diagnosed as psychotic in certain individuals might in fact be episodes of psychic experience.

"Well, it's an interesting theory," Jill said, putting down the article, trying to be polite.

"What would it hurt if you called her?"

"I couldn't do that. Tom would have me committed."

"You wouldn't have to tell him. I could call her for you. I could see her with you, if you wanted."

Shapiro would have a stroke if I went to some psychic, Jill thought with some pleasure.

"You could go just one time to see what she had to say."

Jill looked at Peggy, at her kind, round face, and suddenly it dawned on her: Peggy was not trying to find a simplistic remedy for her illness. Peggy did not think she was sick!

"Alright," Jill said. "I'll do it."

Smiling broadly, Peggy picked up the telephone and called Berkeley information. She got a number for Colleen Murphy, dialed it without hesitation, and passed the phone to Jill. To Jill's surprise, Colleen Murphy answered. Jill made an appointment for the following week.

Jill found Colleen Murphy's home easily. It was a large, older house on a pleasant residential street in Berkeley. Jill took a deep breath and rang the doorbell. The door was answered by a handsome woman, large and solidly rooted to the ground, with grey-black hair worn pulled back in a clip. She looked to be in her fifties and wore a peasant-style print skirt, a black sweater and a magnificent turquoise-and-silver sunburst necklace with matching earrings. "You must be Jill," she said in a voice that was deep and gravelly, yet very pleasant.

Colleen escorted Jill into her living room—a bright room filled with framed prints, plants and book-laden shelves. She offered Jill a seat on an overstuffed couch that had a Mexican blanket draped across the back, then seated herself in a rocking chair opposite the couch. A cat lay in the sun on the broad windowsill.

"This isn't quite what I expected," Jill said, looking around the room.

Colleen threw her head back and laughed. She had a deep, earthy, unashamed laugh. "What did you expect— a dark room with candles and incense burning and pictures of Indian mystics on the walls?"

Jill smiled. She liked the woman, and yet she felt a little stupid being there.

Nervously, Jill took the initiative. She asked Colleen to explain the kind of work she did.

Colleen said that she was a psychologist who specialized in parapsychology—the investigation of psychic phenomena. She also was herself clairsentient, that is, gifted with heightened or extrasensory perceptions—psychic, if you will. In addition, she was a medium—capable of allowing herself to become a temporary channel through which disembodied personalities or entities could communicate with the living.

Colleen said that she had been raised in an Irish family where all of the women had psychic abilities, and she grew up thinking of her talents as being perfectly natural and ordinary. She added that she was on the staff of the California Institute for Psychic Research. Then she explained that she was also a licensed psychologist who worked primarily with people who needed help dealing with their psychic abilities or with sudden or traumatic psychic experiences.

"Now," Colleen said, "what about you? Why have you come to see me?"

Jill hesitated. She did not know where to begin. She really did not want to talk about her psychological problems. She did not want to give this woman the opportunity to say, "I can't help you, because you actually are crazy."

"I have had some strange occurrences in my house— footsteps, music playing, door handles being rattled." What an understatement, Jill thought.

Colleen gave Jill a peculiar look. She seemed about to say something, but then appeared to change her mind. "Where do you live?" she asked.

Jill told her. She had not considered the possibility that the psychic would come to her house, and the prospect made her uneasy. She really did not know what kind of person this woman was—yet, she wanted to trust her.

Colleen whistled. ''I would have to charge you for driving time and mileage.''

Jill nodded. They discussed a fee, which seemed reasonable to Jill. Jill said that she would like her mother-in-law to attend the session. Colleen agreed and then consulted a leather appointment book. ''I could come Thursday afternoon at two,'' she said, seeming pleased. She got up from her chair, held out her hand, gave Jill a warm smile and said, ''I am looking forward to seeing what I can do for you.''

Leaving Colleen's, Jill realized that she was ravenous. Certainly, Peggy—who was minding the baby—would not care if she stopped for lunch. The prospect of that small pleasure left Jill feeling almost buoyant.

The day had turned warm and sunny, and without much effort Jill found a cafe with outdoor tables. She was seated immediately at a table on the patio. As she drank in the details of the pleasant courtyard—the tables with their blue-checkered cloths and fresh flowers arranged in Perrier bottles, the casually well-dressed patrons deep into their luncheon conversations, the clear sky overhead, the gentle breeze—she realized that she felt different than she usually did. She felt alive. Good God, she felt alive and she felt sane!

Like most first-time visitors to Jill's house, Colleen arrived effusing over its beauty. Jill introduced Colleen to Peggy, who could not hide her discomfort as the psychic marveled at everything she saw.

Jill led the way to the living room. At the entrance to the large room, Colleen stopped suddenly, looking perplexed.

"Do you know, did a body ever lay in state in this room? I had a strong picture of a coffin over there," she said, indicating the far end of the room.

Jill shuddered as the image of Ben's grotesquely distorted face overtook her mind.

"What is it?" asked Colleen.

Jill glanced anxiously at Peggy, hoping that she had read nothing in her behavior, telling herself once again that seeing Ben in that coffin had been a hallucination.

"Nothing," Jill said, trying for a casual voice. "I don't know of anything like that, but then, it's an old house."

Colleen shrugged. Jill led the way to the overstuffed chairs in front of the fireplace. Colleen took a small tape recorder from her purse and set it next to her. "What I am going to do," she explained, "is go into a kind of self-hypnotic state. In this state, I am particularly sensitive to other energy forms that are nearby. If there are any entities here, I can communicate—or attempt to communicate—with them telepathically. Then I allow myself to be used as a human channel for them to speak through. It's similar to how a radio works—except that psychic vibrations are at a much, much higher frequency than radio waves. Well . . . Shall we begin?"

Without waiting for an answer, Colleen closed her eyes, dropped her head on her chest, and extended her arms, holding her palms upward. She sat silently for what seemed like a long time while Peggy and Jill glanced nervously from Colleen to one another. Suddenly, Colleen's body jolted—as if she had received a powerful electric shock—and her hands fell to her lap. Her head rose from her chest, although her eyes never opened.

In spite of herself, Jill felt her heartbeat picking up.

Finally, Colleen spoke in a soft but firm voice.

"I want the baby," she said.

Jill was thrown completely off guard. Why would Colleen ask for her baby? Jill had never even told her that she had a baby.

"I don't understand," Jill said. "What do you mean, you want the baby?"

"I told you, I want the baby!"

Although the medium did not raise her voice, her tone was ominous. Jill felt herself panicking. Her baby was upstairs sleeping—alone. What had she done? She looked over at Peggy . . . and gasped. Peggy was deathly white and absolutely still, her face ravaged with terror. She sat frozen and glassy-eyed, staring at Colleen, a hand over her mouth.

"Peggy, what's wrong?" Jill asked frantically, jumping from her chair.

In response, Peggy shifted slightly, but her eyes did not leave Colleen.

"Colleen, we need to stop this!" Jill said, marching over to the psychic and turning off her tape recorder. "Do you hear me?" she demanded, shaking Colleen's shoulder. The psychic was as still as death.

"Snap out of it! Do you hear me?"

Suddenly, Colleen's body jolted and her eyes flew open. Jill recoiled, her heart hammering. Colleen shook her head slightly, then turned to look at Jill.

"Why is the tape recorder off?"

It took Jill a moment to answer. "It's enough for one day," she said evenly.

Colleen glanced at Peggy. Peggy's gaze had shifted inward, from the psychic to some private point. Her hand remained clasped to her mouth.

Jill went to her mother-in-law and knelt in front of her.

"What's wrong?" Colleen asked with evident concern. "What happened?"

Jill was too concerned about Peggy to answer. Gently, she turned Peggy's face toward her. "Are you ill? Should I call Tom?"

Peggy shook her head and then glanced up at Colleen, who stood by helplessly.

"Colleen, please show yourself out," Jill said without looking away from Peggy. "My mother-in-law needs to rest."

Reluctantly, Colleen gathered her things and left.

"Peggy, please talk to me," Jill implored. "Please tell me what is the matter."

"You must not stay here any longer," Peggy said finally. Her eyes were watery and full of fear. *"She wants your baby!"*

"It's alright, she's gone now," Jill said, referring to Colleen. "That was all just a lot of mumbo jumbo. She doesn't really want my baby. Why on earth would she?"

"Because hers is dead! Because she wants everything of mine!"

"Who are you talking about, Peggy?"

"Dora! Don't you understand?"

Jill's stomach clenched as she remembered the condolence letter and the sad little snapshot of Dora with her baby.

"Jill, don't you see that you can't stay here? Not with the baby!"

"Oh, Peggy, Dora can't hurt us—she can't hurt anyone anymore," Jill said, wrapping her arms around Peggy, as much to comfort herself as the older woman. She had to get Peggy up, get her moving around. They both had to get a grip on themselves.

"Come on, I'll make us tea," she said, urging Peggy out of her chair.

Jill led Peggy into the kitchen. Neither woman spoke as

Jill prepared the tea. She placed two steaming mugs on the table and sat down beside Peggy.

"You okay?" Jill asked, squeezing Peggy's hand. She could see that Peggy's color was returning.

Peggy nodded.

"Could you tell me about Dora's baby?" Jill asked after a few minutes, without really being sure of why she was asking. "If you feel up to it, could you tell me what you remember?"

"It was so long ago . . ."

Jill nodded, her expression urging Peggy to continue.

"Well . . . you knew that Ben and I tried for many years to have a baby?" Peggy finally responded. "That there were miscarriages and a stillbirth?"

Jill shook her head sadly. She had not known.

"In the years that we were trying so hard to have a baby, Dora got it in her mind that *she* wanted a baby too. Only she said she couldn't have one herself." Peggy sighed wearily and then continued. "But knowing Dora, I don't think that was the truth. I think she just couldn't bear getting fat, even for a few months. Anyway, she wanted Ben to arrange for a private adoption—private to make sure that the baby had good-looking parents. Finally, Dora got her baby—a very pretty little boy. She played the role of the doting mother to the hilt. We still saw each other in those years, and she played the role with particular relish in front of me. And, of course, she named the baby Benjamin."

Jill sucked in her breath.

"The baby died of the flu while on a trip back East with Dora. That's the whole story—at least all that I know of it. Dora gave a lot of money to children's charities in his memory. But it seemed that she had no more desire to be a mother after he died."

Jill squirmed in her chair. She was both exhausted and curiously excited. Colleen knew nothing about her baby. Jill had never mentioned him and none of his things were in the living room. Colleen could not have possibly known about Benjamin—and, Dora *did* have a baby in this house. A baby that died! Good lord, Tom had even told her that Dora had been clutching a baby blanket when she died. The woman had been dead only a few months when she and Tom moved into her house expecting a baby. A baby that they named Benjamin. Oh God, could it possibly be that there was some bizarre explanation for everything that had happened?

Something that was outside of her own mind?

Chapter Nineteen

TOM ARRIVED HOME LATE THAT EVENING AFTER WORK-
ing a fourteen-hour day. Jill thought that he looked as
exhausted as she felt. As they shared a supper of soup
and cold cuts, Jill groped for a way to tell him about
what had happened that afternoon. With seeming off-
handedness, she brought up the subject of psychic telep-
athy. Maybe, just maybe, she suggested, it was possible
that an individual's psychic energy could remain in a
place after he or she had died. And perhaps it was possible that such energy could react in strange ways with
the psyches of living people.

"Huh?" Tom said, pausing from his meal to look at
her. Then he laughed. "Don't tell me you've been reading
the *National Enquirer* in the checkout line!"

"I know, it's an easy subject to make fun of," Jill replied evenly, "especially if you don't know anything about
it. But have you ever watched a psychic work?"

"No, and I wouldn't want to. That kind of thing drives
me up the wall, Jill, because when people take it seriously
they are likely to get hurt. I have seen people die who did

not have to because instead of going to a doctor in time they went to some faith healer who performed some mumbo jumbo and told them they were cured. I hate thinking about those charlatans and the pathetic people who get taken in by them.''

Jill nodded, sighing. In Tom's mind there would be no difference between Colleen Murphy and a charlatan in a tent. She would tell him when it was over—when she understood whatever it was that was happening to her and stopped it. She changed the subject, wondering vaguely if all doctors were like the ones she had known—constitutionally incapable of grasping an unscientific idea.

Later, as she lay wide-eyed in the dark with Tom asleep beside her, she decided what she would do: She would ask Colleen back to complete the session, but this time without Peggy. She knew Peggy would never want to go through an experience like that again, nor would Jill want her to.

As she tried to settle down to sleep, Jill remembered a segment she had seen on *60 Minutes* about terminal cancer patients who sought unorthodox cures in Mexico. She had watched the film of these ravaged people spending their last dollars for bizarre treatments at seedy-looking clinics, and she had wanted to scream at the set: Don't do it! Was Jill, herself, now about to join the ranks of those desperate cure-seekers—a terminal mental patient in search of a magic doctor? Was Tom right after all?

Jill was extremely restless in Dr. Shapiro's office the next morning. The possibility that there was a connection between Dora Miles and some of the bizarre experiences that Jill had had in her house so preoccupied her that she could think of nothing else. Finally she decided to take a gamble with Dr. Shapiro. Maybe she could break through to him where she had failed with Tom.

"Look," she blurted out, "what if all the things that have happened to me since moving out here weren't really all in my mind? What if I heard footsteps because there actually were footsteps to be heard? What if there really was a woman in my bed that night—an apparition, if you will. I mean, there are perfectly respectable people— scientists—who think something like that may be possible."

"I'm not sure I understand," the psychiatrist said slowly. "Are you talking about ghosts and such?"

Jill took a deep breath. "Well, not exactly ghosts—more like psychic phenomena—paranormal occurrences."

Dr. Shapiro lifted his eyebrows. Jill could not tell if the gesture was one of reflection or one of skepticism. "Perhaps energy takes forms that we don't recognize yet," Jill continued tentatively.

"I hear you saying that you think your house might be haunted."

Jill bristled. "I am *only* saying that I think it might be possible that some of the things that have happened to me weren't in my mind."

"In a sense I agree with you," Dr. Shapiro said after a long silence. "I think you are haunted." The psychiatrist considered his words carefully. "However, you brought the ghosts with you, Jill. No ghost who happened to be hanging around a house you moved into could ever be as powerful as a ghost you know intimately."

Dr. Shapiro leaned forward in his chair for emphasis. "These are *your* ghosts, Jill. Nothing out of the ordinary has happened to Tom in your house or to anyone else as far as we know."

Jill sank in her chair. She should have known better than

to broach this subject with Dr. Shapiro. He was a doctor like Tom.

The psychiatrist continued: "I do think we have to look, however, at why you feel the need to project *your* conflicts onto some exterior phenomenon."

Jill shut her eyes. Why had she bothered?

When Jill got home, she telephoned Colleen Murphy. The psychic was concerned and anxious about Peggy. Jill assured her that Peggy, although terrified by the session, was alright later in the day and that she was fine now.

"I still want to get to the bottom of this," Jill said. "If it's alright with you, I would like us to continue alone."

Colleen agreed to see her the following Tuesday. When she arrived, Jill took her directly into the living room, seating her in the same chair as before.

"Before we start," Jill said, "I want to ask you a question. Is it possible . . ." Jill groped for the right words. "I mean, can we stir anything up—cause trouble for me or my family—by these spiritual contacts?"

Colleen laughed gently and put out her hand in a gesture to stop Jill's train of logic. "You mean, can this process materialize a demon who will wreak havoc on your life? Hardly!" Then Colleen's manner became serious as she considered what she was going to say next.

"Jill, I don't think we are even dealing with the present in these sessions. What we are seeing is like a fingerprint—a fingerprint left by someone long gone. We are also dealing with how you are affected by your ability to see that fingerprint—in other words, by your sensitivity to the past."

Jill was not quite sure that she understood, but she nodded anyway.

"Shall we begin?" Colleen asked, turning on the tape recorder. Then, as before, she held her palms upright and dropped her head onto her chest. Jill waited anxiously as the psychic sat without moving. Then, suddenly and disturbingly, her body convulsed, throwing her hands into her lap. When her body stilled, she lifted her head from her chest. Although the psychic's eyes were closed, Jill felt she was somehow staring at her.

"I want the baby," she said once again.

"Who are you?" Jill asked, trying to keep her voice calm. "What is your name?"

Jill braced herself.

"Ellie Shaw," was the firm, clear response.

Jill felt as if the breath had been knocked out of her.

"Who did you say you were?"

"Ellie Shaw."

Jill had nearly forgotten about the lovely blonde teenager who had ridden her bike to see her so many months ago.

"But you are not dead," Jill stammered. "I saw you. You came to visit me. We spoke . . ." And later at Tom's parents, they all stared at me when I said you had come by, stared at me *because Ellie Shaw was dead, had been dead for years*.

Jill slumped in her chair. The silence was resounding. The sound of her heart beating seemed to fill the room. There was no one to help her.

Forcing herself to speak, Jill rasped: "You are the girl who came to see me?"

"Yes."

"Why?"

"Because I want the baby."

"Why . . ." Jill asked, her voice cracking, "why do you want *my* baby?"

"Not your baby. My baby."

"He's not your baby! What do you mean by that? What are you talking about?" Jill was nearly yelling, her voice shrill, her fear mounting.

There was no answer. Jill took several deep breaths and asked the same questions more calmly. Still there was no answer.

Colleen's body jolted. She dropped her head into her hands and shook it. Finally, she looked up at Jill, exhausted.

"She's gone," she said. Colleen sat without moving for a moment. Then she rewound the tape recorder, saying, "Let's see what we've got."

They both listened in silence. At the end of the tape, Colleen said, "You know her?"

Jill nodded wearily and started to explain.

"Wait," Colleen said, "I want to get this down." She turned on the recorder again.

Jill told her about Ellie Shaw's visit and the subsequent dinner at her in-laws.

Colleen whistled. "Oh, I wish we could have documented her visit at the time, but that's hindsight." Colleen's vitality had completely returned. She sat forward in her chair, energetic, enthusiastic.

"Jill, you obviously had a profound psychic experience with this Ellie Shaw. That sort of thing is extremely rare." Colleen seemed to be trying to contain her excitement. "I'd like to run some tests on you down at the institute and introduce you to some of my colleagues. I think you may have remarkable psychic powers."

"I'm not interested in finding out about my psychic powers," Jill snapped. "I am interested in finding out what's going on here. I want to know who this Ellie Shaw is and why she has attached herself to me."

"Of course," Colleen said, backing down. "I'll do whatever I can to help."

"I didn't mean to sound so testy . . ."

Colleen put her hand out to stop Jill's apology. "I understand," she said.

Jill was quiet for a moment, then she asked softly: "Colleen, do you think my baby could be in any danger?"

"From Ellie Shaw?" Colleen shook her head. "She can't do anything. She has no power except to communicate. She has no efficacy in this world. She can't act. Besides," Colleen added, "I believe that it's not your baby that she wants, but her baby."

The words registered with Jill: *Not your baby. My baby.* Yes, of course, that's what she had meant. Jill nodded, feeling somewhat relieved.

As soon as Colleen left, Jill telephoned Peggy to fill her in on what had occurred. Peggy, although full of questions, was unable to tell Jill anything more about Ellie Shaw than she already knew: that she had been a patient of Ben's and that she had tragically committed suicide as a teenager.

"The most important thing I have to tell you, Peggy, is that there is nothing for you to worry about anymore," Jill said. "There is no way that finding out about this poor girl can cause me any harm."

"Oh, Jill," Peggy said, unable to hide her worry, "I don't know. I just don't know."

On the pretext of doing a favor for Peggy, Jill dropped by Tom's office the next day.

"She wants me to look up something in one of Ben's old files, a birthday. She said she didn't want to bother Mrs. Fisher about it."

Tom smiled. His mother hated to bother the office.

"You can look up front, but if it's an old file, it's probably in the basement," he said, handing Jill a key to the storage room.

In a battered basement file cabinet, Jill found what she was looking for. A manila folder, yellow with age, told her that Ellie Shaw had indeed been a patient of Ben Douglas. The doctor's neatly penned notes showed that at age fifteen the unmarried Ellie Shaw had become pregnant. The pregnancy was uneventful, but the male baby delivered at home by Ben was stillborn. There were no further entries in the chart.

After leaving Tom's office, Jill went to the local newspaper, where she was dismayed to find out that the small weekly had been published only since 1948. Driving past the high school, however, Jill's spirits soared again. Of course, Ellie must have gone to this high school.

Making a hasty U-turn, Jill pulled in front of the concrete and stone building. She found the library without a problem, but as soon as she walked into the large room, she was confronted by the librarian, curious about Jill's business in the school.

Not expecting to attract any attention, Jill was thrown off guard. She said she would like to see the yearbooks for the years 1938–1940. "I would like to look up my mother," she said hastily.

"You're Dr. Douglas's wife, aren't you?" the librarian said, finally placing the familiar-looking woman.

Jill nodded.

The librarian, whose name was Mildred Sparks, thought it odd, very odd, that Mrs. Douglas would be looking up her mother in the Willowglen yearbooks, since she knew that the young doctor's wife was a stranger, without roots in the town. Still, she went into the closed stacks to get the books for Mrs. Douglas.

The librarian returned to the main room and gave Jill the yearbooks. In an attempt to escape the librarian's watchful gaze, Jill took the books to the farthest corner of the room and sat down facing the wall. The yearbook from 1939 creaked when she opened it and the smell of must floated from the pages. Flipping to the index, Jill ran her finger down the list of names.

Her heart fluttered when saw Ellie's name. She turned the pages back, and there toward the bottom of the page was the smiling face of the lovely young girl Jill had met. Jill bent over the picture. Ellie smiled from the page, her blonde hair swept into a ponytail, her loveliness un-dimmed by the years. Yet, she was not quite the same girl who had visited Jill. The girl whose picture had been taken for the yearbook was a living, breathing teenager—a girl who went to football games and dances.

"Oh, Ellie, what happened to you?" Jill whispered to the image in the photograph, as her eyes filled with sudden tears.

"Did you find what you wanted?" It was the librarian, leaning over her.

As Jill nodded, several large tears splashed onto the yearbook page.

"Are you alright?" the librarian whispered. "Can I do anything to help you?"

Such personal attention, Jill thought, wiping her eyes. "Do you have a photocopy machine?" she asked tersely. The librarian pointed it out to her.

Not bothering to hide her irritation at the librarian's intrusiveness, Jill picked up her things and went to the machine. She copied the page with Ellie's photo on it, and then in a sudden inspiration, copied the six pages of students in Ellie's class. Then, Jill hurried out of the library.

Several days later, Mildred Sparks's thirteen-year-old son stepped on a rusty nail and had to be taken to see the doctor. As Tom examined the boy's foot, Mildred remarked, "I didn't know that your wife's mother went to our high school."

"She didn't," Tom said, without looking up from the boy's wound.

"Well, I didn't think that she did," Mildred continued, chattily. "That's why I was so surprised when your wife came into the library at the high school and said that she wanted to look up her mother in one of our old yearbooks."

Holding the boy's foot gently in his hand, Tom looked at the woman quizzically.

"I got her the yearbooks," Mildred continued breathlessly, "then when I went over to see if she needed anything else, I saw that she was crying. I have been concerned about her. Is she alright?"

"She's fine," Tom said evenly. "We just had a baby, and my wife's been very tired. We both have been. But she is fine, thank you."

Tom ordered a tetanus shot for the boy and then patted him gently on the arm. "I think you're gonna live, pal," he said.

Tom said good-by to Mildred, then left the examining room, walked down the hall, and went into the bathroom. He locked the door behind him, turned on the tap and splashed cold water on his face.

He did not need Mildred Sparks's gossip to know that Jill was not getting better. She had been a stranger to him lately, more secretive than ever before. The lifelessness that marked her illness was now covered with a veneer of plastic. Instead of sharing her fears with him, she engaged in chipper, meaningless conversation. He had no idea what she thought anymore. He could not reach her. Every day, she slipped further and further away.

Tom dropped his head in his hands.

Oh, God, was it ever going to end?

Chapter Twenty

IT SEEMED TO JILL THAT TOM WAS PARTICULARLY SLOW IN leaving for work the next day. She tried to hurry him along without being obvious about how eager she was for him to leave. She was obsessed with finding out about Ellie Shaw and could not wait to get to work. A challenging research project always excited her, and this project meant more to her than any assignment she had ever done in her career.

Tom sensed her excitement and wondered aloud what was up.

If you knew, you would have me committed, Jill thought. She told him that she just felt a little better than usual this morning.

"I'm so glad to hear that," Tom said, meaning it with all his heart.

As soon as Tom left, Jill cancelled her appointment with Dr. Shapiro, telling him that the baby did not seem to be feeling well. The psychiatrist was so sympathetic that Jill felt guilty about her fib.

After she hung up, she put her hand on Benjamin's forehead to reassure herself that her baby was fine and happy and untouched by her lie.

Then Jill went to work. She spread the photocopied pages of Ellie's classmates across the kitchen table. Jill counted twenty-eight students in the class—fifteen girls and thirteen boys. Two extra girls, Jill thought, two girls sitting against the gym wall at every dance. But Ellie would never have been one of them. She was too lovely.

Jill started with the girls. Although she knew that they would be harder to locate than the boys, she felt that a female classmate would have more information to offer. But, as she feared, none of the girls was listed in the phone book under her maiden name. Undaunted, she turned to Ellie's male classmates. She found three of their names listed.

No one answered the first number. The second number belonged to the son of the man she wanted. The son's wife informed her that her father-in-law had been dead for many years. The third number produced a man who *had* been a classmate of Ellie's, but to Jill's great disappointment the man said he remembered nothing about Ellie.

Jill returned to the female classmates. She began calling individuals with the same family names as the fifteen girls, hoping to find a relative who could direct her to one of them. It was a frustrating exercise. People were not at home. They had never heard of the girl in question. They refused to speak to a stranger.

Between these calls, Jill continued to dial the number of the remaining male classmate. Finally, a woman answered the phone. Jill identified herself and said she was trying to reach Jim Cleveland.

"I am his wife," the woman said, her tone wary and suspicious.

Jill smiled, wondering if *she* ever sounded that way

when an unfamiliar voice asked for *her* husband on the telephone.

"The reason I'm calling," Jill said pleasantly, "is that I am trying to locate people who might have known Ellie Shaw at Willowglen High School in nineteen thirty-nine."

"Why, I knew Ellie," Mrs. Cleveland responded, her suspicion replaced by the pleasure of feeling important. "We were in the same class at Willowglen. Of course, that was a very long time ago."

Jill's heart raced and she had to take a deep breath to calm herself. "I would like to know anything that you remember about her. She's sort of a lost relative of mine."

Mrs. Cleveland responded with a chatty reminiscence. Jill let the woman talk, prodding her in the right direction with well-conceived questions.

Mrs. Cleveland had not been a close friend of Ellie's. "She was not in *our* crowd," was how she put it. And, indeed, from Mrs. Cleveland's description, Jill obtained a picture of a girl who, no matter how pretty she was, would never have been admitted to "our crowd."

Mrs. Cleveland said that Ellie was a poor girl. She had no father and her mother had to work. Ellie was pretty, but not well dressed, better liked by the boys than the girls.

"She got pregnant in our junior year," Mrs. Cleveland said tentatively, as if she were not sure how Jill would respond to such information.

"Yes, I know," Jill said. "Tell me what you remember about that."

"Well her mother tried to hide it, of course. She kept Ellie at home and told everyone that she had a disease that made her bloat. Of course, everyone knew the truth," she said, a trace of the old in-crowd smugness creeping into her voice. "The next year, she killed herself."

Jill's stomach tightened. Mrs. Cleveland had little else to offer. She did not know who the father of Ellie's baby was, or what happened to the child.

"Mrs. Cleveland, is there anyone I could talk to who knew Ellie well?"

The woman thought for a moment. "Yes, Dick Hampton. He was a couple of years younger, but they were pals. He might have been her next-door neighbor. Anyhow, he owns the Texaco station."

Jill's heart leapt. "Thank you, Mrs. Cleveland. Thank you so very much."

Jill put down the phone and looked at the clock. It was eleven-thirty. She would race over to the Texaco station right now while Mrs. Sanchez watched the baby.

Dick Hampton's Texaco station was small and unpretentious, still retaining the old-style, skinny gas pumps. Except for two small boys pumping air into their bicycle tires, the station was customerless when Jill arrived. She parked her car, walked past the boys, peered into the empty station office and then stepped carefully into the garage. A mechanic worked under the hood of a ten-year-old Oldsmobile.

"Excuse me," Jill said politely. "I am looking for Dick Hampton."

"You're talking to him," he said, without turning around.

Jill introduced herself and explained why she was there, her words pouring out in a nervous rush. Dick Hampton continued his work without comment while Jill waited anxiously in silence.

Finally he asked: "Why do you want to know about her?"

"I think we might be related in some way." It was a lie that was also in a way the truth.

Dick Hampton turned from his work to look at Jill and she returned his gaze. He was a trim man of medium height, undistinguished except for the deep blue and rather sad eyes that now regarded Jill from a grime-covered face. There appeared to be nothing expansive about him. When he finally nodded at Jill, the movement was so silent that it was barely perceptible.

"I don't want to interrupt your work," Jill said, leaning back against a part-strewn counter.

"It's lunchtime," he said, adding, "you're gonna get grease on you."

Jill jolted away from the counter. "I don't want to interrupt your lunch," she said.

"That doesn't leave you with much," he said. Jill stared at him uncomprehendingly until it dawned on her that previously she had said she did not want to interrupt his work.

"All right," he said, pointing to the station office, "meet me in there."

Jill stepped into the cluttered office and looked around. There were a couple of battered file cabinets in one corner. In another was a wooden desk with an old-style adding machine on it. Behind the desk was a wooden swivel chair cushioned with a faded blue pillow. On the wall behind the desk were a clock, a pinup calendar so modest that Jill was surprised to see that it was current, and a faded map of California with Scotch-tape-mended tears. Jill sat down in the straight-backed chair next to the desk.

Dick Hampton came into the office carrying a bag lunch, two cans of Pepsi and a package of peanut butter on cheese crackers from the vending machine. He put a Pepsi and the crackers in front of Jill and then he sat down on his swivel chair with the faded blue cushion.

Without saying a word, the gas station owner opened his sack, pulled out a sandwich and bit into it. Jill murmured a thank-you for the crackers, opened them and took a bite of one. She was so nervous and her mouth was so dry that she nearly choked on the concoction. She gulped some Pepsi and then launched into a monologue that she hoped would loosen Dick Hampton into talking. She explained how she had gone through the high school yearbooks to find Ellie, then how she had searched for her classmates, which led to Jim Cleveland's wife, who suggested Dick Hampton. Eventually, with a great deal of effort, Jill was able to draw him out.

Dick described Ellie as a cheerful, fun-loving girl who was always kind to her younger neighbor.

"She taught me to dance," he said, "but it didn't stick."

Dick confirmed that Ellie was fatherless. "Dead or ran off, who knows," he said.

Jill asked him what Ellie's mother was like.

"Then, I thought she was sour, real sour," Dick said. "Thinking back, maybe she was just worn out."

After a period of silence, Jill gently asked Dick about Ellie's pregnancy.

"It wasn't like it is now," he answered slowly, "with unmarrieds living together and having babies and Lord knows what else."

Jill nodded, wordlessly encouraging him to go on.

Dick told her that after Ellie's pregnancy began to show, her mother kept her sequestered in the house, telling everyone that she was ill—too ill for visitors. Dick was allowed in the house, though, because Ellie insisted—and probably because her mother thought he was too young to draw any conclusions. Ellie never discussed with Dick how she got pregnant or her feelings about being pregnant. She told him that she was going to give her baby up for adoption and then go back to school as if she had just gotten over her illness. But late in her pregnancy, Ellie changed her mind. She told Dick that she had decided to keep the baby. She said she was going to move to a town where no one knew her. She would say that she was eighteen and a widow. She would get a room, a job and find someone to mind the baby while she worked.

Ellie seemed relieved by her decision, but her mother would hear nothing of it. She said keeping the baby would ruin Ellie's life and that Ellie would wind up just like she had. Once Dick overheard Ellie's mother saying that the adoption was all set and there was nothing Ellie could do about it.

On the day that Ellie's labor started, she sent Dick to get her mother from work and to fetch the doctor. When Dick went to bed that night, Dr. Douglas's car was still outside.

The next day Dick heard that Ellie's baby had died. Ellie was sick after the birth and Dick was not allowed to see her. When he finally did see her, she was not the same girl. The spirit had been drained from her and she was brokenhearted. She told Dick that her mother said the baby died because Ellie was just a girl and her body could not properly nourish a baby. But Ellie said that she saw the baby when he was born, and he was round and healthy and screaming.

"The infant was *not* stillborn, then?" Jill interrupted. "He died after birth?"

Dick nodded and continued with his story. Ellie went back to school, but the kids did not treat her well. After a while, she quit school and got a job in the variety store. But she never returned to her old self. She was solemn and sad, always sad. Eventually her mind started to go. She had delusions. She told Dick that she dreamt she heard her baby crying for her every night. Later she said that the dreams were not dreams at all—she heard the baby crying for her when she was awake too. She thought it meant that her baby was still alive, and that since he was alive, she would be able to find him.

Unfortunately, Ellie told these things to other people as well as Dick. Before long the whole town was talking about Crazy Ellie. Shortly before she died, Ellie told Dick that a rich woman had come into the variety store carrying a baby the same age as Ellie's would be. She said she was going to find out if the rich woman's baby was really Ellie's son.

"Did she try to find out?" Jill asked.

"I don't know."

"Do you know who the rich woman was?"

Dick shook his head. A short time after they had that conversation, Ellie ran away. At least, that is what everyone thought. Months later her body washed up from the ocean. It seems she had ridden her bike straight over a cliff.

"I guess she had had enough," he said simply.

Jill took a deep breath. Dick turned to check the clock behind his head. Jill jumped up. "I don't know how to thank you," she said. Dick responded with his barely perceptible nod.

Jill returned to her car, the blood pounding through her veins at an astonishing rate. There was no question in her mind as to where Ellie's baby had gone. Jill knew the date of Ellie's baby's birth from Ellie's medical file. Now she had only to compare that date with the date on the condolence letter that she had found among Dora's correspondence when she cleaned out Dora's belongings. Jill had given all of Dora's letters to Ben. She turned her car toward Peggy's house, desperately hoping that her mother-in-law had not thrown them away.

Peggy was pruning shrubs in her front yard when Jill arrived.

"You've got grease on the back of your skirt," Peggy said to Jill as they walked toward the house.

Jill laughed, explaining to Peggy where she had just been and why. Then she asked Peggy if she still had the box of Dora's personal papers that Jill had given Ben.

Peggy shrugged. "I started to go through some of Ben's papers, but it got to be too much. Do you know," she said sadly, "that Ben kept every letter Dora ever wrote him?"

Jill shook her head and put her arm around Peggy's waist. Peggy took Jill into Ben's study, pointed to the desk, the file cabinets and the boxes stacked in the closet and said, "Help yourself."

In half an hour, Jill was able to find the box of papers she had given Ben. The contents had remained untouched since she had put them in the box. Jill sorted the letters carefully until she found the one she was looking for. The letter was postmarked seven months after Ellie's delivery. It had to have been the same baby. There was no other explanation.

Jill took out the photograph that had been inside the letter and examined it, looking for a resemblance between the sun-bonneted baby and Ellie. She could not examine the photograph, however, without her eyes clouding. Dora looked so happy, the baby so healthy.

Two women—two mothers—suffered the loss of the same baby. Then Jill had moved into Dora's house pregnant and had a son—a son with the same name as Dora's boy. No wonder there was—as Colleen would put it—psychic energy stirred up in that house.

As soon as Jill got home, she called Colleen with her findings. Colleen, every bit as excited as Jill, made an appointment to come to the house the next day.

Jill felt as if a burden had been lifted. She could physically feel a lessening of the weight that had been pinning her down for so many months. She was not crazy. There was an explanation for every strange thing that had happened to her—perhaps not an explanation that would be scientifically accepted, but an explanation nonetheless.

As she had previously, Colleen arrived the next day exactly on time. After brief greetings, the women went into the living room and Colleen repeated her trance ritual.

This time Jill was completely calm—looking forward to whatever might come of the session. Jill stared out the window, her mind wandering, while she waited for Colleen to say something. When Jill turned from the window to look at Colleen, she was stunned.

Colleen, who was staring straight ahead without speaking, seemed to have undergone a physical transformation. An ample, round-faced woman, Colleen now appeared to have an angular face. Her cheeks were sucked in and her neck seemed rigid and attenuated.

"Colleen, is anything wrong?"

"Turn off the tape machine." Colleen's voice was deep and rasping.

Jill looked at her, astonished.

"I *said* turn off the tape machine!"

Not knowing what else to do, Jill got up and turned off the recorder.

"I don't understand why you want the machine off," Jill said when she had returned to her chair.

"I want quiet!" The voice coming from Colleen was a different one from the calm, even voice that had come from her in the previous sessions. This voice was commanding and unpleasant.

"I want peace," the voice continued. "I want you out of my house. You have already done enough."

"Dora!" Jill gasped.

"That's all."

"What do you mean, that's all?" Jill asked with unintended meekness. "I don't understand."

Suddenly Colleen's eyes flew open, grabbing Jill in their gaze. Jill started, as if the eyes of a corpse had opened to stare at her.

"There is more," Colleen said, looking directly at Jill. "I can make things happen in your mind."

"What are you talking about?" Jill screamed. *"What do you mean?"*

Colleen looked up at Jill, her expression taunting, and said in a mocking voice: "Tsk, tsk, such unseemly behavior. Of course, what does one expect from a crazy person? You must remember, my dear, that no one ever listens to a crazy person!"

"Colleen, stop it!" Jill was on her feet, standing over Colleen, screaming at her. As she grabbed Colleen's shoulder to shake it, a searing pain of electric shock jolted her body. For a horrific moment, she was unable to remove her hand from the psychic's shoulder; then she leapt back and collapsed into her chair.

At once, the rigidness seemed to seep from Colleen's body, and her face, although deathly pale, appeared full again.

"What happened?" the psychic asked weakly. "I feel so utterly drained, so ill."

Her voice shaking, Jill told Colleen what had happened. As she recounted what she had seen and heard, Colleen appeared increasingly distressed.

"Multiple entities are not uncommon in a house," she began slowly when Jill had finished. "What disturbs me is the intensity of the energy and the way that it . . ." *Uses* was the word that came into Colleen's mind. Hesitating, she searched for a softer word. ". . . involves you."

Jill took an anxious, audible breath. "Colleen, what did she mean—Dora—when she said that she could make things happen in my mind?"

"I'm not sure," Colleen said slowly. "I think she means that she can communicate a thought to you—even an image, actually make you see it."

"Then it is possible that something I thought was a hallucination was actually some sort of . . . of psychic transmission?"

Colleen nodded. "I think it would be best for you," she said, choosing her words carefully, "to leave here for a while. Then we could deal with all this under more . . . ah, secure conditions for you."

"Are you saying 'For God's sake get out of the house!' like they do on those trailers for scary movies?"

Colleen smiled somewhat feebly and nodded.

Jill shook her head. "The point of all this is for me to *stay* here. There are some things I haven't told you about myself . . ." Things like I see a psychiatrist every day. Things like I have to take medication so I can be allowed to stay home rather than in some mental hospital. ". . . but for now, just trust me when I say that I need to stay here. Besides, I don't think my husband would be very receptive to hearing that we have to move from this house on the advice of a medium from *Berkeley* who thinks that invisible entities are causing my problems.''

''Jill, I want you to understand something,'' Colleen said, leaning forward, looking at her intently. ''Without question, you are the catalyst for the phenomena in this house. A hundred other people could have moved into this place and never had anything happen to them. Something within *you*, something within your psyche is interacting with the spirits of these women, activating them, stirring the residue of their longings and their rage. Without you, they have no power. They need you. *They'll use you.*''

''I don't get it,'' Jill said, anger flashing in her voice. ''Are you saying that this is somehow all my fault? That there is something wrong with me? That I am making all this happen?''

''No, no, no,'' Colleen said, attempting to soothe. ''What I am saying is that you are a remarkably psychic person who has come upon a charged atmosphere. I can't exorcise the spirits from this house, but I *can* teach you to control your psychic abilities so that you won't be victimized by these spirits any longer.'' Colleen paused, hoping that Jill was grasping what she was saying. ''At the institute, we can teach you to close your psychic door on the spirits who haunt this place.'' She slowed her voice for emphasis. ''Without your *compliance* these spirits would no longer have any power.''

Without my compliance? Jill did not need to listen to this. She already had a husband and a psychiatrist who thought there was something wrong with her mind. She did not need to hear it from some medium!

She felt a weight descending upon her. She was at a

dead end. She had no real proof that there was anything going on in this house outside of her own mind; she had only another professional who wanted to fix her. Perhaps she should walk out the door with Benjamin and leave them all behind. Except that she could not be sure the craziness would not start all over again somewhere else. Except that she still loved Tom.

Chapter Twenty-One

TOM HAD NOT HAD A WEEKDAY AFTERNOON AT HOME IN longer than he could remember. The surgery he had been scheduled to assist in had been moved to the following week, leaving him a whole afternoon free. Tom and Jill sat at the kitchen table finishing sandwiches while Benjamin merrily pounded the tray on his highchair.

Tom would have been perfectly happy if Jill—as usual—had not been so distracted. When the phone rang, she jumped up and ran out in the hall to answer it.

"Who was that?" Tom asked pleasantly when Jill returned to the kitchen after several minutes on the phone.

"Just a solicitor," Jill said flatly. It had been Colleen Murphy who called.

"What was he selling?"

"*Time Magazine,*" Jill answered through clenched teeth. A long time ago, Jill would have recognized that Tom was merely trying to make conversation—a long time ago when she had a private life, a long time ago when she was not watched every minute. She felt like tinder—dry, brittle, almost itching for a match.

"Hey, I didn't mean anything," Tom said, sounding a little hurt.

"Okay," Jill said tersely.

"You're taking your pills, aren't you?" Tom asked, matter-of-factly.

Jill nodded, using every muscle in her body to control her anger. She wanted to explode. But, while husbands and wives all over America exploded at one another, without anyone thinking there was anything odd about it, an outburst from Jill would be viewed with alarm. Indeed, any deviation from her pill-induced dullness set up a little red flag of *maybe-she-is-slipping-again*.

Colleen continued telephoning Jill, trying to persuade her to come to her institute where, she said, Jill could learn to control her psychic powers in order to protect herself. Jill, however, had no intention of being worked over by any more therapists. At least, she thought, the coming Thanksgiving holiday would give her a rest from Colleen's phone calls.

Jill had never cared for holidays. They had always been such sad affairs during her childhood. In her memory, all the holidays ran together into a meal where her father and grandmother, feigning gayness, discussed whether the turkey was moister this year or last. The meal was always followed by a visit to her mother. Her mother never even knew what day it was, much less what it meant to a young girl not to have a holiday like the ones pictured in magazines.

Jill and Tom, with the baby, went to Peggy's house for Thanksgiving dinner. It was Peggy's first holiday without Ben, and the pain of his absence tore at all of them. Peggy asked Tom to sit in Ben's place at the head of the table.

When Tom picked up Ben's knives to carve the turkey, his hands—his fine, steady, physician's hands—shook. Jill wanted to reach out and put her own hand over Tom's and tell him how sorry she felt for her silent, accusing anger. But she did not know how to reach out to him anymore. She looked down at her plate and wondered if things would be different if Ben were alive.

Chapter Twenty-Two

THE SECOND MONDAY AFTER THANKSGIVING WAS BENJA-
min's sixth-month birthday. Six months, Jill thought, lifting the baby from his crib and holding him close to her,
just six months—such an insignificant amount of time—
and yet it felt as if this little person had been in her life
forever.

Jill dressed the baby in warm clothes. It was raining
and bitter outside, and the old house was drafty. Winter
in glorious Northern California, Jill sighed. How often had
she wished she were in California as she trudged through
the icy winds and filthy snow of a Manhattan winter? Little did she suspect that Northern California had its own
cruel version of winter—the incessant rain, the mudslides,
the shroudlike fogs. Details that were never mentioned in
the travel brochures.

Maybe the sun was shining in Los Angeles. Perhaps she
should relent and go down there with Tom for the weekend. He had a day-and-a-half conference to attend on Fri-
day and Saturday. He had made plane and hotel
reservations for both of them—without consulting Jill.

What Tom thought—Jill assumed—was that she could lie around the hotel pool, go shopping, or do some other wifely thing while Tom was at his conference. Then, the happy couple could spend Saturday afternoon and the rest of the weekend together.

When Tom had first discussed the plan with her several weeks before, it had seemed like a good idea, but as the time grew nearer, she had found herself not wanting to go.

"I have never been away from the baby that long," she told him. "It's too long to leave the baby with your mother; it will be too hard on her," she said. The real reason Jill did not want to go—although it was hard for her to admit it to herself—was that she did not want to spend that much time alone with Tom.

She did not want him to touch her. Lately, in the night when she bumped against him, she felt her flesh almost recoil. She could not remember when it had started—when the pleasure she had felt from his body turned to distaste. During the day she could fake it—pretend that things were like they always had been between them—but not at night. She could not fake anymore at night. No, she would rather hang around in the rain than face a romantic weekend in a hotel with Tom.

At least, the rain got her out of her appointment with Dr. Shapiro. God, how she hated seeing him. How she hated Tom's insistence that she see him. Tom wasn't the one driving all the way there. He wasn't the one who had to sit for an hour talking to the psychiatrist. Sometimes she refused to say anything to Dr. Shapiro and the two of them would just sit there in silence with the meter running. She could not talk to him about anything that was important to her.

Oh, he was a little helpful in regard to the growing

distance between Tom and her. "Stress," he would say, adding: "Outside of Walt Disney movies, stress does not bring people closer together."

But, Jill never got anywhere trying to make the psychiatrist understand the source of their stress—that Tom was silently accusing her of being insane. Anyway, what was the point of discussing it with the great doctor? *He* thought she was crazy, too.

On the phone that afternoon, Tom and Jill had another argument about the trip to Los Angeles.

"I am just not comfortable leaving the baby that long," Jill said. "Please go ahead and go without me."

"Well, I am just not comfortable leaving *you* alone that long," Tom shot back. He had meant to ask her to join him on Saturday, but the tone in Jill's voice had angered him into retaliating.

Tom's comment made Jill bristle. He treated her like an eight-year-old, except when it suited *his* needs to treat her like a woman.

"All right," Tom said after the chilly pause in the conversation. "If you don't want to go to L.A., I'll go down just for the conference and fly back on Saturday. I'm sure my mother can stay with you while I'm gone."

"I have already asked Mrs. Sanchez to stay," Jill said icily.

Actually she would have loved Peggy's company, but she would be damned if she was going to let Tom get away with getting a babysitter for her. She had not asked Mrs. Sanchez to stay with her. She had not even thought of it. Indeed, Jill had told her not to come at all until the weather improved. Tom was only going to be gone for two nights! She had lived alone for years before marrying him, and she was not going to stand for being treated like a child.

The next day during her appointment with Dr. Shapiro, Jill asked the psychiatrist if she could stop taking the pills he prescribed. In his usual fashion, he asked her why she wanted to stop taking the pills.

"Because," she said, "taking a pill every day makes me feel like I am sick, and I don't feel sick any more. Also, I'm tired of Tom's asking if I have taken my pill, as if I am some sort of child. Besides, everything has been normal with me for months now."

"Well, Jill, the medication has helped to *make* everything normal," the psychiatrist said. He elaborated on the uses of medication in a case like hers, why Jill still needed it, and what it had done for her, but Jill tuned him out.

He sounds like an ad for a pharmaceutical company, Jill thought. She pictured Dr. Shapiro discussing her case with his drug salesman, while Colleen discussed her case with her colleagues and Tom figured out all by himself what was best for her. Meanwhile, no one bothered to listen to what Jill had to say about herself.

Later in the day, Jill wondered if there was any area of her life that was private. At least, she thought as she walked into her bathroom, she could still go to the bathroom by herself. No—correction—when Benjamin refused to be put down, she had to carry him in with her.

Jill stood staring at herself in the mirror of the medicine cabinet. She had lost her privacy *and* her free will. Well, what was she going to do about it?

With great deliberateness, she opened the medicine cabinet, took down her bottle of pills, and spilled them into her hand. They were pink and candy-coated. What an insult! At least if they were going to make her swallow her free will, they could give her a big fat chalky pill that would make her choke.

Jill stared at the disgustingly pink capsules a moment,

then turned around and dumped the entire supply into the toilet. With great pleasure, she flushed the toilet and watched the army of pills disappear. Then she refilled the pill bottle with vitamins. No sense in having Tom notice an empty bottle and bringing her more.

Jill smiled. She felt great. Really great.

The weather got worse on Wednesday. Flights in and out of San Francisco International were halted and Jill wondered if Tom would be able to take his trip the next day.

In spite of the gloomy weather, Jill felt marvelous—renewed and charged with energy. She updated her resume and sent proposals for free-lance articles to two magazines. She did all the laundry, vacuumed the living room, and even cleaned out the kitchen cupboards. She felt as if she had been revived from a coma. She did not even stop to eat.

She cancelled her appointments with Dr. Shapiro for the rest of the week, using the weather as an excuse. The three hours a day spent on the psychiatrist—two for commuting and one for the visit—robbed her of her energy. Just look at what she got done without that intrusion in her day!

Jill did not sleep well Wednesday night, but she did not care. She was going to regain control of her life. If the price was a few sleepless nights, then so be it.

On Thursday morning, the news reports said that the airport had reopened. Tom was leaving for his flight directly from the office, so the couple said an icy farewell after breakfast. When Jill returned to the kitchen to do the breakfast dishes, she saw something on the counter that made her cringe—a cockroach, a big brown cockroach.

She had battled cockroaches for years in New York and they still frightened her. She hated the way they lurked in the plumbing and under the woodwork waiting to dart out when you least expected it. And there was something terrifying about how difficult they were to kill.

Jill knew that one cockroach meant that there were others. Feeling a little shaky, she rolled up a newspaper and positioned it over the bug. It was then that she noticed that the brown body on the counter belonged to a coffee bean—a harmless, lifeless coffee bean.

Jumpy. Why was she so jumpy? She felt foolish and annoyed with herself, yet she could not make the creepy sensation on the surface of her skin go away.

The baby was fussy and irritable the entire day. Worried that he might be catching a cold, Jill decided against taking him out, even though there was a break in the weather. When Tom called just before his plane took off, Jill felt a twinge of regret for not going with him.

Another storm hit with a vengeance in the evening, bringing a harsh wind and rains that pounded against the windows.

Jill watched television indiscriminately all evening—one mindless sitcom after another—needing the company of the images on the screen. A girl in one of the programs looked a little like Ellie Shaw. She had a television mother who looked to be no older than Jill. That can't be right, Jill thought, but then she realized that of course she was old enough to have a daughter Ellie's age. She tried to imagine what she would do if she were the mother of a pregnant fifteen-year-old who wanted to keep her baby. She shook her head. It was just too much to contemplate.

As she always did when Tom was away for the night, Jill compulsively checked and rechecked the locks on the windows and doors before going to bed. Although she had lived alone for years without being nervous about it, she realized how easily she had become dependent on having another body in her bed at night. Checking the windows in her bedroom, she saw something that startled her. A car, long and black and decades old, was parked in the driveway below. Astonished, she watched the rain pelt the car for a second, then, incredulous, she glanced away and looked again. There was nothing there. The window in front of her had begun to cloud from her breath. She rubbed the window and looked again. Nothing. An illusion, she told herself, a trick of the rain.

After checking on the baby, she turned out the lights and got into bed. She tossed for a while, and then, after arranging the pillows to fill up Tom's space in bed, she finally fell asleep. And, deep in the night, she began to dream.

Benjamin was crying. She forced herself up, struggled to his room and reached into the crib. It was empty. Frantically, she flipped on the light and searched the room. He was not there. She went from room to room, searching. There were so many rooms, rooms adjoining rooms. The rooms got bigger and still there were more rooms. All the while, as she searched, she could hear the baby crying. He was so close to her, perhaps a room away. Endlessly.

She went to Peggy's house to see if she had him. "What are you talking about?" Peggy said. Her face was hard and her eyes cold. "Your baby is dead."

Jill ran from Peggy's to Tom's office. Ran all the way, her heart pounding.

Tom was at his desk, his back to her. She told him what Peggy had said, her lies. The chair swiveled around and it was not Tom who sat in it, but Dr. Shapiro.

"We are going to have to lock you up, Jill, if you don't cease with this baby nonsense!" He glared at her. "Once and for all, you don't have a baby!"

Jill backed out of the room and saw Tom at the end of

the hall. Flooded with relief, she went toward him. Then something made her stop. He was with Colleen. His face was buried in her neck and his hand groped inside her blouse. Colleen looked up at Jill and laughed, her mouth gaping and full of teeth.

This can't be, Jill thought, this can't be. She tossed and turned under the blankets, desperate to wake up.

The setting had changed and Jill was working behind the counter in a store. It was an odd store stocked with household and grocery items from fifty years before sitting incongruously beside modern aerosol cans and bright boxes of dishwasher detergent and instant breakfast.

Suddenly Dora Miles came into the store. She was young and beautiful and she carried Benjamin in her arms.

"He cries all the time," Dora said wearily to one of the women there.

"You've got my baby!" Jill cried out from behind the counter. "You've got my baby!"

Dora and the others in the store looked at Jill, then turned to one another, shrugging.

"What can you expect from a girl whose mother is crazy?" one of the clerks said to Dora.

"Like mother, like daughter," a customer said.

Dora shook her head. "Tom could have married any one of a number of girls. Why he picked *her*, I'll never know."

Everyone clucked in agreement, then Dora marched outside with the crying baby.

Jill turned to Dick Hampton, the gas station owner, who had suddenly appeared, and pleaded with him: "Please go after her. She is taking my baby!" But Dick merely looked at the grease under his nails.

Jill could almost hear the rain pounding against the bedroom windows, then she was submerged again. Although it was cold in the bedroom, under the blankets she was soaked with sweat.

Perspiring heavily, Jill rode her bike up the long road leading to Dora's house. Her chest heaving, she rode around the house to the back. A long, black car packed with suitcases sat in the driveway. *Where had she seen that car before?*

Jill parked her bike. As she was walking toward the back door, Dora, dressed in a suit and hat, emerged from the house. She carried the baby wrapped in a blanket in her arms.

''What are you doing here?'' she hissed, her voice cutting into Jill's brain.

''I just want to see the baby again. I want to see if he's mine.''

''You're crazy!'' Dora shrieked. ''If you don't leave this instant, I'm calling the police!''

Let her. She did not care. She had to find out. She moved closer to Dora and suddenly—very suddenly—she yanked the blanket from the baby's face. Then she screamed. Dora was carrying a doll in her arms, a lifeless doll with huge, unseeing eyes.

''Where's my baby?'' Jill was pleading now. ''What have you done with him?'' she screamed through her tears. She was beside herself. Hysterical. Wailing. She dropped to her knees.

''Shut up!'' Dora was screaming above her. ''Shut up!'' The doll fell to the ground, its eyes fixed on Jill. Dora reached for something leaning against the house. Out of the corner of her eye, Jill saw that it was a shovel, a shovel bearing down at her head. Before she could scream or cry out, it smashed into her, exploding her skull.

Her heart was hammering horribly, but she did not wake up. She was still on the ground, twitching, bleeding, choking on her own blood. And then she saw the shovel come at her again.

Jill bolted upright in bed, screaming and drenched in sweat. For a very long time, she sat still trying to regain control of her breathing. Finally, she pulled her legs to the side of the bed, stood up, and unsteadily made her way into Benjamin's room. He slept peacefully, his head making a beautiful arc against the sheet. She watched him breathe for a moment before returning to her own room.

She turned on the lamp on her dressing table and sat down. Mechanically, she picked up a brush and began pulling it through her hair. Then she took an elastic band and arranged her hair in a ponytail—a ponytail just like the one Ellie had worn.

She put her head on her arms and rested, and when she looked up, Ellie Shaw stared back at her from the mirror. Her loveliness and her youth were heartbreaking. "Oh, Ellie, she killed you," Jill said, breaking into sobs. *"She killed you."*

At some point in the night, Jill crawled back into bed. When she awoke the next morning, she had a blinding headache. At first she thought the headache had been caused by the elastic band that was pulling her hair so tightly at the back of her head. Then she remembered the dream. And the sound of the dream—the sound of a skull being smashed, heard from the inside.

Fighting nausea, Jill wrapped herself in her robe and made her way to the kitchen. She turned on the oven for heat and boiled water for tea. Then she took a pencil and paper and sat with her tea at the table. She took a few sips of the tea, hoping to calm her queasiness. Then she forced herself to write down her nightmare exactly as she remembered it. When she finished, she began recording in a frenzied shorthand all that she knew about Ellie Shaw and Dora Miles.

Although she felt as if she had barely slept, her mind, wildly alert, raced, and her writing hand ached from the effort to keep pace with her thoughts. Suddenly, she saw it all before her and everything made sense: Dora Miles would not have wanted to adopt just *any* baby. She had to be certain the parents were attractive. Her doting brother Ben arranged for her to adopt the baby of an unmarried teenaged patient, the blonde and blue-eyed Ellie Shaw. At the last minute, however, Ellie decided that she could not give up her child. And Ben—Jill could only hope that he believed he was doing the right thing—gave the child to Dora, telling Ellie he had died.

But Ellie sensed that the baby was alive. She *knew* it. My God, she heard it crying for her! She traced the baby to Dora, confronted her, and Dora killed her.

And later, when her broken, battered body washed ashore, no one—not a single person in this town—ever suspected that her death was anything other than suicide.

But why the doll? Where was Ellie's baby?

Oh, God. She knew the answer.

Jill tried to block the images forming in her mind, images of a screaming infant helpless in the frenzy of a crazed woman.

Of course the trip out of town was to hide what Dora had done. Except that Ellie arrived as she was leaving. Dora must have cleaned up after Ellie, disposing of her body—and her bicycle—as efficiently as she did everything else. *Then*, she left town, in her suit, in her hat, cradling her fake baby, letting people see them leave, pausing to chat, smiling. After a time, she wrote some sad letters, then returned home, carrying on as always and, in her grieving, admired more than ever.

Dora had washed Ellie's blood from this place. She had cleaned up the bits of her brain tissue and the shards of her skull. She had pushed her body over a cliff into the ocean. She had gotten rid of the human matter, but she could not get rid of the rest. The physical evidence of Dora's crimes may have been removed, but the psychic evidence was still here.

The tragedy of those three lives—Ellie's, Dora's and the baby's—had permeated the very structure of the house. Colleen was right. Jill would have to learn to shut her psychic door if she wanted to live in this house. Except that she did not want to live here anymore. She knew what she needed to know for herself. She no longer needed to prove anything to anyone else. Tom could come with her, accept her as she was, or he could stay on without her, clinging to the truths of his medical faith.

She felt absolutely clearheaded and profoundly sad. Yet, deep down, was a kind of numb relief.

It was over.

Chapter Twenty-Three

AN HOUR LATER, AT EIGHT-THIRTY, BENJAMIN AWOKE with a cold, fever and congestion. "It's no wonder in this weather," the pediatrician said when Jill called him. He told her to use Tylenol drops for the fever and to run a vaporizer. "If he gets worse, I'll get to your house," the pediatrician said. "Don't risk taking him outside."

Caring for her sick baby completely absorbed Jill for the rest of the day. At four o'clock, Tom called, telling her he would be home the next morning at ten.

"I am glad you have Mrs. Sanchez with you," he said. "I would hate to think of you all alone in that storm."

"Yes," Jill responded weakly.

By late afternoon the baby seemed better. When he fell soundly asleep at five o'clock, Jill went downstairs to the library to scan the shelves for something mindless to read. She did not want to do any more thinking that day. On the top shelf she saw just the type of book she was looking for, a 1960s bestselling potboiler. She had seen the movie version so she wouldn't even have to bother creating images of the characters in her mind.

When Jill stood on the couch to reach for the book, she saw the box of photographs from her father that she had shoved up there months ago. She took the box and sat down. She would take just a minute and glance at the pictures again.

The photograph on top of the pile was a picture of Jill, her mother, and her father sitting on the couch at home. Jill was about sixteen and wore the ludicrous hairdo that was so *au courant* when she was in high school. Her father, looking not all that much younger than he did now, sat smiling in a suit with the pant legs too short and his white socks showing. Her mother, posed between them, sat prim and smiling in a crisp Harriet Nelson-like shirt-waist dress, her hair neatly permed.

Jill was aware of the physical sensations in her body— a tightening of the stomach, a prickling in the back of her head—seconds before her mind was able to grasp that something was terribly wrong. The setting of the photograph was unquestionably their old house. The people in the picture were definitely Jill, her father and her mother— except that her mother had never worn a crisp shirtwaist dress, or had a neat permanent, or worn an all-American mother's expression on her face.

Jill had never seen the picture before—nor could she have ever seen it—because, as she slowly grasped, the picture *had never been taken*. When Jill was in high school, her mother was in a mental institution. On the rare occasions when she was allowed to visit home, she wore a shapeless dress, her hair lank and unstyled, and an expression of impenetrable blankness.

Her heart racing, Jill stared at the photograph, desperately searching for an explanation, groping for some under-standing that would halt her mounting panic. She flipped the snapshot over and saw the Kodak markings, the ordi-

nary Kodak markings. Ordinary paper for film that re-
corded the images of dreams.

She turned the picture back over and looked again.
Blood rushed from her head and roared in her ears. Her
image in the photograph had changed. The face was now
cast down, unsmiling, eyes hiding from the camera.

"No!" Jill screamed, as she tore the picture again and
again, shredding it into tiny pieces, and throwing the
pieces into the wastepaper basket. Icy sweat poured down
her face. The room seemed to close in on her. She had
been wrong. Incredibly foolish. She was not well. Not
well at all. She should never have stopped taking those
pills. She had to reach Dr. Shapiro.

In near-blind panic, she made her way to the telephone
in the hall and picked up the receiver. There was no sound.
The phone was dead. She clicked the receiver, hung the
phone up and tried again. There was nothing, only heavy,
dead silence. She jiggled the wires to the phone, tightened
the metal plate underneath, but even as she did these
things, she knew her actions were futile. She heard the
wind howling, heard the rain smashing against the house.
The phone lines were down.

Her hand still clutching the dead telephone, she tried to
control her wild breathing. She had to get ahold of herself.
She tried to think.

Suddenly, she understood. She heard the voice from that
last session with Colleen as clearly as if it were speaking
to her now. *I can make things happen in your mind.*

Jill lowered her head and began to laugh. Her laughter
was bitter and close to tears.

"Very good, Dora, or whoever the hell you are," she
said, sending her words down the long length of the hall.
"You transmit quite a picture. But I'm turning off my set."

Jill released the phone and walked toward the dark living room. She wanted a drink.

The dead have no power except to communicate, and then only if you let them.

Well, she wasn't going to let them. She was tired, exhausted really. She had let down her defenses. She was not crazy, but psychic, as Colleen had been trying to tell her all this time. Psychic. She saw and she heard. There was no reason to be afraid. She was not crazy, and the dead have no power.

A brandy would calm her nerves.

Jill hesitated a moment at the entrance to the living room. The room was pitch black. God, how she hated dark rooms. Moving quickly, she found the switch for the overhead light and then went to every lamp, turning each on to its fullest wattage.

They kept their liquor in one of the cabinets beneath the shelves bordering the fireplace. Opening the cabinet, Jill realized that she had not had a drink of anything stronger than wine since she had learned that she was pregnant with Benjamin. There was a full array of liquor bottles inside. Strange, so much liquor for people who never entertain, Jill thought as she began searching through the bottles for the brandy she wanted. As she looked, the reflection from a silver picture frame on the shelf above the bottles caught her eye. Dora had lined the fireplace shelves with framed photographs, mostly of herself. Jill had tossed the photographs into this cabinet when they moved into the house.

She found the brandy, then idly picked up one of the framed photographs. The picture, which looked to have been taken during the 1940s, was of some man handing a plaque to Dora, who wore a nurse's uniform. At first, Jill could not grasp what disturbed her about the photograph; then she flipped the frame over. Attached to the back was a yellow newspaper clipping dated 1942 that said Dora had been honored for her work in setting up a volunteer nurse's aide program at County Hospital. The hospital in which Benjamin had been born. The hospital in which a nurse wearing that uniform had tried to kill her.

No, it wasn't possible. The dead have no power. She had been alone in the morgue. Isn't that what they all told her? She had been sick. She had let Dora into her mind and it had made her sick.

Oh, God, her logic was the logic of the asylum!

Jill put her head in her hands. Being alone in this place during this awful storm was doing strange things to her. She had to get out of here. Get the baby and get out!

She shoved the photograph back into the cabinet and slammed the door. Then she picked up the brandy, took a swallow directly from the bottle, and hurried upstairs.

Benjamin was sleeping fitfully in steam from the hissing vaporizer. She felt his head. It was blazing.

She grabbed the small bottle of Tylenol drops from his dresser, and—her hands shaking—measured three-quarters of a dropperful. Then she woke Benjamin, took him in her arms, and inserted the dropper in his mouth.

Please let it work.

She rocked him for an hour, cupping his burning head in her hand. As she waited desperately for his fever to cool, she listened to the rain smashing against the nursery windows and knew without doubt that she could not take Benjamin into this storm.

After Benjamin fell asleep in her arms, she put him back in his crib. She stood over him, stroking his head softly. Then, finally, she went into her own room.

She turned on the television and sat on the end of her bed. Images of disaster filled the screen—washed-out roads, mudslides, downed power lines, uprooted trees, people huddled in Red Cross shelters. Power was out in large sections of the area, the report said. Phone lines were down. In some sections, people were virtually stranded in their homes.

She turned off the television, wiping desperate tears from her face. She had to remain calm. In control. She could not risk taking Benjamin into the storm. Surely, she could keep her wild fears at bay until morning. For Benjamin's sake, she had to.

She would do something ordinary, something constructive to pass the time. Jill glanced at the closet. She had been meaning to organize it for a long time. With forced determination, she took several armloads of clothes and placed them on the bed. Then she straightened each garment on its hanger, and returned it to the closet, hanging blouses with blouses, skirts with skirts, the busywork steadying her nerves. As she neared the back of the closet, something caught her eye. It was the royal blue Saint-Laurent evening gown that had belonged to Dora Miles— the gorgeous, impractical gown that she would probably never wear, but that had been too lovely to give away. She lifted the gown from the closet, allowing herself to be soothed by the seductive rustle of its satin. The color of the gown was so vibrant, the blue so alive, that the fabric felt almost warm to the touch. No longer bothered by the cold of the room, Jill took off her clothes and slipped the dress over her head.

She zipped the back of the dress easily. Good God, had she lost that much weight? When she had tried the dress on months ago she would not have been able to zip it halfway. She looked at her reflection in the mirror. She was thin! Positively skinny, elegant! She had not even noticed. Of course, it was no wonder. Her life these days left her with precious little time for herself.

She turned from side to side, basking in the pleasure of her reflection. Then, being careful not to crush her dress, she sat at the dressing table and began brushing her hair. As she swept the brush through her hair, she could not help admiring the reflection of her raised arm. Arms were so difficult. A good arm had to be soft, yet thin, but not so thin as to appear skinny. The arm must be well formed without the look of muscle, and perfectly pale. Her arms were just right, one of the many things in her life that she had gotten just right.

Making a perfect, straight part down the middle, she pulled her hair tightly around her head and into a smooth twist at the back. Pleased with her hair, she rummaged through her makeup drawer looking for the right shade of foundation. Irritatingly, she had to make do with one that was not pale enough. She worked the foundation into her skin, and then covered it with powder to obtain the pallor she wanted. Then she pushed a black pencil over her eyebrows until they were thick enough and black enough. When she finished, she took the pencil and created a beauty mark beneath her right eye; then she applied mascara. She had to hunt through tube after tube of lipstick before she finally found a red that was right—dark enough, deep enough, the color of liver. Using a brush, she extended the natural line of her lips, then worked the color deep into them.

She examined her hands. They were a mess. She had them in water far too often now. Perhaps she should cover them with gloves, but she had always preferred to go barehanded, because it complemented the severity of style that was her hallmark. She rubbed lotion into her hands, deciding not to bother with them further. She was, after all, a mother. She would wear the roughness of her hands as a badge—a flaw that attested to her perfection.

She rose from the dressing table and looked at herself in the full-length mirror. For a woman in her circumstances, who got as little sleep as she did, she looked marvelous. She would even forgo jewelry tonight. She was that confident of how brightly she shone.

She glided out of the bedroom and downstairs. It bothered her that she could not find her Baccarat ice bucket, but rather than risk upsetting herself before a party, she made do with an ordinary ice bucket and an ordinary glass. After considerable searching, she found the gin. Her irritation that the liquor was not in its usual place was soothed by the sound of ice cracking in her glass as gin splashed over it. It had been so long since she had heard that sound—too long. She held the glass to her lips, letting the scent of juniper fill her senses, savoring the moment, before taking a sip. Finally she allowed the liquid into her mouth. She had forgotten the pleasure of that taste, the pleasure of warmth in her throat.

She went to the record player and put on a recording of Dietrich. No one sang like Marlene. She shut her eyes and let the party begin.

Every eye was on her. The women envious. The men wanting, but not in a vulgar way. She was very nearly unattainable and they knew it. Still, they admired her, coveted her as they would a perfect piece of art. So lovely, they said, so serene, so perfectly in control. Of course, that kind of perfection took work, but she never let it show.

He crossed the room toward her. Women reached out to him, trying to slow his progress toward her with a light hand to his arm, a whispered greeting. Unfailingly polite, he spoke to each one, but she knew, without having to look, that his eyes were on her. The moment was sublime: the laughter, the clink of fine crystal, the rustle of expensive gowns, the smokey music, the envious eyes upon her as he walked toward her. Her happiness was absolute.

Then suddenly, with nerve-shattering pierceness, the baby started to cry, his screams crashing down upon her.

He never gave her any peace. He never let up.

The sun lighting Peggy's dream was brilliant. She was climbing a ladder to the roof of the garage. Jill was up there already. The two of them were going to cut the branches that were bearing down on the garage roof. It was the sort of job that Ben or Tom would have taken care of had they been alive. But now Jill and she were without husbands and they had to do everything themselves.

Reaching the top of the roof, Peggy saw that the growth was much thicker than it looked from below. Massive limbs hung over the roof, engulfing it in shadow. Vines snaked around their feet and curled around their ankles. Taking an ax, Peggy joined Jill cutting and hacking. They worked until Peggy thought she would drop, but they made no progress. The growth had only gotten thicker, surrounding them in jungle.

Vaguely, Peggy was aware of buzzing. The buzzing grew louder and more insistent. Suddenly the air was black with insects swarming over them. Wasps! A microsecond separated the realization from the attack. They bore into her in a mad frenzy. Screaming, she flailed her arms. My God, the wasps were hanging from her arms.

"Jill!" she screamed.

Jill stared at her impassively, a pulsating wasps' nest cradled in her arms.

"Oh God, Jill, look! Look what you have in your arms! Toss it over the roof! Throw it fast!"

Jill looked down, and then she too began to scream.

Still screaming, she hurled the nest over the side of the roof.

And then Peggy saw. Floating in front of them, suspended in the air, staring at them with a look of profound astonishment, was tiny Benjamin. Time resumed, and he fell kicking and screaming from her view, his terrified screams ringing in her ears.

"I didn't see him in your arms!" she wailed at Jill. *"I didn't know you were holding him!"*

Jill, dressed in tatters, stared back at her with dead eyes.

Peggy awoke gasping for breath. Clutching at her heart, she tried to slow its fierce hammering. Jill! The baby! They were up there alone in this storm. And something was wrong! She never should have gone to bed. Something was terribly wrong at Jill's house.

Peggy sat up in bed. Calm down, she told herself. She had merely had a bad dream, that was all. Jill was probably in bed sleeping soundly. The electricity wasn't out everywhere. Jill was far enough away—she could still have power. And Dora's house was solid.

Grabbing her robe, she made her way to the light switch—still no lights. She found the telephone—still dead. Settle down, she told herself. There is no panic like that of a hysterical old mother. But she could not settle down, because she knew in her bones that Jill and the baby were not alright. She had to get to her.

She dressed quickly, pulling on warm clothes. Grabbing a flashlight, she opened her kitchen door and fought her way toward the garage. It was a chore to lift the heavy garage door against the blowing rain—she was barely able to do it. Soaking wet, she got in the car and backed carefully out of the driveway. Once on the street, she found it nearly impossible to see. Torrents of rain pounded her windshield and there were no lights anywhere—not even traffic lights. She crept toward the main highway. Once on the highway, she knew there would be those reflectors in the road and the lights of other cars to guide her.

She tried to concentrate, tried to estimate where she was. She hoped to see the lights of a patrol car. She could ask the police to take her to Jill's. Fear for herself was mingling with her fear for Jill. She tried to remain calm; panicking would not help anything.

Somehow, she did not know how, she managed to make her way onto the main highway leading through town. At least, she *thought* it was the main highway. The traffic lights were out here too, and without the traffic lights and the lights of the town, she could not really tell where she was. She was completely disoriented but she kept on going. She could not see anything at all ahead of her, but there were other cars on the road—she could hear them.

She heard the screeching of its brakes, but she never saw the car that plowed into her.

The baby was lying on his back in his crib, screaming, his head thrusting from side to side.

She looked down at him and sighed. Nothing she did made any difference. He never slept. She never got a break from the screaming.

He stiffened when she touched him and began screaming even more loudly. She picked him up and put him on the changing table. He continued to scream, his face red, his knees pulling into his chest, his little fists clenched.

She hated him.

He squirmed and kicked on the table, making it an ordeal to diaper him. His screams cut into her head. She couldn't stand the noise. She just couldn't stand the noise. The incessant noise.

She should not have tried to take care of him without

help. But she had always detested hired help. They never did their jobs correctly. She had to do their work for them, and then pay them to boot. It wasn't worth it. But what she had not known was that caring for a baby was not like keeping house. At least if you had help with a baby, you could get away from the screaming once in a while.

He refused his bottle. She put him on her shoulder and walked the floor with him. Across the nursery. Up and down the hall. Her arms ached. Still he would not stop crying. She tried the rocking chair, the bottle again. Still he kept it up.

She would not get any sleep again tonight. She knew it. It would be just like last night, and the night before, and the night before that. She never got the sleep she needed. The sleep she *had* to have. Her face was being destroyed.

She began to cry. She just couldn't do it again tonight. She just couldn't go another night without sleep.

She put him back in his crib. What else could she do for him? Her legs giving way in exhaustion, she collapsed into the rocking chair and put her hands over her ears to shut out the screaming. She did not have the strength to move, and even if she did, what difference did it make? She could hear him screaming in every room of the house.

Eventually his screams became sobs. Then, finally spent, he was quiet.

She had been drifting and now she was finally back at the party. The Negro musician was at the piano. He sang as he played, and she had never heard anything as sweet as his music. A butler passed a silver tray laden with cool drinks in crystal glasses. She took another and held it to her lips, the cracking ice creating a fine juniper mist that cooled her face. The circle of admirers around her was large. The colonel, resplendent in his dress uniform, worked to entertain her with his droll stories. Her eyes wandering from the colonel, she saw that *he* was nearing her at last. In an electrifying instant, their eyes met and they reached out their hands to one another. He to take her hand in his and bring it to his lips bowing. She to receive the kiss . . .

Then, like a buzzsaw through her brain, the screaming started again.

Half asleep, she was on her feet and over him. "Be quiet!" she screamed into his face. "I can't take any more!"

His screams became even more piercing, hacking through her nerves, filling her head with searing, unbearable pain. She had to stop the noise. She had to make him shut up.

His small pillow was in her hands coming down on his face.

Just a few seconds of silence. She had to stop the pain, just for a moment, just for an instant . . .

From out of the corner of her eye, Jill saw an image reflected in the window that nearly stopped her heart. She saw herself, her face contorted in murderous frenzy, about to grind the life out of her tiny child. Jill stood motionless above the baby, a pillow in her hands, her heart exploding as her mind grasped the horror of what she had nearly done. The pillow fell from her hands and bounced harmlessly into the crib. Her terror was absolute. She had very nearly killed her baby without knowing it. She remembered nothing before that awful moment when she had caught sight of herself shoving a pillow at her baby's face. Shaking uncontrollably, she stared at Benjamin crying beneath her, imploring her for help. In another moment he would have been dead.

Terrified of touching him, she moved away from the crib to the far wall of the nursery. Then she pounded her fists into her face, striking herself with blow after blow, until she collapsed sobbing to the floor. She remembered nothing. Nothing! She was out of control, capable of doing anything without even knowing that she was doing it.

She had to get away from the baby. Now! Get out of the house and get as far away from him as possible. She could not risk being alone with him another minute.

"Oh, God, oh, God," she murmured, sobbing.

No! She could not give in to her desperation. There was no time. She had to get control of herself. She had to think.

She would go to the police, turn herself in, and send someone back for the baby. She would have to leave Benjamin here alone. She had no choice. She had to. But what if something happened? What if he got sicker? What if there were a fire? Smoke? What if she blacked out on the way and never got to the police? Then he would be alone up here for hours and hours. He could starve. He hadn't eaten anything. No one would know he was alone up here and in this storm . . .

No. She could at least get to the highway. She could at least get that far. She would flag down a car. She could at least do that.

She pulled herself to her feet and saw that Benjamin had cried himself to sleep. She wanted to go to him, check on him, make sure he was alright. She wanted to hold him one last time. But she could not. She could not allow herself to touch her own baby. The gravest threat to his life this night came from her. His own mother. The mother who loved him more than anything else in the whole world.

Sticking close to the walls, she fled the nursery and ran into her own room. She talked to herself as she looked for her shoes and purse, as if she could force her mind to remain present.

She picked up her shoes from the floor, stood upright, and as she did so, she saw herself in the mirror. Her breath caught in her throat. For a fraction of a second, she thought that she was seeing someone else, someone not alive, someone—something—that had crawled from the grave. And then she realized that the thing was her. Her true self. The outer mask had been ripped away to reveal the face of her soul—its lips murderous and huge, smeared red with the blood of her own child, its eyes hollow, and ringed with the blackness of depravity.

Her filthy, rotten body was draped in an evening gown. Oh, my God, the dress. She remembered putting on the dress!

Shaking, the satin of the gown burning into her flesh, she groped for the zipper at the back, and half pulling and half ripping, she freed herself from the dress. Then, shivering, naked except for underpants, she opened the window and hurled the grotesque garment into the storm.

Moving as quickly as she could, she threw on her clothes and hurried from the room. She paused at the door of the nursery, leaning into the room just far enough to see that Benjamin was still sleeping.

"Good-by," she whispered. "Good-by, my precious angel."

Wrenching herself from the sight of her baby—she dared not linger—she headed down the hall to the stairs. Suddenly she heard a door open, and then footsteps. Loud, clear, distinct footsteps.

Tom! Tom was home!

"Tom!" she screamed, running down the stairs. "Tom, thank God, you are home!"

There was no answer.

"Tom!" she shouted, as she searched through the downstairs looking for him. She paused, her heart pounding. Tom was not there, but *someone was*. She was certain of it. She had heard the footsteps, unmistakable footsteps. Slipping quietly into the kitchen, she reached for the knife rack and pulled out a butcher knife. Tom's favorite knife. The knife he honed to perfection, pulling it back and forth across the sharpening stone, lightly mocking Jill's fear of sharp knives, saying it's the dull knives that cut you.

Turning out the kitchen light, she pushed her back against the wall next to the doorway. She lifted the knife above her head. Sweating and shaking, she listened and waited.

Chapter Twenty-Four

COLLEEN MURPHY, WHO HAD NEVER IN HER LIFE FEARED death or much else, sat in her bed, frozen in terror, a hand clutched to her heart. The noise was overwhelming. The pounding and smashing of the storm and the violent hammering of her heart had merged into a single mind-shattering racket. Then Colleen heard a dull beat punctuating the din, the sound of footsteps coming toward her.

I am not ready, Colleen thought, the pain in her head blinding. I'm not ready to die.

Her body rigid, she watched the bedroom door open toward her.

Colleen stared in astonishment when she saw the person who had come for her.

"Jill!" she gasped. It was Jill who had come to take her across!

But how could that be? Jill was not from the other side. She was alive.

The younger woman stopped at the foot of Colleen's bed, a look of profound desperation on her once lovely face.

"I don't understand," Colleen whispered.

Jill said nothing.

Then Colleen saw what Jill was holding in her arms. She saw the small bundle, the tiny blanket caked with dried blood.

"Oh, no! No!" Colleen sobbed. "Not the baby! Oh, no!"

Jill stared straight ahead, the bloody bundle silent and motionless in her arms.

"I tried to help you," Colleen said, weeping. "I did everything I could."

She could have done more.

Colleen looked at Jill, her eyes pleading for Jill's forgiveness. "I should have seen . . ." she stammered.

Jill's stare returned nothing.

Then, as if the weight of it were no longer bearable, the bundle slipped from Jill's arms and landed with a soft thud on the hardwood floor. Jill's arms fell slack to her sides, and Colleen, stifling a scream, saw for the first time the ugly wound in Jill's belly.

"Oh, my God!" she cried, scrambling to Jill's side.

The wound was spurting blood. Frantic, Colleen did the only thing she could think of to stop the bleeding. She plunged two fingers deep into Jill's abdomen.

Somehow she would pull Jill with her to the phone. She reached behind Jill's back to support her. Jill went limp in her arms, her head falling backwards like a giant rag doll's. Blood splashed against Colleen's face, and with numbing horror, she saw, for the first time, the gash in Jill's neck.

There was no hope. There was nothing she could do. Sobbing, she collapsed with Jill to the floor. She pulled her fingers from Jill's body and held her close. Jill's blood flowed over her, binding them together.

And then, all of a sudden, Jill was gone. Vanished. Colleen lay alone on her floor, embracing air.

Gasping, Colleen stumbled to her knees and looked wildly around the room.

It had not happened! She had seen! Merciful God, it *was* a vision! There was still time!

She pulled herself to her feet. She could get help to Jill! She could.

Shivering, Colleen glanced at herself. Her nightgown, soaking wet and sticking to her body, was drenched in blood.

Screaming, the pain in her head blinding, she pulled at the soaking garment, tearing it off. Then, stumbling naked and wet toward the phone, she collapsed in a blaze of light, a blood vessel bursting in her brain.

Chapter Twenty-Five

OUTSIDE, THE WIND TORE A TREE BRANCH LOOSE and hurled it against Jill's kitchen window. Inside the kitchen, back against the wall, Jill waited, the knife held high in her shaking hands. Icy sweat fell from her face. Despite the storm, despite the awful cold, the kitchen seemed hot and stuffy, as if the walls had closed in on her, compressing the room into the size of a closet.

Whoever was in the house with Jill was moving around quite openly now, not even trying to conceal the sound of footsteps. And whoever it was, was playing a little game with her. Footsteps coming closer, then stopping, an interminable silence, then coming at her from another direction.

Blood rushed in Jill's ears and her breathing was out of control, but she was determined to remain standing. The wooden handle of the knife slipped in her soaking palms. Her arms ached painfully above her head.

She shut her eyes against the pain, really only blinked them, but it was enough. She had let down her guard.

In an instant, Dora was there, in the room with Jill,

pressed against her, using fierce strength to pin Jill's arms high above her head, her powerful grip pressing the soft undersides of Jill's wrists into the wall.

The knife fell from Jill's hands. Her legs buckled beneath her and for a horrific moment she endured the pain of having her body hang from her wrists. Desperately, she pushed her feet back onto the floor, willing her legs to support her. Her wrists felt as if they had been snapped in two.

Dora's face was pushed so close against her own that Jill's breath had nowhere to go. She tried to scream, but she could make no sound.

The next moment, the dead woman's lips were upon Jill's, hungrily joining hers. Jill tried to turn away, but she could not. The kiss was overpowering and she gave in to it. It pulled at her whole body and she forgot everything else. The excitement of that embrace was beyond anything she had ever known, beyond anything human. Transcendent, it sucked the breath from her body, pushing her higher and higher into the dazzling reaches of the universe.

Her body melted into Dora's. Pleasure and agony were indistinguishable. As the embrace pushed her on and on, building toward a final shattering spasm that would at last release her from this world, Jill thought: So this is what it is like to die.

And with that thought came a sharp jerk, as if life were grabbing her by the neck and pulling her back—and accompanying this wrenching fall toward earth was the awareness that she was being suffocated.

Reflexively, she jerked her head back, smashing it into the wall behind her, and with all the strength that she had left within her, she turned her face to one side and gasped for air. Her attacker stepped back, letting go of Jill's wrists.

Jill filled her lungs with great gulps of air. Then she turned to look at Dora Miles.

"Tom," she murmured. The photographs she had seen did not show the remarkable resemblance. Dora looked just like Tom, or how Tom would look as a woman.

Dora remained motionless as Jill studied her face.

"Why?" Jill asked finally, staring into the depths of the dead black eyes. "Why are you doing this to me?"

Dora stared back at Jill for a long time, her eyes holding Jill's in their hypnotic gaze.

"You torture me," she said finally. "I hear your thoughts, the baby crying. Incessantly, day and night. Forever. I get no rest. The torment never ends."

The voice stunned Jill. Rasping, deep, unearthly, but there—there in the room with Jill. Not in Jill's head, but in the room, in the air. Dora Miles was speaking. She had flesh and she had dimension. She existed. She stood in front of her, for anyone to see or hear.

"You keep me alive," Dora said. "Alive and in pain."

"You are not alive!" Jill gasped. "You are not alive and you have no power!"

Suddenly Dora was gone and a fraction of a second later Jill's own mother stood before her, ravaged by an eternity of illness, eyes blank, tubes hanging from her nose, her hospital gown stained with urine.

"Oh, no, no, no," Jill cried, staring helplessly, unable to shut her eyes. "No, no, no," she pleaded, crying, her control gone.

A moment later, her mother was replaced by Dora, her expression coldly triumphant.

Beaten, Jill collapsed to the floor sobbing.

"Don't you see, Jill, that there is no barrier between us?" Dora said, kneeling next to Jill, stroking her hair. "That our thoughts are open to one another?"

Jill sobbed, unable to fight off the dead woman's ca-
resses. Then, from upstairs came Benjamin's hungry cries,
sharp and desperate.

"Stay here," Dora whispered to Jill. "I'll take care of
him. I'll take care of everything."

Numbly, Jill watched her leave the room and head upstairs. She wanted only to die, and in dying to escape her
unbearable horror.

Then Dora's words suddenly registered in Jill's brain.
Propelled by panic, Jill grabbed the knife from the floor,
struggled to her feet and ran into the hall and up the
stairs, taking them two and three at a time. Blindly, her
heart bursting in her chest, she ran down the hall and
into the baby's room.

Dora leaned over the baby, her hands inside his crib,
her arms rigid with tension. In one furious instant, Jill
plunged the butcher knife deep into her back. Then with
wild strength, she pulled the knife from the muscle and
stabbed her a second time at a third. But as she lunged
a fourth time, the knife met no resistance. Dora Miles was
gone, and Jill saw with a horror beyond reason that she
had been thrusting the knife into her baby's crib.

She leapt forward and looked into the crib. Benjamin
lay on his back on the far side of the crib, screaming but
unhurt. The thick, padded crib bumper leaked stuffing
where it had been slashed.

Sobbing, hysterical, she dropped the knife and picked
up her baby. She held Benjamin in her arms, trying to
control her sobbing as she felt his warmth against her.

Carrying him tightly in her arms, she took him with her
to the kitchen for a fresh bottle, then returned to the nursery and fed him in the rocking chair, holding him against
her. As she held him, she tried to imprint her memory
with the milky sweetness of his scent.

When he fell asleep, she put him in his crib and covered him tightly. For a moment, she lingered, stroking the soft down of his head; then she picked up the knife from the floor.

She tiptoed from the nursery and into the bathroom. She turned on the light, shut the door, walked to the sink and looked into the mirror. In place of her own reflection, Dora Miles stared back at her, her dark eyes boring into Jill.

Jill turned her back to the mirror and sat on the floor. Then, without fear, without emotion, she brought the knife across her wrist. She winced as she sliced through the flesh, but, she thought vaguely, it really did not hurt that much.

Without her, Dora could do nothing to her baby. Jill was certain of that. She needed Jill's body to accomplish her ghastly plans.

Woozy, Jill lay on the floor. It was three or four in the morning. Benjamin had taken a full bottle. His fever had broken. Tom would be home in six or seven hours.

She had to do it this way. It was the only way to keep her baby safe through the night.

Chapter Twenty-Six

THE TILE BENEATH HER FACE WAS COOL, COMFORTING. Her wrist throbbed, and she shifted slightly. Vaguely, she was aware that she was not alone in the room. She did not care. She wanted only to sink back down, to slide away.

Someone was grabbing hold of her wrist and the pain pulled her to the surface. She opened her eyes. Above Jill, her blonde hair freed of its ponytail and cascading over her shoulders, was Ellie Shaw. She held Jill's wounded wrist in her hands.

"It's not deep," she said.

Jill lay on the floor watching dully as Ellie cleaned and bandaged her wrist.

"You must get up and come with me," Ellie said when she had finished.

Jill nodded. I am dead, she thought.

Effortlessly she got up. Then she saw that her body had remained motionless on the floor. Yes, she thought, I am dead.

Suddenly, and without Ellie doing anything that Jill was aware of to get them there, they were under the house.

How strange, Jill thought. Is this where we are to going to live?

"Do you know where you are?" Ellie asked.

Jill nodded. They were in a crawl space under the house in an area that contained the water heater and the main plumbing connections. A wooden wall separated this area from the rest of the basement so that plumbers could get at the pipes without having access to the house.

"You see this wall?" Ellie asked.

Again Jill nodded.

"On the other side of this wall is the cement wall of the basement. This wall, however, is not original." Ellie pointed out some rotting boards along the bottom, as if to underscore her point. "It was put in long after the house was built. There is space between this wall and the cement wall of the basement. In that space is where you must look. You do that for me and you do it for yourself. You have no choice."

Jill did not understand, nor did she try to understand. A powerful thought had overtaken her. She was not dead, but she would be if she did not return.

Feeling cold, Jill reached for the covers, and as she did so she was aware of the hard floor beneath her. Her eyes flew open. In the light of dawn, the first thing she saw was the knife, then the pool of reddish-brown blood against the white tile floor. Her eyes moved to her aching wrist. It was tightly wrapped in layers of gauze bandage.

Slowly, unsteadily, she first sat, and then pulled herself to her feet. She felt no relief that she was alive, no confusion over the events of the night before, and no fear. She felt only a grim sense of purpose.

She tiptoed into the nursery, checked on Benjamin who was sound asleep, and then went downstairs. She pulled her boots and parka from the hall closet and put them on. Then she made her way out the kitchen door through the pouring rain to the toolshed.

She easily found what she needed—a battery-powered lantern, a pick and a shovel. She had to accomplish her task quickly—she had only a few hours until Benjamin would awake. She did not question that she *had* to do the task. She had heard Ellie's words and she knew them to be true. She knew it absolutely. She had no choice.

Jill lugged the tools to the crawl space at the side of the house. She opened the door, crouched, and entered, pulling the tools in behind her. Keeping her head low to avoid bumping into any pipes, she carried the tools over to the wooden wall. Working clumsily at first, then with smoother effort, she removed enough rotting lumber from the bottom of the wall to create an opening large enough to crawl through. Stretching her lantern into the darkness behind the wall, she saw that she had uncovered an area that was about six feet long and four feet wide—the size of an ample closet—the bottom of which was about five feet lower than the ground on which she now knelt. She lowered the lantern into the cavity, followed by the pick and shovel. She took off her parka. Then, crouching on all fours, she backed through the opening in the wall and lowered herself into the hole.

Without pausing to think, she took the shovel, pushed it into the damp earth and began digging. The work went slowly, miserably. Her whole body ached, but she dared not stop. She just kept digging, piling earth around her, creating a deeper pit. The dirt was alive with crawling worms, but she did not let her revulsion slow her pace. The skin on her hands blistered and tore, and fresh blood soaked the bandage on her wrist. She kept working, as if in shock, no longer feeling any pain.

She had no idea how long she had been digging when her shovel hit something mushy. She moved the lantern closer so she could see what it was. It appeared to be some sort of decomposing fabric. She bent down and picked it up. But as she did so, the aged, filthy material came apart in her hands, revealing something yellow and hard in the center.

She knew what it was. She had known all along what she was looking for, but she had been unable to admit it to herself.

She held the remains of Ellie's baby in her hands. She fell to her knees, cradling the little bundle in her arms. She lifted out the tiny skull and held it to her breast, sobbing convulsively. She grieved for the death of a baby she never knew, and she grieved for her own lost childhood.

She had been crying for a long time when she suddenly became aware that the rain was coming down even harder, sounding like an army of angry people stomping above her head. Still clutching the tiny skull in her hands, she struggled to her feet. It was then, when she stood, that she noticed that there was no light coming from the opening through which she had crawled. A second later she realized that there was no light because there was no longer an opening. She picked up the lantern, and wildly disoriented, swung it around looking for the opening she had made in the wall. It was gone.

"No!" Jill screamed, grabbing the pick and using it to hack desperately at the wooden wall just above her head. She was confused, frenzied, the pit airless. The wood cracked and splintered from her blows. When she could no longer lift the pick above her head, she tried to pull at the boards with her hands.

Suddenly there was a hideous noise, an awful creaking sound, as the wooden wall of the basement began collapsing on top of her, knocking her to the ground. A second later she was buried under a hail of dirt and wood. Screaming, she clawed at the rubble engulfing her, but each blind thrust rained more debris upon her. When she could no longer move, she screamed. She screamed until the dirt was so thick in her throat that she could scream no more.

The sound was high-pitched and strange. Where did it come from? An animal? Was there an animal somewhere in the debris with her? A rat? Did rats sound like that? She felt something sharp cutting into her leg. She was being bitten by a rat. She tried to move her leg, but she could not. She would have to lie there while the rat continued to gnaw. The high-pitched sound intensified. She did not know that what she was hearing was the sound of her own moaning.

She felt warm, cozy. She was in her own bed. She saw the pattern of her sheets clearly—white with tiny blue flowers. The down quilt was over her. She was in her own bed and she had been dreaming. She did not remember what the dream was, except that it had been horrible. She would snuggle back to sleep. She was so sleepy, so incredibly sleepy. But something was keeping her from going back to sleep. A rock. The jagged edge of a rock was digging into her hand. Jill's eyes opened. She saw the darkness of the pit and knew she was dying.

Chapter Twenty-Seven

FROM VERY FAR AWAY, JILL HEARD VOICES. BUT THE voices were not far away, Jill was. There were people close by—possibly just a few feet away. She had to make some noise or they would not know she was in here. She was so sleepy though, and it was so pleasant floating like this. She could go on drifting forever. Everything looked so beautiful! She was engulfed in a dazzling bouquet of light, heading toward the sun.

Why should she wake up? The baby? But, the baby was in her arms, sleeping too, his little head snuggled against her breast. She felt the top of his smooth head—smooth head? But her baby had soft hair covering his head. *This was not her baby. Her baby was somewhere out there— alone!* She had to wake up. She had to pull herself back.

She tried to make a sound, but her mouth was full of dirt. With great effort, she produced a slight cough, but that was all. No matter how hard she tried, she could not make a sound loud enough to be heard. People, a lot of them, were on the other side of her tomb. But no one could hear her. No one would know she was there.

She tried to move, but she was almost completely pinned by the rubble. The only parts of her body she could move at all were her right arm and her head. Desperately, she began moving her arm and shaking her head. As she struggled, she tried to scream, but the only sound she could make was a faint and high-pitched moan.

Finally, her desperate movements shifted some debris. A fraction of a moment later, more dirt rained down upon her face.

She no longer heard voices. Nor did she see the slender ray of light coming toward her.

A savage blow struck her chest. And then another. Someone had his mouth over hers and someone else was pounding his fists into her chest. She felt herself gasping and sputtering. Then she heard someone say, "*All right! We've got her!*"

An oxygen mask was placed over her nose and mouth. She opened her eyes and looked around. She was outside. The police were there, with firemen and paramedics.

She tried to lift the oxygen mask from her face, but someone clamped it back. She gestured with her arm as intensely as she could manage. Someone eventually understood. A fireman came and knelt beside her. Benjamin was in his arms, wide-eyed with delight.

Jill gestured at the oxygen mask.

"Don't try to talk," the fireman holding Benjamin said. "Part of the basement wall collapsed, trapping you. The supports had rotted and all the rain leaking in finished them off."

Two days later a police detective came to Jill's hospital room. After a brief introduction, he got right to the point. "What were you doing under the house?" he asked.

Jill looked away from the policeman. She did not want to answer him. She did not want to have to talk about any of it. She knew, though, that if she did not answer his questions now, she would just have to do it later.

She looked back at the detective. The whole story was too complicated to explain, besides he would not believe her. So she tried to make her answer as simple and as plausible as possible. "I dreamt," she said slowly, "that there was an infant buried under the house. I went down there because I had to find out."

"Did anyone tell you that a baby might be buried there?"

"No," Jill answered.

"Did you find any diaries, or letters, or anything at all in the house that might lead you to suspect that there was a baby buried there?"

"No," Jill answered.

The detective continued to apply logic to a situation that had none. And, Jill continued to answer his questions with a simple, but firm, "No." Finally, the detective gave up. He saw no point in pursuing this case any further. After all, he knew from the lab reports that the remains of the infant found buried with Jill Douglas were more than forty years old.

He thanked Jill and headed for the door.

"Wait," Jill said. "I have a question for you."

"Yes," he said, turning around.

"How did the police know that I was buried under the house?"

"We got an anonymous tip."

"From a young girl?"

"Yes," he said, "as a matter of fact."

Epilogue—Six Months Later

"I DON'T KNOW, IT JUST DOESN'T SEEM RIGHT MAKING SO *much* money from the sale of one house," Peggy Douglas said to Tom and Jill as they sipped iced tea together in the afternoon sun of her big backyard. "And, it makes me uneasy getting so much money from something that belonged to Dora Miles. It has just got to be bad luck."

"Mom, look at it this way," Tom answered. "The money didn't come from Dora Miles. It really didn't have anything to do with her. This money came from the crazy California real estate market."

Jill shut her eyes against the sun. The money they received from the sale of Dora's house did not make Jill the least bit uneasy. Dora's house was an architectural triumph—at least to someone who did not know much about Dora. The couple who bought the house—or rather the partnership that backed them—had made a small fortune operating a trendy-cuisine restaurant in Berkeley. They planned to turn Dora's house into an elegant bed-and-breakfast inn and an exclusive restaurant. They were even planning to grow all their own produce on the property.

Photographs showing the couple clutching a leg of lamb and an armful of leeks had already appeared in at least one glossy magazine.

"Still, so much money . . ." Peggy was saying to Tom.

Jill smiled. The money wouldn't change Peggy's life. She would go on being Peggy. Maybe when she was completely recovered from her car accident, she would take a nice trip with Lucille Banks or one of her other friends.

Nor would Tom and Jill be changed by having money. After what they had been through, nothing as trivial as money could have an effect on them. So much had changed. Ben was gone. Colleen was gone. So many of their secure assumptions about the world were gone.

Wary of one another at first, near to being strangers, she and Tom had started over. No longer the same people as before, they had begun building new lives together, taking each day as it came.

Jill opened her eyes at the sound of Tom's and Peggy's laughter. Little Benjamin was toddling around on the lawn with a Tupperware bowl on his head for the amusement of his elders. The baby was healthy and happy and—unlike Jill and Tom—would carry with him no memory of the past year.

Jill and Tom had moved into a ten-year-old ranch-style house in a newer section of the small town. Jill had always hated ranch-style houses, preferring the charm of older homes. But now she found the characterlessness of her new house comforting.

On the way home from Peggy's, Jill asked Tom to stop by the cemetery. He parked outside the gates, then reached his hand across the seat to clasp hers.

"Do you want me to come with you?" he asked.

Jill shook her head. It was something she liked to do alone.

"I won't be long," she said, getting out of the car. Jill walked through the lovely, old willow-shaded cemetery, making her way to the familiar spot.

Next to the grave of Ellie Shaw lay the new resting place of her infant son. Jill put her hand on the simple headstone she had purchased for them. *Mother and child together in peace at last*. Then, Jill picked up the leaves that had accumulated since her last visit. The sky overhead was a brilliant blue. A soft breeze rustled through the willow trees. It was such a peaceful day.

"IF YOU WANT THE YOU-KNOW-WHAT SCARED OUT OF YOU . . . JAMES HERBERT WILL DO IT!" — STEPHEN KING

HAUNTED

A country home so haunted by an unspoken horror from the past, that even David Ash, a skeptical psychic investigator, cannot dismiss the chilling sound of a child's distant laughter. As Ash quickly discovers, this is no laughing matter.

___HAUNTED 0-515-10345-4/$4.95

SEPULCHRE

Deep in the English countryside, a house is filled with the dark, terrible secrets of Felix Kline—a man who commands the respect of Hell itself. But an evil even more sinister than Kline's rises up to challenge him, and no matter who wins, it will be an evil victory...

___SEPULCHRE 0-515-10101-X/$4.95
